PRAISE FOR
THE SECOND SHOOTER

"One of the best conspiracy thrillers I've read in a long time. Think Michael Marshall's *The Straw Men* meets *Fringe* but highly original in its own way. Clever and addictive."

Robert Swartwood, *USA Today* bestselling author of *The Serial Killer's Wife*

"A brilliantly original and very funny commentary on modern American life. It's Lethem meets Amis, in a journey into paranoia about the corrupt and byzantine machines that made us tick."

Sarah Langan, author of *Good Neighbors*

"Nick Mamatas has looked at the paranoid landscape of conspiracy theory and come up with a novel that manages the difficult trick of being both deeply disturbing and very funny. I liked it a lot."

Dave Hutchinson, author of *Europe in Autumn*

"A brilliant, brutal and highly entertaining thriller."

Cara Hoffman, author of *So Much Pretty* and *RUIN*

"A magic trick of a book, where it seems like every turn of the page blasts you off into an entirely unexpected direction—and yet, Mamatas keeps you rooted with great characters and a maddeningly relevant plot."

Rob Hart, author of *The Warehouse*

"A psychedelic thrill ride with layers of mysteries, in which the twists and surprises never stop coming."

John Appel, author of *Assassin's Orbit*

PRAISE FOR NICK MAMATAS

"A trippy, imaginative treat."

Kirkus Reviews* on *Hard Sentences

"Unafraid to explore some deeply weird places."

Tor.com* on *Sabbath

"Among the best... Mamatas plays fair with the mystery elements, the stakes keep rising, and it all builds toward a satisfying conclusion."

Locus Magazine* on *I am Providence

"Mamatas writes in a witty, sassy style that invigorates his narrative."

***Publishers Weekly* on
*The People's Republic of Everything***

THE
SECOND
SHOOTER

First published 2021 by Solaris
an imprint of Rebellion Publishing Ltd,
Riverside House, Osney Mead,
Oxford, OX2 0ES, UK

www.solarisbooks.com

ISBN: 978 1 78108 926 2

A CIP catalogue record for this book is available
from the British Library.

Designed & typeset by Rebellion Publishing

Printed in the United Kingdom

THE
SECOND
SHOOTER

NICK MAMATAS

SOLARIS

1.

MIKE KARRAS USED to worry that his habit of flicking his pen would annoy his interview subjects, but none of them had ever seemed to care, so he felt free to indulge now. Ex-cops didn't seem to care about much. They indulged him too, but only to a certain extent.

Karras knew the script, the patter, the cliché.

How can I help you?

I didn't keep copies of my old case files or anything.

What is this you're working on again? Ex-cops had a dozen ways of asking that one, and tried it over and over again. *Now about this book…? So, who is going to publish your study?* and *Well, which is it: a book, or a study? You got a publisher for your book?*

But cops only had one way of saying that they'd given up.

I'm not a cop anymore.

Karras had developed a tic; two quick flicks of his pen when he heard that. He did it now.

"I'm not a cop anymore," Lurlene Grutzmacher said.

Karras flicked his pen twice. She licked her lips twice. Her kitchen smelled only a little like tobacco. Like the doctor had found a stain on an X-ray and told her to quit, so she had.

"It's a rough job," Karras said.

"It was a rough day," she said, shifting her weight as she spoke. "Even after Columbine, and Virginia Tech, you don't think about it. My beat was the public library downtown. I wasn't even supposed to roust the unhoused guys when they parked in front of the computer with their garbage bags to look at porno all day."

"The First Amendment," Karras said. "Freedom of speech."

"Something like that."

Lurlene Grutzmacher wouldn't have been much of a cop. The public library was her speed. She was a sausage-shaped woman, her face mannish except when it burst into a wide all-teeth-*ten-hut* smile. A lunch lady with a gun.

"I was there mostly to be the friendly face of the police for kids." That smile.

Karras smiled back. "You saved Da'shawn Kishimoto. Shielded him with your own body."

Lurlene casually lifted her shirt. She had a belly roll on her, and revealed a gibbous moon of plain white bra. Three bruises in a row on her flank. Yesterday's paintball game, or real bullets three years gone by. This was part of the script too; showing off old war wounds. Then...

"You ever been shot, Mister Karras?"

"Can't say that I have, Ms. Grutzmacher." He flicked his pen, knew that she was going to say...

"There's video of the second shooter," she said. "There *was* video."

Karras dropped his pen, then snatched it back up. She sneered for a moment, then said, "You can call me Grutz. Everyone does." She was back to the patter now. Finally. But what she was supposed to have said was *Good, you keep it that way* or *I can't say I recommend getting shot.*

Not that there was video of a second shooter. That there had been video of a second shooter.

"What did he look like?"

"I think Bill's nearly done with our steaks. Follow me."

Lurlene had definitely quit smoking only very recently, because Karras didn't smell the lighter fluid, or the steaks, until he followed her into the backyard. Husband Bill was dark-skinned, with an easy smile and a two-tined fork held aloft. "Hey, Mister Karras, I hope you like 'em raw inside and burnt outside," he said cheerfully.

"It's the only way I know how to grill, myself," Karras said.

"The male of the species is patently inferior," Lurlene Grutzmacher said, easing herself into a deck chair. She nodded for Karras to claim the one next to her.

"Look," she said quietly, leaning over. "See that?"

"Bill's apron?" he said, quietly as well. Bill could surely hear them anyway as he was no more than two yards away, but he politely declined to notice.

"The heat shimmer over the grill," she said.

"Yeah."

"Well, yeah," she said. "That's what the second shooter looked like."

Karras turned and peered at Lurlene, at a loss. Whatever cop script she had been performing had been thrown out and a new coke-addled screenwriter brought in to punch up the third act with a high concept and a twist ending. Karras's knack for knowing what a person was about to say had failed him. Was Lurlene having a stroke now, right in front of him?

"Not just face to face. On the video, too. It's why they buried it."

Karras swallowed a smile. "Buried the video. You've seen the video?" Lurlene didn't smile back for a long moment, then she did.

"The bullets, too. Gone by the time I was brought in to the ER. How do you think I lived through that shit?

You think I wore a bulletproof vest to the library?"

Bill spoke. "Steaks are up!"

Karras didn't mind keeping his mouth full for the next twenty minutes.

2.

LURLENE GRUTZMACHER HAD cancer, definitely, Karras decided. That's why she had once smoked and no longer did. She must have been given massive amounts of chemotherapy, or had a tumor in her brain somewhere. Cognitive issues, even dementia, weren't unusual in such cases. Maybe she was in remission now, or just resigned to an early death and happy to munch on overgrilled steaks, but she wasn't a cop anymore, she was a nut.

It happened. Karras had been on the road for three months so far, researching what he called 'persistent believers' in second shooters. Almost all early media reports of mass shootings, whether the gunman was politically motivated or working through some personal psychosis to deadly effect—or both—included details about a second shooter.

There is almost never an actual second shooter. The fog and night of war in the microcosm explained nearly every sighting. Even police don't routinely face fire from an AR-15. Sounds echo, witnesses panic. Everyone looks like the perp. Any handbag or umbrella could be a gun. One assailant uses two guns of different calibers, so cops and civilian witnesses hear two shooters.

Plus, who wants to admit that in a deadly game of kill-'em-all, the home team of twenty—with huge advantages in coordination, communication, and firepower—so often fumbles against a solo player?

Second shooters vanish when the AP updates its story and sends the new version over the wires. Even the conspiracy theorists don't care overmuch for the phantom second gunmen. The whole phenomenon was just a massive false flag operation with no shooters, no victims, and an endgame of disarmed peasants trudging their way to the FEMA camps under the mournful whip-whip-whip of black helicopters hovering in the federally-owned sky.

But there were a handful of true believers. Eyewitnesses who wouldn't recant, despite facts and evidence. Even police officers. No, *especially* police officers, despite their training, the demands of their superior officers, and the widespread understanding that eyewitness testimony is unreliable. They were happy to talk, and Karras to listen. He was interested in the psychology of the believers more than the specifics of their claims.

Lurlene Grutzmacher had probably seen *Predator* on Netflix the night before. Bill looked like the kind of guy who would have voted for Jesse Ventura for President if given half a chance. Her story could be a sidebar: *A Real Phantom Shooter*.

Karras just had to decide whether Lurlene had been messing with him purposely or as an artifact of some mental problem. No, he didn't even have to do that. He could hear the voice of his editor in his head already.

When in doubt, Sharon Toynbee liked to say, *cut it out*. A surprisingly ethical stance for an editor pulling a paycheck from Little Round Bombs Books, an independent publisher specializing in books about ninja throat-strikes, Trilateralism, and 'radical composting,' among other topics. Then she'd wink and say *Save it for later*.

Three months of interviews, crisscrossing the country in an increasingly filthy Nissan Sentra, Mike Karras had cut out a lot more than he had kept. Karras kept himself busy and gas in the car with SEO work and borrowed Starbucks wifi. His advance was already budgeted for the cheapest motels along his sawtooth route across the middle of the country.

No coastal elites, Sharon had told him when assigning him the book. New York and LA only bought the weird shit on psychedelics, memoirs of obscure shoegaze musicians, and vegan cookbooks. True crime and conspiracy business was pure flyover territory stuff, so the book had to be focused there. Little Round Bombs Books was conveniently located in an old warehouse in Ann Arbor, Michigan, and had a foot in both Americas. *Rumors of a Second Shooter* needed to be middle-of-the-road gonzo: yes to near-pornographic descriptions of firearms and bodies chewed to pieces, yes to picking apart shooter manifestos and even invisible shooters and phantasmic bullets. No to anything that might upset Auntie Becky and her church group, but also nothing that would play to the far-right. *We're college-town late-night stoner-conversation radical,* the late publisher, known by his pseudonym Viktor Surge and for his Gandalfian beard, had written in Little Round Bombs's famously casual submissions guidelines. Keep it simple: a discussion of alienation under capitalism, or toxic masculinities, or even the ubiquity of selective serotonin reuptake inhibitors. *If it's bullshit, make it deep. If it's deep, throw in some bullshit.*

WHAT KARRAS NEEDED, he thought in darker moments, was another mass shooting, preferably one within three hundred miles of wherever he happened to be. Lurlene Grutzmacher lived right outside Dallas, and now Karras was stuck in rush-hour traffic. Bill's steak had alchemically transformed into something closer to mercury than meat, and it was filling up his GI tract.

This was one of his darker moments. *Come on, special boy! Get angry!* A slaughter close enough to drive to, with plenty of witnesses ready to talk about the tightly coordinated team of gunmen who had just torn through a school, or church, or shopping mall. He had the news on the radio, and the police scanner app running on his phone. Despite the shocking number of mass shootings out there, America was still a great big country, and on a daily basis a lot more people were dying of heart attacks and car accidents than they were at the hands of crazed gunmen.

He called Sharon, who answered. Little Round Bombs didn't have secretaries or a phone tree.

"Hey..." Karras said.

"Hello," Sharon said. She was all business. *How are you* might artificially extend the conversation.

"Just talked to a kook."

"These people are bound to be experiencing all sorts of mental difficulties after what they went through."

"Maybe," Karras said. "Or maybe she was just messing with me." He relayed Lurlene's claims.

"Huh." Then nothing. Karras was about to prod her for more when she said, "Could have been an ultrathin invisibility cloak."

"What?" he said.

"Scientists at UC Berkeley created one back in 2014. Volumetric distribution to bend light around

19

an object under the cloak. Sort of like wearing a sheet made of a funhouse mirror. Or tiny fish-scale mirrors. Nanoantennae, if you understand what I mean."

"What? Well, if it's real why don't we see them…" Karras caught himself and laughed. "Why don't we *hear* about them all the time?"

"You know. Berkeley's just the tip of the iceberg. It was a tiny cloak—eighty nanometers in length—but that's what went public. It's not unusual to slowly reveal first-generation technology via press release while developing nth-generation technology in secret." Karras thought how strange it was to hear someone actually say *nth*. "You don't want to know what the President's smartphone is capable of," Sharon said.

"And the bullets?" Karras said.

"Does she have X-rays? Documentation from a physician?"

"Probably not."

"JPC."

"JPC?" Karras said.

"Just Plain Crazy. Even if she encountered a shooter with a hyperadvanced invisibility cloak doesn't mean she isn't a kook."

"What are the chances of the Dallas Library Killer having a confederate with a hyperadvanced anything? David Wayne Cunningham was living out of his car," Karras said.

"Low," Sharon said. "But greater than zero. Sidebar

it; save it for later. When in doubt…"

"This book is going to be seventy-five percent sidebars." Karras was joking but Sharon's voice went granite: "It had better not be, Michael."

The staff at cheap hotels still hadn't gotten used to someone walking into the lobby while using a Bluetooth so he said a quick good-bye, checked in and quickly retired to his room to type up his notes. The room service selection was just a bunch of local take-out place menus in a three-ring binder, and there was no free wifi, so Karras just organized his notes without Googling *"invisibility cloak"+real*. He could do it later, on his phone. Data overages were a write-off. Meat and heat got to him quickly enough, so he kicked off his shoes, stretched out on the planklike bed and closed his eyes.

Within Karras's laptop, which was not connected to the internet, or any private networks, or even plugged into a wall outlet, the pointer was removed from the file named LURLENENOTES and then overwritten with near-identical information.

3.

PEOPLE WANT TO *talk*. Karras was forty, just old enough to have been one of the last journalists to learn that lesson, right before the Internet took over and reportage was replaced by embedding tweets into listicles for Flavorfeed.com. He had broken into the business the old-fashioned way: obituaries. The dead can't sue for defamation, and grieving survivors just *want to talk*, so a new reporter gets to hear all about how Uncle Lou was in the Big One, or how Grandma Tully enjoyed show tunes and even met Wayne Newton on the *Queen Mary* once.

Fact-checking obits, that was the tricky part. Did Lou buy his Purple Heart from a pawn shop; did Wayne Newton ever even perform on the *Queen Mary*? Karras wasn't so great at that. But then again, who was anymore? Facts were tricky things. For every fact there was an artifact of identical mass and velocity. When they made contact, boom! No more mainstream journalism for Mike Karras. There were easier ways to make $21,000 a year anyway. He didn't have any of those jobs either, but traveling the county to write a book was pretty fun.

Except for today, when the keyless fob to his rental car malfunctioned, locking Karras out. He had rented via app as well, which made getting a human being on the phone nigh impossible. Leaning on the 0 didn't help, nor did screaming, "Human! A human being!" into the phone, but tweeting at the rental company did, and soon a tow truck came to take the car, and the fob, away. Another would be arriving… sometime.

There was nothing to eat at a Super8, not even three-dollar Pop-Tarts from a vending machine. It hardly mattered to Karras, because he wasn't staying at the hotel, not really; he just stored his meat there. Karras lived online. His laptop, his phone, they were portals. Mike Karras felt like he lived everywhere at once, except that he occasionally had to eat a bowl of soup, then piss 75 percent of it out two hours later. That brought him back to himself, his body, every time.

Karras made the best of it. He was the only one at the lunch counter not peering into a phone, into a newspaper, or into space. *People want to talk.* He turned to the guy on his left and smiled, purposely.

"Hi, Garn," Karras said.

"Hello," Garn said back. Good. Not an idiot—Garn remembered that his shirt came with a nametag. Not a wild homophobe either, for a down-home blue-collar type. A man can smile at another man. Garn's smile parted his mustache and beard; he had pretty good teeth.

"I'm Mike," Karras said. "What do you think?" He waved his spoon at the front page of the daily paper Garn had been worrying over.

"Nice to meet ya, Mike," Garn said. "I, for one, am entirely against this…" he poked at the photograph of the President signing a renewed assault rifle ban into law, "bi-business." Garn looked back at Karras with a new intensity. "Where you from?"

"Chicago, originally," Karras said.

"Yeah, I figured. You got a bit of an accent on you," Garn said. "Pretty strict gun control laws in Chicago, right?"

"Well, there used to be—" Karras said. Garn quickly followed up:

"And there's lots of shootings too, yah? Gang shootings. Drive-bys. Chi-raq, they call it."

"I guess there aren't enough good guys with guns to shoot the bad guys with guns," Karras said. "Plenty of bad guys shooting bad guys, though."

"Can't complain too much about that, but this is bullshit." Garn gestured toward the newspaper again. He planted his coffee cup over the President's smile. "You ban eighteen-inch barrels, they'll just manufacture seventeen-point-nine-inch barrels."

"To skirt the law?"

"To comply with the law," Garn said, punching the word *comply*. Com-plaah. "But until they pass a law, which they can't"—*cain't*—"saying that you can't manufacture a gun that shoots bullets, a gun is going to shoot bullets. And unless they come to everyone's door and take away all the guns that shoot bullets, there are going to be millions of guns out there. I got four myself. Two for me, and two for my wife." He took a sip of the coffee. "I'm on the road all the time. She needs a gun. A long gun for varmints, a hand gun for personal self-defense."

"They say a gun in the home ups the chances of someone being shot," Karras said.

Garn chuckled. "Like I said, I'm on the road all the time. Honestly, I feel like Trish would shoot my pecker off in a hot minute if I had a job around the house. You married, Mike?"

"Can't say that I am," Mike said. "Never been. Got a kid, though. A boy." That was a lie, Karras knew what was coming and joined in when Garn spoke.

"*Talk about needin' gun control!*" they said as one. Garn liked Karras again, and patted him on the back.

That's what Karras was good at. Sometimes—not all the time, but often enough—he could tell what people were about to say and do. It was a party trick, more than anything else. People were like amoebae on a slide, reacting to stimuli. And unlike amoebae, people carry their stimuli with them: how they dress, how they hold themselves, their race and age. Open books, and Karras could sometimes peek one page ahead. He couldn't tell if they were lying, or crazy, not any more than anyone else could, but what they were about to say, it was usually obvious. Anyone could train themselves to do it, except that most people never bother. They're too busy thinking about themselves—their own *subjectivity,* to use a term Karras had picked up in his single abortive semester of grad school—to care at all about the meat in the next stool over.

Karras didn't have a kid. He had a few pics of his sister's boy on his phone though, just in case.

"So, Mike," Garn asked. "What's your opinion?"

"I think that if anyone tried to pass a law eliminating all guns that can shoot bullets, or hell, even all semi-automatic weapons, there'd be a liquid ton of shoot-outs between formerly law-abiding citizens and militarized police," Karras said.

"Heck, that'd be no good," Garn said.

"Well, on the other side of that river of blood, I'm sure there would be a peaceful utopia," Karras said.

"You read about that guy with the machetes?"

"Which one?" Karras had read about both of the guys with the machetes, the one who tried to go apeshit on the mayor of Newark, New Jersey, and the one who decided to take out the one-dollar Chinatown bus from lower Manhattan to Atlantic City. Machete #1 was unlucky; his knife got stuck in the mayor's secretary's skull, and the mayor herself was carrying and blew him away. Machete #2 managed to kill six people and injure fourteen before the bus tipped over.

"Both. What if someone on the bus had been carrying, like Mayor Terhune?"

"Probably pretty hard to shoot the right person on a crowded bus full of screaming people with a gun."

"Harder *without* a gun," Garn said. And that was it. Something inside Garn wound down; he would speak no more on the topic. There were all sorts of logistical issues worth discussing—what if two passengers had been carrying? What if the machete-wielder had had a gun too, but simply preferred the visceral satisfaction of the blade? Garn would not discuss them. Maybe he would talk sports, but Karras didn't follow any.

Karras had met a lot of men like Garn on the road. 'Wind-up people,' he called them. They had player-piano rolls in their torsos, and when the roll was over, they stopped talking. Wind-up people were almost invariably male; women knew how to change the subject to keep a conversation going, and how to extract themselves from rhetorical alleyways before hitting the far wall.

One little side bit of the book—and the book was beginning to feel like it was made up from nothing but secondary material and sidebars—was going to be a barometer of American opinion about guns.

The kookier the ideas the better. But nobody Karras encountered had any original thoughts to offer on the topic, no brave or even stupid demands to make of the President or Congress.

Nobody he could get to talk, anyway.

Somewhere, though, there had to be people with ideas. Not just policymakers and 'influencers,' but thinkers from the grassroots. *Organic intellectuals.* The people making the Facebook memes that spread so quickly, and planted themselves so resolutely in the minds of the folks listening to Karras now loudly slurping his soup.

He tapped at his own phone, half-heartedly looking for confirmation emails from the mass-shooting survivors he hoped to interview. Karras was a traveling salesman now, carving out a haphazard route across the country, selling a service: he'd come over, accept hospitality, dress up or down as necessary, nod seriously either way, and only ask questions that made it sound as though he believed the interview subject.

Two messages were waiting for him. One was from Rahel Alazar, most famously a survivor of a church massacre in Berkeley, California. It was a Lutheran church that rented space to a local Oriental Orthodox community comprised mostly of immigrants from Ethiopia. The shooter, Lee Nam-jin, was a Korean student of electrical engineering at the nearby university, and apparently had some objection to the rental agreement. He hadn't left a manifesto, but after shooting four members of the congregation immediately after Sunday Kidase he had taken the rest hostage—turned out his gun had jammed. He bluffed, then ranted about some of the finer points of Protestant theology to his captive audience until the police showed up. He charged them, ran right into a Taser, and then was shot by a cop while incapacitated.

Nobody was happy with that result.

Alazar wanted to talk about the second shooter. The one who she encountered, when she ran onto the altar and through the curtain past which she was not allowed, for that spot was the Holiest of Holies, where are kept the tabot, replicas of the tablets Moses brought down from the mountain. The shooter's assault rifle also jammed and so he fled out of an open East-facing window—the Eastern windows are always propped open during the service, for which Alazar thanked God.

Not a trace was found of the second shooter, and Lee Nam-jin wasn't talking, but Alazar remained committed to her story. *And because you too are perhaps an Orthodox Christian after a fashion,* Alazar's lengthy response concluded, *you might understand.*

Karras hadn't been to a church in ten years and that was for a midnight Easter service he remembered mostly for his cousin Athena's hair going up in flames thanks to a candle. Even his mother, who had cried and cried till he agreed to accompany her, said, "See, I knew there would be something interesting for you here." Greek Orthodox and Ethiopian were different anyway, though he'd need to Google to understand how or why. Everyone's three clicks away from a PhD in ancient African theology.

Rahel Alazar he wrote back to right away. California, sure, but this girl was black, the daughter of immigrants, some kind of religious nut—hardly a coastal elite. It would be a long drive, but Karras was ready to visit a place with a bookstore that wasn't just three shelves of bestsellers in the Walmart. Plus, weren't invisibility cloaks being created in Berkeley?

The second email was from Chris Bennett, the radio show host and YouTube personality. Karras was never up early enough to listen to Bennett's syndicated AM radio show, *Year Zero*, and no station running it was foolish enough to run it any time after four o'clock in the morning. But it was about UFOs and false flag operations and such, like the right lane of the highway that Little Round Bombs occupied on the left. The YouTube channel just played the radio show, with video, which betrayed Bennett as having all the charisma of an empty chair. On the radio the man was gold, but get a look at him and the only thought one had was *But why won't you shave those random patches of hair off your cheeks?*

Bennett's choice of subject header: *Our Fake Fight.* As if there had already been some sort of agreement made. Bennett had suggested a fake fight once before, two years prior, when Karras was working on Misinformation.com as a contributing editor. The idea was to get a lot of publicity and social media traction by publicly critiquing each other's work, and then descending into personal insult and caricature. "If we do it right, we can get all our Twitter followers riled up. I got a lot of college kids following me, and older guys on SSI and stuff. They need some direction in their lives, ya know?" Bennett had said. They were both at Book Expo America, at one of those tedious publisher parties where men still wore business jackets over T-shirts, and kept their hair in ponytails. Karras clutched his drink and had been about to ask about Bennett's recent promise to his fans to quit Twitter forever because of some Politically Correct/ Social Justice Warrior 'censorship' controversy, when another, more dangerous question had escaped his lips instead.

"What's the difference between a 'fake' fight and our real disagreements?"

"It's obvious, isn't it?" Bennett had responded. "We'll be friends." Bennett's eyes looked so hopeful that Karras had said he'd think about it.

Now, more than a year later, this email. Bennett had dropped off Twitter as threatened, but still had plenty of social media pull with his videos. He'd finally painted himself into a corner with one video series called *Everything is a False Flag—Peace Is At Hand*

and needed Karras to bail him out. Once 9/11, mass shootings, ISIS, the death of Queen Elizabeth, the great glacier crack-up, and the extinction of the bald eagle were all declared hoaxes created thanks to the "metacognitive collective conceptualizations of the hypermediated holographic illuminated universe," Bennett had pushed himself out of the conspiracy theorist berth and had accidentally rebranded as a full-blown candidate for the lunatic asylum.

Mike, we need to begin Operation Fuss-Up, the email began. Bennett spelled out a fairly extensive script. Karras would forlornly describe Bennett as a former friend and colleague who seemed to have succumbed to mental illness. Bennett would fire back, using 'PC judo' to complain about Karras being 'ableist and oppressive.' It all got worse from there, with R. D. Laing and Thomas Szasz getting dragged into it, a supposed death threat from a third party that would just be 'attributed' to Bennett. Then Bennett would drop off the internet, set all his accounts to private—*so people will know that I'm alive, or that I am probably alive*—and then... Karras started skimming.

He was tempted to just write back, *So you want to do a false flag operation?* but he deleted the email instead. Amazingly, despite his paranoia, Bennett was an optimist. A world where every atrocity was a hoax and all witnesses and victims just well-paid 'crisis actors' was essentially a utopia. Even if the government or the Illuminati were behind all these stunts, what harm was there in letting them play their games, if the only thing wrong with society was the fact of imaginary crises? Bennett usually just muttered something about Walmarts becoming prison camps.

The phone buzzed in Karras's hand. He had all sorts of notifications set up—shootings, mass killings, assassinations, his own surname, a few other things he was interested in, even some SEO stuff (air conditioning units in Dayton, Ohio was one)—but for all that, the phone rarely started vibrating while he was holding it.

Stillwater, Oklahoma. Not a mass shooting. The guy had a truck and was driving it through the middle of Oklahoma State University.

In a moment, Karras's dark mood, that cynical summoning of a special boy, fled from his brain and settled in his stomach, where it burned like thick tar.

4.

Garn WAS QUIET during the ride. Karras had nudged him and showed him the news story, and Garn had volunteered that he was headed that way, and it was only about a five-hour drive, including a stop to unload the truck. It was surely against all sorts of rules and insurance policies and laws, but Garn didn't even tell Karras to duck out of sight if a cop car came into view, or to climb into the surprisingly neat sleeper area of the cab. Garn didn't even have a comment about guns.

Karras felt the need to explain himself, to fill the empty space. Updates were coming in quickly via social media, and with only slightly less alacrity and slightly more accuracy than the wires. The truck had been stolen. Ten dead, fifteen injured. Reports of shooting and, indeed, of a second shooter. The truck-driver traded fire with campus police, and then somehow the police had been outflanked by a sniper atop one of the taller buildings on campus. It took an hour to kill the trucker, but no details were being released. Through all this, Garn was silent, as he was through Karras's exegesis on second shooters, the inevitability of screencaps from Facebook replacing news-gathering and Chit-Chat threads being ignored by so-called journalists, and whether the attack itself might have been inspired by frequent chatter about the lethality of non-firearm weapons that erupt after every mass shooting. If Garn had opinions, he didn't betray them. He fiddled with the radio, then apologized for interrupting.

Finally, as they crossed the state border, Karras confessed.

"You know, there's this impulse which I've had to fight," he said. "When something like this happens, I've been almost too open-minded. Like a lot of liberals"—there were air quotes around that last word—"I'd force myself to think 'Maybe it was the Klan, or a right-wing Christian.' But then, it would be someone with pretty obvious Muslim roots. It took me a while to train myself out of tweeting 'Don't jump to conclusions; this attack could be a special white boy!'"

Garn spoke. "Timothy McVeigh was not a Christian."

"What?" Karras said. "Uh... I know."

"He was agnostic."

"I read the biography."

"His background was Roman Catholic," Garn said. There was a hint of solemnity in his voice now. "He took last rites before his execution."

"Better safe than sorry, eh?"

"Yeah," Garn said.

"Anyway, it's a dangerous reflex, and frankly it makes the left look a little stupid sometimes. There's plenty of right-wing Christian terrorism out there, but I've noticed that it tends to stick to the red states. For whatever reason, skinheads and Klansmen don't travel to San Francisco or Boston to carry out their massacres. But Stillwater... I'm thinking maybe right-winger, or maybe just a college kid who couldn't get laid. And he may well be a right-wing Christian white boy, just demographically."

"They're always either Muslims or nerds," Garn said plainly. Karras could see how the conversation would unfold. He'd object—abortion clinic bombers, racist lynchings, etc. Plus, can't Muslims also be nerds? Garn would counter: those weren't the sort of mass slaughters he was talking about. That's not what people think about when they hear the word 'terrorism.'

And then Karras would say, "Of course. They think Muslims." And Garn would say, "Exactly," and both would think that the other player in the conversation was missing something obvious.

So he jumped ahead. "Are you carrying?" He knew Garn would be cagey.

"We don't have fifty-state reciprocity for concealed carry yet." Which of course was not an answer to the question, but it was also not 'no,' which meant that it was necessarily 'yes.' Now it was just a matter of understanding what Garn was carrying. Perhaps a pump-action shotgun; even just the sound of the pump is a sufficient deterrent most of the time. Probably some sort of knife, maybe carried in his boot. He could casually reach for it to slice a piece of fruit in front of the sort of truckstop hangers-on that make people like Garn nervous. Neither would be an issue for concealed-carry licensure.

Did Garn want to play good-guy-with-a-gun? Diesel duelist? One way to find out.

"So if things get hairy...?"

"I'm just dropping you off," Garn said. "I'll admit I'm a bit of a curiosity-seeker. You see a lot of strange things on the road, and hear about them too from other guys, on the CB, on Facebook, whatever."

"Looking for a coffee-shop anecdote, then?" Karras asked.

"Somethin' like that," Garn said. A compliment was forthcoming, Karras could feel it.

"I met a reporter today and everything."

"I'll definitely put you in the book," Karras said. There were two possibilities emerging now, like a fork suddenly happened upon in the middle of a seemingly straight highway.

All good things, I hope.

Or

You're right you will.

Garn could go either way. A reversion to pleasantries or vague belligerence. Whatever got him what he wanted—a convivial companion for two more hours on the road, or a whimpering city slicker he could socially dominate, with just enough irony in his voice for some plausible deniability.

Then Garn came to the fork and took the straight-ahead path into crazyland. "When you're a trucker, you see the whole world pass by. You're never really anywhere, you understand me, Mike? And this country is so big and so great—God bless it, truly, God bless it—but something's happened in the twenty years I've been on the road. Everything's vanished, everything's gone. I used to have a mild accent. Now I've a thick one," Garn said, exaggerating. *Ivva thikun.* "It's all Walmarts and Denny's and Denny's analogues now, no more local stores. Highway signs used to be a little different, depending on state and county. Now they're all the same. *We're* all the same. We're a little gray dot sliding over the surface of a big gray puddle, Mike Karras. You understand me?

"That's why I want to see this. I'm not condoning it. I'd never do it. If I had the means and the opportunity, I'd put two taps center-mass in the son of a bitch running those college kids down, and I don't even like college kids, but I get it. Not that I understand it, I 'get' it," Garn said. "If you're a Muslim, if you're a nerd, if you're whatever, sometimes you just feel the impulse as a little gray dot on a big gray puddle to make some ripples, add some color. Is Allah real? Is, I dunno, the Force real, or is Game—you know what Game is?"

"Of course I know what Game is," Karras said. "I'm a man in my 30s."

"What if Allah ain't real? I know he ain't, but what if you believed, but then suddenly realize? Same with Game." Garn took his hands off the wheel and gestured broadly at the entire world. "In a flash of lightning, you understand you've been wasting your time. You can live like some sort of moron, knowing that you made a huge mistake, or you can insist to the whole world that, no sir, you are right and Allah is the truth or the Game does too work but the bitches refused to play along," he said, excited.

"Anyway, I just want to take a look," said he finished.

Garn had drifted to the edge of Situationism, just like that. Karras considered for a moment bringing up Raoul Vaneigem, *The Revolution of Everyday Life*, the concepts of spectacle and animality and other half-remembered French bullshit that sometimes kept him warm at night. It was all supposed to be for the proletariat anyway, and Garn was armed. He was already halfway to revolutionary, maybe. But there were many miles to go and Garn had already shown himself to be highly unpredictable, so Karras dredged out a line of Vaneigem's from memory: "My sympathy for the solitary killer ends where tactics begin."

"Yeah, me too," Garn said. The truck engine roared.

5.

IT WASN'T A crime scene; it was several tableaux of medical personnel and twisted metal, all ringed by yellow police tape. The taped-off areas were themselves ringed by satellite trucks, and small but high-powered lighting rigs. Garn eased the truck as close to the scene as he could; the long line of carnage and press drifted by the huge windows casually, like a kiddie ride at Disneyland. He drummed his fingers against the steering wheel. Karras knew what he was thinking—*I could do this. I could do this with my truck, any time.* Thankfully, Garn shivered at the thought, and Karras felt a surge of both relief and the satisfaction that comes with confirmation of an intuition.

"It's not like I can park easily," Garn said. "You need to step out?"

"No, let's go together. It's a college campus in chaos. We'll just park in a lot and take up a dozen spots. Every cop in town is here, but they're all busy, aren't they?"

"Sure enough," Garn said, his smile reckless. It was nearly a mile before they found such a parking lot, and it was deserted, but the walk back toward the scene was diverting—flashing lights, the squawk of radios, a TV news van passing them as they walked, then turning back, then passing them again—and the night air cool.

"You got a press pass?" Garn asked as they entered the edge of the crowd.

Karras shrugged. "No. It's not like a press pass is a badge or something anyway. We'll just see what we can see." It was Oklahoma; saying "Excuse me" and looking both authoritative and nervous worked to part the crowd. Garn, in his flannels and hat, was being read as somebody's concerned father, and Karras in his casual, wrinkled polo shirt maybe an adjunct instructor or some sort of insurance adjuster.

"Well, there's something," Garn said. The truck was on its side, the container behind it torn like it was made of papier mache. "Full trailer. Harder to turn than a semi. No wonder."

"Yeah," said Karras. "No wonder."

People want to talk. The trick was to find out why: the cop who wants to feel important, the bystander too anxious to shut up, the casual liar who finally had an interested audience. Wanting to talk and telling the truth are two different things. Karras just needed a talker to get closer to the scene. He went for a cop. An older fellow, a bit too hefty to chase down criminals. In a uniform—he'd never made it to detective. He wouldn't know much, but he'd talk.

"Officer Colligan," Karras said after a subtle glance at the man's chest. "What's the story?"

"He's alive inside the wreck," Colligan said. He gestured broadly. At the far end, there were a few cops in body armor crawling over the tractor unit like beetles. A firetruck stood nearby, and an ambulance, but the firefighters and the EMTs were hanging back. Some small idiotic part of Karras couldn't help but look at the scene as theater—the lights on the rescue vehicles, the choreography, the awkward silence punctuated by barked jargon that wasn't for him to understand, and most of all, the crowd of onlookers pressing in, eager for some epiphany, some catharsis.

"What do we know about him?" Karras asked.

"What makes you think it's a him?" Colligan asked, his tone now sharp. Garn opened his mouth to say something, but Karras smirked.

"It's a him," he said.

Colligan broke into a smile. "Just testing you. Yeah, we don't know he could actually handle a big rig. We're running licenses, looking at rental records. He may have stolen the thing; maybe the Saudis bought it for him."

"Could be anything," Garn said.

"Could be anything," Colligan repeated. He adjusted his belt.

"Did he work alone?" Karras asked.

"We have reports, witnesses..." Another expansive gesture.

"A second driver, or a second truck?" Garn asked with a guffaw. Colligan didn't like that, which didn't surprise Karras. The game being played was that of an avuncular authority figure holding forth; the cop didn't want to deal with a pair of bratty nephews.

"We got men on nearby rooftops. A helicopter is coming. Nobody is getting away. Nobody," Colligan said.

Karras felt his phone buzz in his pocket. It was probably a notification about the scene he was already visiting. Garn was talking to Colligan about the challenges of maneuvering a truck without experience—had they called the local trucking schools?—when the phone buzzed again. And a third time. Karras hadn't tweeted in days. He surely wasn't going viral right this second, was he? Colligan finally glared at him, and he retreated a few steps to check it.

An actual phone call, from Sharon. Three in as many minutes. And as he moved to thumb the screen, the phone rang again.

"Hey," Karras started. "What—?"

"Hi, honey," Sharon said. "I just wanted to let you

know that I love you and miss you, and that the pot roast is in the oven."

"Oh… great." Sharon had set up a handful of codes with Karras before he hit the road. Little Round Bombs was fairly into security culture, or as into it as any company that accepted mailed-in manuscripts from crackpots on how to mint one's own perfectly legal coins could be. Karras didn't take the codes very seriously, so had to rack his brain for a long moment.

"Love you and miss you…" Check the server his notes were on, as it may have been hacked.

"Pot roast is in the oven…" Stay away from the office.

"Uh, okay, hot stuff," Karras said. Probably nothing, Karras decided, but he'd check his notes when he got settled in a motel somewhere. And ridiculous; anyone bugging the phone would already know that he and Sharon had a purely professional relationship. And then an explosion tore through the tractor unit, and a screaming human wave rose up against his back. Karras was pretty fast, but he was also too calm and the crowd possessed a speed fueled by blind panic. "The whole truck's gonna blow!" someone shouted, which Karras immediately realized was false. Clearly the driver had some sort of explosive on his person, and set it off manually when there were enough cops in view to maximize the media-friendliness of the atrocity.

"Mike!" Sharon shouted. "What was that?" She said other things too, but Karras couldn't hear them. He swallowed the reflex to shout back "Call 911!" and pushed the phone back into his pocket, and realized that he had been as well trained as anyone else. The police were already there. A few of them were dead. And he was running for no other reason than that everyone else was running. Karras planted his feet and angled his shoulder to make a wedge. The running crowd split around him; the scene wasn't quite a panic yet and a couple of the students even said "Excuse me" as they squeezed past.

It wasn't that the scene was safe now; it was that danger could come from any direction, not just from the truck. The killer probably set off the bomb in the tractor unit manually—did he have the brains and backing to have prepared a second bomb that would go off automatically, but not immediately, after his death, and one that wouldn't have just detonated thanks to the first bomb?

"No, probably not," Karras said aloud, though he couldn't even hear himself. The best bet would be—

And then the shots were fired, popping like firecrackers from seemingly everywhere at once. Karras had to fight off another reflex; his own nervous system tried to pull itself free from his flesh and hit the ground, but that would definitely be fatal in the middle of the ruckus. He didn't want to run into the path of the fire either, and surely the ambush shooter, or shooters, had formed a perimeter to pick off people as they fled in waves from the flaming tractor trailer.

Then another thought came into Karras's head. *Will there have been a second shooter tomorrow?* He pushed ahead as well as he could, edging back toward the trailer, toward the police. Maybe the shooters, like the driver, wanted to maximize the number of dead cops, but in a way that might work to protect Karras. The cops dressed like targets in their uniforms, and ran toward danger. He held his messenger bag, a particularly useless shield though it was dark and his shirt light, in front of him. Security through obscurity might keep Karras from being shot, pushing against the currents of the fleeing onlookers might keep him from being hit by bullets being randomly fired into the crowd.

That was the story he told himself, anyway, as he pushed back toward the truck. A line of police and rescue personnel held the perimeter immediately around the flaming truck. Karras wasn't sure if that was standard operating procedure or not. He took it as a sign that the immediate area was safe, and cast a look around for Garn.

"Hey," someone said. He was very close, right behind Karras's ear. "Fucking move." He grabbed Karras, and then Karras's feet were off the ground, and then Karras was face-down on the asphalt. The cuffs fit perfectly.

6.

ONE THING THE local police did not care about at all was the right to a phone call Mike Karras was sure he had coming to him. Secondarily, they were entirely uninterested in allowing him to use his cell phone, or to get ten seconds on a computer to recall the number of his publisher. Nor did they want to give him back his wallet so he could look at his own business card and use the number that way. *Memorize an emergency contact number next time you go traveling, sir* was just another way of saying that Karras could fucking stew, with his story about being from California to write a book and hitchhiking with an untraceable trucker just to check out the scene like some kind of media vulture.

Three of their number wouldn't be returning to their

families after the terrorist attack the night before, after all.

Year Zero was on the radio at three o'clock that morning. Karras had a little cell to himself—the sort an especially annoying but presumed innocent arrestee about to be fingerprinted might be kept in. The officer at the desk didn't seem all that interested in Bennett's droning about the 'Oklahoma terror truck' until he mentioned Karras's name.

"And we have information from a top-secret but absolutely impeccable source," Bennett said, "that Mike Karras, author of such books as *Trilateralism, Neoliberalism, and Surrealism* and *The Imperial Citizen Handbook* was on the scene during that horrible motorized atrocity. And he has not been heard from since. Now, listeners, some of you know Karras. A few of you readers might even own his books—"

"Heh," Karras said. "Very few."

"That you Mister Bennett's discussing, is it?" the officer said. "I didn't know you were famous."

Karras shrugged helplessly.

"How do you think he knows you're here?"

"Maybe my editor got in contact with him?" Karras guessed. It made sense. He was incommunicado, but Sharon Toynbee had probably rung his cellphone to pieces, and then decided to pull out all the stops to find Karras, up to and including dropping Bennett a juicy tidbit.

"—a peculiar and dangerous man. Intellectually dangerous, I mean," Bennett said on the radio. "You know, some folks are just too smart for their own good. Did Karras know something? Did Karras do something?"

The cop raised his eyebrows. "Well. Did you?"

"Do you listen to Bennett every morning, then?" Karras asked.

"Every day," the cop said. "I prefer the UFO stuff." He shrugged. "I like the science fiction, have since I was a kid. This guy is just an entertainer. You can't take it too seriously."

Karras didn't say anything. The cop said, "So, what's he like?"

"Oh, well, of course…"

Karras didn't even make anything up. Bennett was a clever guy, and did read a lot, and was very good on the radio, and a patient interview. One time he even had a lucid moment on air and helped talk a guest down from suicidal ideations, and paid for an appointment with a therapist.

"The therapist was also some sort of kook, it turned out," Karras finished. "Past-life regression therapy. But whatever works, right?"

"Yeah, whatever works," the cop said. "Listen, at shift change I'll get you your phone and read off the number you need."

Karras licked his lips. "Maybe."

"I'll let you punch in your passcode."

"Well…"

The cop shrugged. "Yeah, maybe I'll watch carefully. Maybe I won't. Just consider your situation, sir."

"Oh, I've been doing that."

When the shift changed, Karras got his phone back and thankfully it still retained enough charge to send a text to Sharon giving her the details of his… 'capture' wasn't quite the right word. Detainment. He went with it, even though THESE ARE THE DETAILS OF MY DETAINMENT pained him to type. *Always a writer, Mike,* he congratulated himself. He ran through the basics, and then added LOG ON TO MY GOOGLE ACCOUNT AND CHANGE THIS PHONE'S PASSWORD THX to the top so she'd see that first, then handed back the phone. Karras's heart rate spiked; Sharon was generally always online, somehow, but there is a first time for everything. She needed to change the password immediately. It wasn't that there was anything *strictly* illegal on the phone, but there were enough texts about esoteric and fringe subjects, the usual sets of nudes that one collects while on the road and away from one's lovers, and the like. A lot that wouldn't go over well in Oklahoma, that might lead a judge to raise bail to an unreasonable amount and—

"Darn it," said the police officer with Karras's phone. His eyeglasses were balanced atop his forehead as he squinted at the screen. "I was sure it was 2774…" He was even verbally processing his attempt to break into the phone. Karras bit his cheek to keep from laughing. "What did you do?" he demanded of Karras.

Karras shrugged, then sat on the bench to wait. That Sharon, she always had it together.

But even Sharon couldn't work miracles. It took time to reach out to her contacts, find a bail bondsman to put him on alert; time to dig up an attorney, time to write and distribute a press release and tweet some tweets for the alternative media. For Karras it was another day of Hardee's for dinner and police officers murmuring about him while he did his burpees and sit-ups.

Monday morning, early, Colligan showed up, and took Karras to an interrogation room.

"I'll get right to cases," Colligan began. "We spoke to your friend. We also made some inquiries. We know what you're doing."

"I'm not having this conversation without a lawyer."

"You're tracking shootings, mass killings."

"Lawyer."

"Don't you think it's a little strange? Showing up at a mass murder site and asking all sorts of questions—what can we do better next time, eh? Your friend said that you told him some story about writing a book," Colligan said. "It's like the old days when some schoolgirl would catch her daddy in an embrace with the babysitter, and Dad would stammer out, 'Oh honey, we're practicing our lines for a play.'"

Karras had lots to say. He wasn't divorced from the psychological reality that *people want to talk*. He wanted to talk—to tear apart Colligan's insinuations, to persuade the police officer to be a good guy, to take another look at what had happened, to agree to just let Karras go and chalk it all up to being in the wrong place at the wrong time. But that's how cops work. They know, like journalists know, that people want to talk.

"Lawyer," he said.

"Listen," Colligan said. "You actually did... what? You were on the scene. A crowded scene. There were dozens of people there, correct? We both know you're being held here because you're a... city slicker." Colligan chuckled at his own choice of words. "Just answer a few questions, and we can process you on out of here."

The cop wasn't very good at this. He switched his pitches too quickly. Karras smiled, and opened his mouth, but then thought better of it. Was Colligan just laying a trap? Did it even matter? "Lawyer," Karras decided.

"All right," Colligan said. "We'll do this when you have a lawyer present. It'll be a public defender unless you carry an attorney in your, ah, belly button, Mister Karras. And make no mistake; our PDs are good, professional people, but nobody is interested in defending a terrorist, or a terrorist enthusiast, or a snotty writer. We lost a lot of people yesterday. Our hearts bleed, Mister Karras, and you're telling me you don't want to help."

Karras didn't say a word. He prayed, not to God, but to Sharon Toynbee of the Infinite Resourcefulness and Reach. His prayers were answered. While the public defender dawdled, the attorney Sharon had dug up rolled in, made demands, jabbed a finger at the cell in which Karras stood, and even whipped out his cell phone and threatened to call his personal friend the local judge. Karras exchanged looks with Colligan and the two other cops on the other side of the wire mesh bars. It wasn't that the lawyer's act was all that persuasive, or that his threats of leave without pay and false arrest charges were meaningful, but it was now universally understood that keeping Karras around would be a bigger headache than letting him go.

Stillwater had people to bury. Karras would have stayed, to interview survivors, maybe even find where Garn had gotten off to, but he had to go. The book was a wreck, he still didn't have a car, and the police would make sure he wouldn't find a warm reception at funerals or wakes. He got his phone back. Sharon had bought him a plane ticket to California. One way. It was coming out of the second half of his book advance, which by this point was rapidly approaching double-digit territory.

And Karras's email inbox was bright red with urgent emails from Chris Bennett.

7.

Karras was extremely surprised to be greeted at San Francisco International Airport by Rahel Alazar, and by her brother who asked to be called 'Tony.' They were beautiful people, like a pair of models one would see in an upmarket fashion magazine eager to prove its anti-racist bona fides. Tony was tall and lanky, with thin locs spilling down his shoulders. Rahel, barely five feet tall, wore a brass nose ring and had dyed the tips of her curls to match. They dressed almost identically in jeans and light shirts, like they were members of the same gospel rock band, and offered hearty handshakes to go along with their enormous smiles.

"We read about you on the news!" Tony said.

"Facebook!" Rahel said. "You must be exhausted.

The publisher told us you were coming, so I decided to pick you up. My brother insisted on coming with me. He's so excited to meet Mike Karras, the famous writer." Tony actually looked a bit more suspicious than enthused, but he played along with his sister's claim. "Let me take your bags, Mister Karras." Karras gave him the duffle, but kept his messenger bag. "Laptop," he said, patting it.

Karras was too distracted to tune in to their wavelength and guess what they'd say next. Bennett's emails had been interesting, in the way that listening to some nutcase talking to himself on the bus was interesting—in small doses. The truck driver had been identified as Bilal Salhab, a Lebanese-American with 'no links, supposedly' to radical Islam. Salhab's father was a semi-prominent business person who Bennett had described as a government contractor who worked closely for the Pentagon, but some quick Googling with the airplane's too-expensive wifi showed that Salhab senior was basically a food import/export guy that had supplied some foodstuffs and ingredients to other contractors, who in turn produced MREs.

The road outside the terminal was choked with cars. That was a new thing. Yellow taxis had all but disappeared over the past few years, thanks to Uber and Lyft, and now even those were being superseded by the domed self-driving electric vehicle—colloquially called 'ladybugs' over the objections of Volkswagen—

Silicon Valley had designed and Shanghai had built. The Alazars led him past a brace of ladybugs to an aging blue Cadillac likely just on the right side of California's emissions testing. The thing even had bench seating in butter-brown leather. *Oh*, Karras said to himself. He wanted to pull out his phone and post a photo of it to social media.

"Yes, it's obvious," Tony said. Rahel nodded in agreement. They had been talking during the entire walk up to the parking lot roof, but Karras had just read from his phone and grunted. "A self-driving truck."

"And a remote-control bomb," Rahel added.

Karras opened his mouth to object, then caught himself. There was no particular reason *to* argue with Rahel, whose confidence he required, or Tony, who at least was giving him a free car ride to Berkeley. People want to talk, so let them.

"Who is responsible then?"

"The federal government," the siblings said as one. They were more Berkeley than Karras had expected.

"Okay, I'll bite," Karras said. "A false flag operation. To what end?"

"I was hoping you'd be able to tell us," Rahel said. Her eyes were large in the passenger-side visor mirror. She kept eye contact with Karras, guilelessly.

Karras couldn't resist a meaningless academic question. "Hmm, well, the most obvious answer is to inspire even greater Islamophobia in the red states.

Most of these minor terror attacks by a lone Muslim guy happen in immigrant-heavy communities on the coasts."

"Is it accurate to call it Islamophobia if they're really killing us, Mister Karras?" Tony asked. "What do you think of Turkish people?"

"You can ask my papou—my grandfather—if you want a rant about the Turks," Karras said. "But anyway, it hardly matters. If it's a false flag, then Bilal Salhab wasn't trying to kill anyone, and wiring a bomb to him and strapping him into a self-driving tractor trailer is all about making sure that people are afraid of all the other Muslims who aren't trying to kill…" Karras paused for a moment. "Us."

Tony grunted, satisfied.

"Or it could have just been practice for something else. Did the federal government"—here Karras found himself raising his hands and twitching his fingers to make air quotes, which he hated when others did it and which made no sense anyway as he was talking about the actual federal government, not some ironic one—"just snatch up Salhab at random, cuff his ankles to the bottom of the seat, and let the truck drive itself over the crowd to see if they could send drone vehicles down any road they wish, to kill—or maybe even round up—American citizens? Maybe the supposed Muslim tie-in is itself a distraction. While we're all looking for the feds to bring back the registry and drop the hammer on immigrants, what they're really planning is a giant fleet of cattle cars to bring us all to the camps."

The Alazars grew quiet. Whether they were seriously thinking about the possibility or just realized that Karras was indulging their fancies he couldn't tell, because there was nothing to read in their faces and expressions. Neither of them was even thinking about speaking, so there was nothing to predict. Karras started feeling nervous, so he looked out the window.

"This new Bay Bridge is pretty amazing."

Then he sensed something from the front seat.

"The Chinese built it to collapse," Tony said. Rahel nodded solemnly. "If we get a quake that's even just a five point five on the Richter scale…" he continued.

Rahel quickly turned to face Karras. "You believe me, don't you? About the second shooter, the man I faced who ran away? The Lord sent you to me, yes? I never check my email, but that day I did, and you had reached out to me. Do you believe me?"

Karras tensed his throat to physically swallow the cliché answer bubbling forth—*I believe that you believe*. Rahel would probably direct Tony to stop the car and throw him over the side of the bridge if he said such a thing. So Karras forced himself to relax, ignored all strategy and psychology, opened his mouth, and surprised himself.

"I do believe you. There is something going on, and you're going to help me find out what it is."

8.

KARRAS WAS GLAD the Alazars drove past the numerous Ethiopian restaurants on Telegraph Avenue. He still wasn't keen on sitting in restaurants full of gape-mouthed strangers. Then they pulled into a driveway, and parked. Rahel sang out, "This is home!" then turned to Karras and said more quietly, "I have a large family."

"I'm used to it," Karras said. "I have a million crazy Greek cousins."

"God bless," Rahel said.

Rahel and Tony's parents were enthusiastic, all smiles. Mother Bruk shook Karras's hand firmly and told a brief anecdote about how her own father still taught English back in Africa, though he was nearly one hundred years old, and had published poems in a newspaper. Father Samuel winked and smiled and offered Karras a beer, which Karras was glad to accept. A mass of cousins and other relatives Karras was introduced to lined up to shake his hand, but he instantly forgot their names except for the youngest, a girl named Yayu who made Karras shake hands with some sort of Transformer toy, and then bellowed, "I'm glad you're here, sir! We're having pizza because of you!"

Tony and one of the other cousins brought out some pizza boxes from the kitchen. Everyone gathered around two long folding tables that took up much of the living room and passed out slices, beverages, a large bowl of salad, and spices in a pair of glass jars. Bruk prepared two slices with the spice and handed the paper plate they were on to Rahel, who passed them on to Karras. "Better this way, please try it."

"Pizza *is* not better this way," said Yayu, who had seated herself on the other side of Karras, the Transformer on her lap.

A murmur went up around the table, and strangely everyone ended up looking at Tony for a final judgment. He shrugged expansively and said, "Try it, please, Mike."

Karras liked the first bite, but pretended to love it. "Oh, man, this is amazing."

"It is *not* amazing," Yayu said, completely disenchanted with both pizza and Karras.

"So you're writing a book about our daughter," said Samuel. His voice was low and deep. Casual, but enough to silence the room.

"I'm writing a book," Karras said. He took a bite of his pizza to buy a second to think things through. The family seemed cool; Rahel's generation was clearly largely assimilated into US culture, her parents educated. But there was an undercurrent of patriarchy, and a collectivist impulse. He was being judged. He swallowed. "I'm writing a book about a uniquely American horror, and your daughter's tragic experience is part of it."

"It wasn't tragic," said Bruk. "It was a miracle."

"I was a boy during the civil war. These horrors are not uniquely American," Samuel said. "It's man's inhumanity to man, I say."

Karras quickly mentally reviewed what he knew of the Ethiopian Civil War. There had been a coup against Selassie—Samuel's family had surely been supporters of His Imperial Majesty, given his daughter's religious sentiments—and somehow the army was Marxist and Eritrean nationalist guerillas had been involved. That's all Karras had. Samuel wasn't launching a Berkeley-style political argument, whatever he was getting at. One of the cousins said something in what Karras guessed was Amharic to Samuel, but Samuel shrugged.

"I agree," Karras decided on diplomacy. "War is terrible, always. But I mean specifically the idea that when there is a mass shooter or other mass slaying—

like the truck the other day—all the early news says that witnesses see multiple attackers," Karras said.

"Karras here was involved in the truck attack," Tony offered.

"I was there, I wasn't involved."

"That's an interesting coincidence," Samuel said.

"There is no such thing as coincidence," Bruk said.

"Do you ever listen to the radio?" Samuel asked.

"Bennett, eh?" Karras said, trying to keep the spice in his belly from rising back up and out of his throat. Before Samuel could even respond, Karras had his phone out. "Something you might want to see…" He found Bennett's latest email, made it full screen, and passed it along the chain of relations to the head of the table.

Samuel's eyebrows went up. "Ah, you know him…?" Then he frowned and started jabbing at the screen. "It went away."

"Let me have it…"

Rahel said, "Tony!" She put her hand on Karras's outstretched arm. "Tony's so good at phones." The phone went around the other side of the table and ended up in Tony's hands. He tapped away at the screen with both thumbs.

"Can I just—?" Karras started. There was more Ahmaric from around the table, aimed at Tony, who answered back with an impatient cluck. Karras had nobody to even make eye contact with except for Yayu, who had liberated a slice of pizza from his plate and was dusting off the spices with a napkin.

"Give me a sip of your beer, please, sir," said Yayu.

"How old are you?"

"Just one sip?" Karras peered at her. "I'm eight."

Karras shrugged, nudged the bottle closer, and averted his gaze.

"Yes, that email is entirely gone," Tony said. "But I can confirm that you correspond with Bennett."

"I'd just like my phone back now," Karras said, more testily than he wanted to sound. "I do know Chris Bennett. He emails me frequently. I'm sure he's saying some terrible things about me on his show, but it's an act."

"An act!" said Samuel.

"Like…" Karras paused. "Like professional wrestling." One of the cousins, or maybe she was someone's aunt, hooted and nodded, her hair suddenly everywhere.

"Ah, so you're friends, and the radio show is political entertainment, is that right?" the woman asked. What was her name… Gelila or something?

"Yes." Karras felt that tug in him. He wanted to talk, just like everyone else.

"I think you might have some malware in here," Tony said. "Or spyware."

"Wait," Samuel said. "It's fake news, then? You're working with Bennett? I love his show…" Karras must have made a more extreme face than he wanted to, as Samuel added, "…but I don't take it very seriously. It's just interesting to hear what weird people think."

"You can just walk outside and read the bumper stickers on the cars here in Berkeley for that," Gelila said.

"There's definitely something wrong with this phone…" Tony muttered. Rahel looked expectantly at Karras.

"I don't really have anything to do with Bennett. He keeps trying to cajole me into some scheme. If I'm mentioned on his show, it's because he's hungry for material. Ever since smartphones came out, nobody believes in UFOs or Bigfoot anymore. So he dove into politics. And here's what sells when it comes to politics: tell people what they want to hear, namely that everything is fine."

"That's not what he says on the show, though," Samuel said. "He speaks of endless conspiracy theories: the government, the New World Order, FEMA camps and the United Nations intercepting all my letters home, the Illuminati…"

"Yeah, but conspiracies to what end? To manufacture mass shootings and terrorist attacks. If they're all false flags, then there have been no mass shootings and no terrorist attacks. And it's not like his listeners are anarchists ready to dismantle the state, right? Most of them just rush off to vote for more government—left-wingers for gun control, right-wingers for a border wall and a Muslim ban—even though that is supposedly what the government wants."

"Your book sounds like it will be very interesting,"

Bruk said. "Very insightful!" She shifted in her chair. Karras realized that she was stepping on her husband's foot. "Who wants to bring out the shisha?"

Yayu said, "Me!"

"Not you," said Bruk.

Karras snatched back his beer and took a swig. The kid really had only taken a sip.

Tony brought out a big shisha pipe and filled it with tasty tobacco limned with molasses and lemon. It was a long relaxing smoke session, with little chatter. Eventually, the various cousins said their goodnights. Yayu had Optimus Prime kiss Karras good-bye on the cheek as her parents left. Karras felt the hour catching up with him, but his eyes widened when Bruk announced, "All right, everyone, it is getting late and our guest needs rest. Tony and Rahel, bring the tables to the back porch and I'll set up the futon."

"What? No, I can't stay here..." Karras said.

"Why not?" Samuel asked. His kids were working around him to collect plates and glasses.

"There are plenty of motels around here."

"Pah!" Samuel said, swatting away the very notion of motels with the back of his hand. "You want bedbugs? You want someone to slit your throat in the night?"

"Nobody is going to slit his throat in the night," Rahel said as she tugged on the corner of the far table. Karras moved to help her, but Samuel clamped his strong hand on his wrist.

"She's fine. She can do it," Samuel said. "You're the guest."

Rahel shot him a smile as she folded the table legs. "It really is fine. And please stay."

Karras wasn't sure what the smile meant, or rather he completely understood that she was just being friendly and and just trying to navigate the patriarchy, and perhaps had already grown suspicious of Karras, and certainly wasn't going to slip downstairs for either a serious interview or a make-out session, but Karras couldn't help but daydream for an instant. It was a good smile.

They want to keep an eye on me, he realized. "Do you have wifi?"

"Of course we have the wifi. Tony, give him the wifi number," Samuel said.

"I will, Pops, I will," Tony said, just having returned from taking the other table away. "Do you want to sit in the kitchen and have coffee?"

"It's near midnight," Karras said.

"Church tomorrow," Rahel sang out. "You'll come with us, won't you?"

He would now. "Yes, but I really need some sleep." He and Samuel were sitting on a pair of folding chairs in the middle of the now empty living room, like they were on a primitive cable access talk show. "Are you really going to drink coffee after midnight, Tony?"

"It's in tiny cups!" Tony and Rahel both said. Then they both laughed.

"My kids are good kids," said Samuel. He offered his hand to Karras again, shook, then excused himself to the kitchen, taking his folding chair with him. Now Karras felt like he was being made to wait in a police station. Bruk appeared from somewhere and huffed her way through extending the futon and putting bedclothes on it.

"Only one night," Karras said. Bruk looked at him from over her shoulder, nearly glaring. "I mean, I have to write, you know. Creation requires solitude."

She nodded. "My own father said something like that once. Please sleep well, Karras. What sort of name is that?"

"Greek," said Tony.

"It's my last name. I'm the kind of person people like to call by his last name. My first name is Michael."

Bruk scrutinized him for a moment. "Yes, I understand why."

Karras shrugged. "Maybe one day you can tell me."

"You don't look like a Michael," Rahel said. She was still smiling, and about to say something else, something either flirty or devastating, but Tony and Bruk both stiffened. "Good night," she said instead. Bruk said something in Amharic and the children went dutifully into the kitchen, like a pair of surprisingly well-behaved seven-year-olds.

"You have a serious face, Mister Karras," Bruk said. "That's why. Sleep now. Church is early and the service is long."

"Most Greek people skip the first hour or so and show up closer to communion."

"So do some Ethiopians," said Bruk, "but not this family."

Karras was left alone as night crawled into the living room. The sheets were freshly laundered, and it had been a while since Karras had stretched out on so comfortable a mattress. But he couldn't sleep. He gripped his phone like it was a rock he was about to throw through a window, wary of checking it. Would the wifi allow Tony to spy on him? He wanted to check the news, check in with Sharon, maybe even tap out a few notes. Yayu and the beer bottle would be good for some flavor. He used to try to cage sips from guests, rather less successfully, when he was a kid too.

They were still talking, in the kitchen. Karras presumed the occasional 'Grikya' or 'Grikinya' was a reference to him—'the Greek.' The Alazars lived in a duplex, but Karras doubted there was a flight of stairs leading up to the bedrooms from the kitchen. They'd have to tiptoe through the living room to get to their beds, and Karras would have to pretend to sleep through it. He dare not even masturbate to relieve the tension of the past few days.

Unconsciousness finally snuck up on him, and waking took him too soon thanks to a pair of sharp hand-claps by Samuel. The family was already dressed and ready. It was still dark outside.

Karras had packed a decent shirt. People like to talk to a man in a button-down. It was wrinkled, but Bruk offered to iron it. "I have time," she said and she inspected the sleeves. "I don't make breakfast on Sundays. You know we cannot eat until after communion."

"He knows, *imama*," said Rahel. She was dressed in slacks and a conservative blouse, and had in her hands a long white scarf.

"Yes, I know he knows. I said that he knows when I told him," Bruk said, pointedly. She wrapped her own scarf around her head and body. Tony and Samuel appeared from upstairs as well, both draped in white. Tony flashed an embarrassed smile and said, "Don't worry; it's not mandatory for you." The family and Karras walked three blocks to the church, like a collection of ghosts.

The service was familiar enough to Karras. He skipped the prostrations, but took off his shoes along with everyone else, and entered the church proper. Orthodoxy engages the senses, through chanting, incense, and ornate decoration. The walls were entirely bare of icons and murals as the church was Lutheran, but the small congregation made do with easels for smaller paintings, and a folding screen for the altar. Some of the men were in typical businesswear, but most men and women wore the great white shawls, and all the women kept their heads covered. The use of ornately decorated umbrellas during processions surprised him. "It's a symbolic dome," the man standing next to him whispered.

Karras stood one row behind Tony and Samuel. The women stood across the aisle. There were pews, but only the elderly and mothers with tiny children sat. Just like when he was a kid, he tuned out the liturgy—he couldn't understand a word of it, but knew the beats and the rhythms—and focused on Rahel. She seemed... fine. Almost everyone Karras had encountered thus far had been transformed, for the worse, by their encounter with mass violence, even if they managed to survive physically unscathed. PTSD and all the attendant anxiety, paranoia, detachment, and depression were only the most obvious symptoms. His sources all had baggy gray eyes from insomnia, rambled to avoid specifics, or focused on jejune details like "I'll never forget that one of his shoelaces was untied. If only he had tripped..." or "My ice cream was melting, so I drove even faster than I knew I could..." to the exclusion of everything else.

Was it the Church, her tight-knit family, her belief that a miracle had saved her from a second shooter? Or maybe she'd crack during the interview process. Something twinged inside Karras at the thought of it. He rocked on his feet, the droning chants of the priest and cantors lulling him. The man standing next to him jabbed him with an elbow, but smiled apologetically.

Finally, there was a brief homily on the importance of fasting, then communion was offered. The women formed a line and went up first, all except Rahel. Now her smile was gone, and something was stirring in her stoic expression. It couldn't be the first question, but Karras would have to ask if she was being excluded, or if she had excluded herself, for the sin of running behind the altar during the shooting.

Karras did the math; it had been twelve hours since he checked his phone. It had been years since he'd gone so long without it. It felt heavy in his pocket, like a dead thing. He'd set it to Utterly Silent, not even Vibrate. He was a boy again, wearing a scratchy collared shirt, clouds of incense stinging his eyes, bludgeoned by keening in a language he couldn't understand. He half expected Bruk to walk down the aisle from where she was receiving Holy Communion to grab him by the ear and threaten him with being given over to the priest as an altar boy if he didn't stop daydreaming during church.

There was strong coffee served in the back building after the kidase; there the shawls came off, the genders mixed. Tony hovered around Rahel for a moment before excusing himself to show an older parishioner how to delete spam email. She was alone again, at a table for six, by herself.

Karras sat down, but before he could speak, she did: "What did you think? Was it familiar to you?"

"Largely, yeah. Language, the umbrellas, the sign of the cross going from left to right—those were different. But otherwise, it was pretty much like the

Greek church I'd go to on Easter and Christmas."

"And for weddings and funerals?" She raised a taunting eyebrow.

"Weddings and funerals," Karras said. "And baptisms. I have a lot of little first and second cousins once removed."

"Oh, bless them," Rahel said.

"Speaking of blessings…" Karras saw an opening. "About the shooting. How have your fellow parishioners been dealing with it?"

"We pray."

People want to talk.

"And Lee Nam-jin?"

"I pray for him too," Rahel said.

"Even though he's…" Karras trailed off purposely, to let Rahel draw some conclusion. *Even though he's a killer? Or Even though he's dead?*

"Dead, Mister Karras," Rahel said, "though nothing we can say to God can change the killer's fate. But God isn't bound by time, is He? The prayers we make now can be heard by God in the past. So maybe…"

"Do they pray for you?" Karras asked, gesturing broadly at the room.

"Of course," she said. "That's why I'm here talking to you."

"They're giving us room to talk, then?"

"Yes," Rahel said, a little too plainly.

"Tell me about the second shooter." That's what Karras really wanted. Seal off one line of questioning, and a source will be happy to talk about the actually important topic.

"He was in a ski-mask. All in black. About your height. Brown eyes, too. He held his gun like a soldier would, pointing down," she said. "He aimed at me when he saw me."

"Did he say anything?"

"He did, but his voice was weird." She gulped down some coffee and put her chin to the top of her chest. "He sounded like Batman," she said, dropping her voice an octave. Then, in her normal voice, "But I couldn't understand him at all. There was so much blood rushing in my head, all I could hear was something like a wave, or the ocean, and it sounded like he was on the surface, shouting at me while I was swimming deep underwater."

Was Rahel crazy too? She clearly believed in imaginary beings, but that was hardly enough on its own to make someone insane. But the stress of the shooting, and finding herself breaking a taboo for which she might be punished for eons to come...

One way to find out.

"Was he Asian?"

"What does that have to do with anything?" Rahel asked. "Anyway, he was wearing a mask."

"If I put on a mask, could you still tell I was white?"

"Are you white?"

"Greeks are white. European."

She smiled, meanly. "Greece isn't Europe. It's

79

practically Asia Minor. Perhaps you look Turkish. Is the Turk a white man? You could be Syrian."

"The reason I am asking if the second shooter was Asian is because there are a number of theories about second shooters. One is that the media drops all references to them down the memory hole in order to promulgate a narrative of mentally-ill lone wolves," Karras said. "All the better to start locking political dissidents up without due process—rubber rooms instead of prison cells."

Rahel sipped her coffee.

"Another is that the second shooters are handlers of some sort; that the government is brainwashing the killers, and the second shooters are just there to make sure the attackers hit the right targets, and then to make sure they don't survive the experience," Karras said.

"Michael," Rahel said, "Mister Karras. Karras. I read the Internet. I know all these things. You asked me last night to help you. My family opened our home to you. How is this... interrogation going to help you?"

She peered at him for a long moment, comfortably waiting for an authentic answer. There were many to choose from. Karras decided to try them all, plain and businesslike.

"I ask because if the second gunman was Asian, it might be a clue to his identity, or tell us something about the planning of the operation.

"I ask because I'm writing a book, and even if the

theme is a bit breathlessly presented, I want to offer as many facts as possible to my readers.

"I ask because the basic profile of a mass shooter is still a heavily alienated white man with a spectrum disorder or a history with psychiatric medication."

Then he lowered his voice, leaned in a bit, laced his fingers, and licked his lips. A sincerity gambit, and easy enough as he was actually sincere.

"I ask because I've heard some very strange stories so far, as I'm sure you can imagine."

"Like what kind of strange stories?"

"The voice you mentioned—it reminded me of a survivor in Texas who couldn't quite see her second shooter. She described him as a sort of transparent blur."

"She's crazy," Rahel said.

Karras nodded. "I don't doubt it, honestly."

"I'm not crazy."

"I don't doubt that either."

"I don't think he was Asian, Karras," she said. "When I first saw him, I thought he was African."

Karras had a tell. The top of his left cheek, right by his nose, twitched whenever he heard something unexpected. It didn't happen often, because he rehearsed his conversations down various thematic paths, and often ruminated about worst-case scenarios, but now he twitched.

"East African. Not necessarily African American," Rahel said. "I thought at first the shooters might have been Eritrean, that it was a political issue. I didn't even see the Korean man's face until I was shown his picture by the police after. My back was turned when he opened fire. I know what guns sound like. I just ran."

"Onto the altar area. Is that why…?" Karras started.

"Why what?"

"Is that why you're sitting here alone?"

"I'm sitting here with you."

"But this table was unoccupied," Karras said.

Rahel laughed. Her smile was toothy, joyful. "Everyone is leaving me alone because you're here. My mother texted three ladies and by the time we arrived at church, everyone knew."

Karras's cheek twitched again.

"Is it all right that I'm here?"

"It's important that you're here," Rahel said. "You're someone we can point to and say, 'See, someone still cares about what happened here.' But tell me, Karras, *why* do you care? Is it the money?"

Karras snorted despite himself. "It's certainly not the money. Little Round Bombs isn't exactly a big publisher, and even big publishers pay small advances. I just want to know things."

"No money? How are you living?"

"All the hotel rooms and airplane tickets are a write-off for the publisher. When I'm done traveling, I'll have to find an apartment or a roommate situation."

"You're *unhoused?*"

"I'm… on the road," Karras said.

"Is your book going to have you in it? Sleeping in our living room, or eating dinner in front of a gas station microwave?"

"Or witnessing a mass murder and being taken into custody?" Karras said, an edge in his voice. "Yeah, I'll be a character, in places. It's called New Journalism."

"I don't want you to write that I'm crazy, Karras. I'll be very upset. So will my family. You said you wanted my help, so how can I help you? I can only tell you that I saw a man in a mask, that something was wrong with his voice, and when he raised his rifle to shoot me the bullet didn't come out. He looked down at the gun in his hands, then at me, then I ran out the back door of the church. I heard his footsteps running in the opposite direction. I hid in here, actually, and called the police from the phone in the kitchen. I guess he ran out the front of the church before the police came."

"Well, of course you called—"

"When I called 911, they told me police were already on the way. They instructed me to barricade the door and hide. I spent an hour in the cabinet under the sink, my knees touching my ears, and a pair of butcher knives in my hands. I thought I'd have to spring at him like Wolverine from the movies.

"When the police swept the room, they heard me under the sink and demanded I come out. They wore helmets and vests, carried assault rifles. They nearly shot me." Her eyes glistened now. "It reminded me of my father's stories from the war."

That part of Rahel's story hadn't made the news. That part made Karras lick his lips. It wasn't a tell; he did it deliberately to show that his interest was piqued. People talked more when he licked his lips at them.

"I thought the man in the mask had come back, with reinforcements. That they were going to wipe out the entire congregation and blow up the church. My eyes were so full of tears I couldn't even read the word POLICE on their vests. I even thought they were ISIS for a moment. They shouted at me to put down the knives, or they'd"—she leaned in and whispered—"'shoot my effing head off.'"

Karras frowned. "I'm sorry that happened to you. I'm sorry for all of this madness, but, the police—"

"Karras."

"I mean, the cops are there to—"

"Stop."

He stopped. She didn't start. Finally.

"What, Rahel?"

"I know all about the police. The police did not surprise me with their behavior. I'm a black woman in this country, with a black family. Maybe not what they call 'African American,' but I've never met anyone who hates brown skin and makes such nuanced distinctions. Don't give me your canned speech about the police you tell some poor white idiot in Connecticut. You said you wanted our help yesterday—what happened to that?"

The coffee hour was winding down, and families were exchanging extended good-byes. Some of the older children were tasked with bussing the snack trays and coffee cups. Karras turned his head and cased the room. Nobody was looking his way, nobody cared. Even Tony was occupied, nodding along to some story Samuel was telling. *Probably about me*, Karras decided.

"I do need your help," Karras said. "I need to talk to someone whose claims I can't dismiss. You need to make me believe that there was a second shooter, and that the voice phenomenon you experienced was real as well."

"How am I supposed to do that?" She got up, collected her own cup and saucer, flicked her gaze apologetically over to the gray tubs already filled with tilting stacks of cups and plates and flatware.

Karras followed, almost lurching over. "New Journalism style. I build a story where you seem trustworthy to the reader, even if your experience was incredible."

"Isn't that what your friend Chris Bennett does on his radio program?" Rahel asked. She let the cup and plate fall from her hands, seeming to enjoy the noise. "Sell his personality to sell his cockamamie conspiracy theories." There was something about her word choice—who under the age of seventy even had *cockamamie* in their vocabulary anymore?—that made Karras want to kiss her. That, and the fact that she'd never go for it.

"Bennett wouldn't bother to interview you; he'd just find some news footage, draw red circles around shadows on the screen, and call you either a government plant or a space alien," Karras said. "The guy almost never leaves his house."

"I heard it was a compound in Nevada," she said, over her shoulder, as she walked to join her family.

"Are you talking about Mister Bennett's compound?" Samuel said. To Karras: "Have you been there?"

"It's not really a compound."

"It looks very nice."

"It's his girlfriend's parents' condo," Karras said. "Bennett can't afford a cabana and a pool."

"You were on the show again, Karras," Tony said. He was thumbing the screen of his phone. "I'll be right back; stay here, everyone." Karras barely had time to exchange looks before Tony was back. "Okay, we can leave now." His mother especially peered at him expectantly, so he added. "Bennett announced on Twitter and Facebook that you were at an Ethiopian church in the East Bay, and that anyone who wants to 'help with the investigation' should head on down."

"But nobody came?" Karras said.

"No; they all went to Oakland, to Mekane Selam," Tony said. Everyone murmured some assent, save

Karras. "It's the cathedral. Our congregation is a bit off the map, since we don't have our own building and all."

Tony was full of questions, and the answers to them. Obviously Karras's phone was tapped somehow, but it wasn't proper spyware, as Bennett didn't have access to the phone's GPS. It must have been something that controlled the mic; could Bennett have heard the church service and put two and two together... and get three point five?

"Tony, walk faster. I'm getting hungry for breakfast," Samuel said. To Karras: "Do you like waffles? From an iron, not a toaster."

"I have to set up my laptop, put together my notes," Karras said. "I've already imposed enough."

"Did you complete your interview with my daughter?"

"I didn't know you wanted waffles, Samuel," Bruk said.

"No, I have plenty of questions for Rahel. It's why I'm staying in town. I need to talk to the Berkeley police department as well, other witnesses..."

"What app do you use to record interviews?" Tony asked. It didn't matter what Karras was about to say. "Whatever it is, delete it from your phone. Any app that requires access to your mic and camera, really."

Rahel was being quiet. Karras thought of Scylla and Charybdis. Her father was the six-headed sea monster that could tear him apart by forbidding Rahel to communicate with him any further. Her brother, the endless whirlpool of paranoia and technical fidgeting. Her mother seemed to have decided to resolutely ignore Karras outside of her home, perhaps due to some singular notions of hospitality and house-pride. She had to be nice to guests; on the streets, he wasn't one.

"I know shorthand." He didn't. "And have an eidetic memory." It was pretty good, but no. "And why don't you accompany Rahel, Tony, when I conduct the interviews? I have no secrets."

"You definitely don't," Tony said.

"What kind of young man knows shorthand?" Bruk said. She had a key ring in her hand and opened the security gate, which Karras thought was as notable as a young man knowing shorthand. Maybe Samuel didn't wear the pants in the marriage after all.

"My mother was a secretary," he said, which was true and thus felt true, "and she was also a little behind the times. She was convinced that if I knew shorthand, and how to touch type and change typewriter ribbons, I could always get a job in an office somewhere." The bit about the typewriter was true too. The tiny lie embedded in a more significant truth, and wrapped up in a family story.

It worked. Bruk said, "All right, go with her, Tony. Is that all right?" and then looked at Samuel, who nodded and grunted in assent, like a figurehead monarch stamping an act of parliament.

"I want to shower and stuff," Karras said. And nap, and play some mind-numbing game on his tapped phone. Eat a fast-food hamburger.

"Do you need to borrow a phone book, to find a hotel?" Bruk said. Karras decided not to spend much mental energy on deciding whether that was an offer of assistance or a verbal nudge out the door, but just waggled his phone and said he had everything he needed. There would be no waffles. Karras stepped into the home only to grab his luggage. Thirty-five minutes later, he was across town, ensconced in a pink cardboard doughnut box of a motel room he hadn't paid for. The old trick of checking for an open door during morning maid service to have a few minutes of privacy, grab some free coffee, take a shit, or in this case, make a call. Karras looked like the kind of guy who stayed in motels, and could nod and talk fast and shrug helplessly with the best of them, so it usually worked. Worked this time too.

He turned off his cell phone, took out the battery, and called Sharon on the room's landline. Who knew what the motel would do when they found that someone had made a call between check-ins—maybe bill whoever just checked out? Blame a maid? He tossed a $20 bill on the still messy bed just in case.

"Every phone is tapped," Sharon said, instead of hello. The 510 number likely showing up on her caller ID was the giveaway. "Viktor Surge has lowered himself to throwing pebbles at my bedroom window at 3am when he wants to hold an editorial meeting. He won't even come into the office these days. Anyway, the real question is how does Bennett, or anyone else, have access to the information gained by the tap?"

"You've been listening to the show?"

"I have no time to listen to the radio. It consumes too much of my attention, plus sometimes people stammer or hesitate before they speak and that drives me insane. The clipping service sent me transcripts. I read them in one browser tab while doing research and editing," she said. "Have you been listening to the show?"

"I've been to church."

Sharon guffawed.

"The Alazar shooting."

"The Lee Nam-jin shooting, you mean. She didn't shoot anybody," Sharon said. "Did she?" Karras heard her typing.

"I always think in terms of the victims, Sharon. Any hack can give a murderer a sixteenth minute of fame with a jailhouse interview."

"More like a Ouija board interview in your case. Bang, bang."

"I think I might have to go off the grid," Karras said.

"Is that even possible in this day and age?"

"It's not like I have one of those Great Beast 666 microchips embedded in my—what is it, on the palm of my right hand?"

"You mock, but *Crash the Cyberpocalypse* is in its ninth printing. That book is why you have a travel budget. Also, it's the back of the left hand."

"But anyway, off the grid…"

"Did you rent your hotel room with a credit card?" Sharon said. Karras didn't have the chance to explain how clever he was being before she continued. "Good luck finding one that'll even take cash these days. Did you cross an intersection to get to the hotel? You were probably recorded by CCTV. Did you spend any time at all within a five-foot radius of someone with a smartphone in their pocket? That might have recorded your conversations, without you, or them, even knowing. Forget accidents and coincidences— ever been within *twenty* feet of someone with a smartphone in-hand? You've been recorded. Then there are drones, undercover police, fans and fanatics—"

"I get it," Karras said.

"The grid isn't a grid anymore, it's a 10,000-thread cotton sheet," said Sharon.

"Yes, Sharon, I read the Wikipedia article on the panopticon too—"

"That's not what I'm saying, Michael." Sharon could sound like a schoolteacher when she wanted to. "It's not a matter of the panopticon—that concept still implies some central, if anonymous, authority surveilling you. But you, and all of us, exist in a stratum of horizontal coveillance. Sociveillance. What

I am worried about for you is *anti*sociveillance; social co-equals plotting against you for nefarious ends."

"Nefa*rrr*ious," Karras said, rolling his Rs. "Anyway, expect paper missives."

"Expect late nights messing with carbon paper then. I'm not extending your deadline," Sharon said. She hung up without saying good-bye. Karras put the battery back in his cell for lack of any other convenient place to store it, and in a moment of muscle memory conquering conscious thought, turned the phone back on.

Berkeley, California, perhaps thanks to the major research university downtown, or maybe due to the various Luddites and eccentrics that were still hanging on in tiny apartments or precarious collective households in the dicey neighborhoods, was home to two stores that specialized in typewriter sales, supplies, and repairs. Karras strolled down University Avenue to Classic Typewriter, which he guessed stayed in business because of some state-mandated university forms that had never been turned into PDFs. Plus it was closer to his motel than California Typewriter on San Pablo Avenue, and who knew what kind of typewriter he could afford with the petty cash in his wallet? A forty-pound colossus would be murder to wrestle back to the Alazars'.

What was happening in Karras's head was this: he decided to pretend to be spooked. *I'm spooked*, he thought. *I'll try being spooked.* When he glanced at the passing traffic, how many drivers, passengers, already had their gazes upon him? All of them, he decided, even if they were somehow using mirrors to do it. Waiting for the light to change on the corner, the lamppost he was standing next to was buzzing just a little too loudly. The men speaking Spanish to one another; he was the topic of conversation. The mannequins in the large but oddly untrafficked sarong store hid cameras; as he passed, their necks swiveled, recording his gait and sending it all to some distant, poorly protected cloud database that dozens of Russian hackers had already compromised. He might as well have been taking a selfie under every street sign he passed and posting them to Instagram.

Karras didn't *feel* spooked, no matter how hard he tried. He remembered being a kid, and having his first-grade teacher explain to the class that they all had skeletons inside them. It was Halloween, there was a Dollar Store decoration called Mr. Bone-Jangles hanging off the door, limbs akimbo, fleshless face forever smiling, eyes a pair of flame-red points in black sockets. The seven-year-olds were freaked, and Mrs. Braunstein informing them that the room was full of skeletons, and that the skeletons were within them, didn't help.

But Little Mikey thought something different. It had since become a first-date anecdote. Little Mikey raised his hand and said, "I don't think so, Mrs. Braunstein." His mother encouraged such smartypantsness, so he wore it everywhere. "I am my brain. So the skeleton isn't inside me; I'm inside my skeleton. I'm the bus driver and the skeleton is the bus and my whole rest of the body is the passengers." He usually ended the story there, but there was more to it.

The other smartypants in Mrs. Braunstein's class, a girl named Dana, raised her hand. Without even waiting to be officially called upon, she blurted out, hand still in the air, "But Mikey isn't like a bus driver. A bus driver can leave the bus, they *have* to leave the bus to go to the bathroom. Mikey can't leave his skeleton; he's trapped inside. We're all trapped inside our skeletons!" Kids burst into tears, howled for their mamas, then howled louder when someone shouted, "My mommy is trapped in her skeleton too!"

But Mikey, like the kid in the cereal commercial, liked it. He didn't feel trapped in his skull; he felt free inside it. Not a prisoner, but a monk or a hermit drawing on the walls and contemplating the mysteries of the universe. Same now. Let them take his picture, record his conversations, take note of his interactions with others. In his mind, he'd always be free. While the other seven-year-olds around him panicked about the inevitability of their own lives in human bodies, little Mikey enjoyed the privacy of having a true self far from the demands of the world.

Classic Typewriter looked exactly like a typewriter store in the third decade of the twenty-first century would look like. The vintage pieces prominently on display, all with small index cards with the words NOT FOR SALE typed—of course!—on them mounted on the typewriters' space bars. Old machines shoved haphazardly on aluminum shelving racks lining the walls, as likely to be cannibalized for parts as sold intact to an individual. Nobody comes in to browse, or to be convinced to buy a typewriter. In the back of the small room, a display case held paper, boxes of ribbons, loose carriages, and the like. The whole place smelled like an exploded pen. And like one would imagine, Karras was the only one in the place.

"Hello?" he tried. "Hello!" He walked to the display case, looked for a service bell or something. There was a door leading, he presumed, to a back area or supply closet. A bell did ring, then, but it was the little cat bell hanging off the entrance. Karras turned around, to see a pair of young men coming in, clearly not looking to purchase a typewriter. They—a taller Asian kid in a Warriors jersey and a squat white one with a scraggly beard and an unseasonal leather duster—smiled nervously when they met Karras's gaze. Then an older white man stepped in from the back area, and asked, boredly, "Yes?"

Karras turned back. The man spoke first. "Are you three together?"

"No."

"Yes," said the Asian kid.

"We are," said the white kid in the duster.

"In a way, we're all together," the Asian kid said. "Hey, Karras."

"They're fans," Karras said. "I need a typewriter."

"Nobody *needs* a typewriter, Mister Karras," said the white kid. He had his phone out, and pointed it at Karras.

"No mobiles in here," said the salesman. The kids giggled. "I'm serious," he said. "Put it away, son, or leave. If you don't leave, I'll call the police right now."

"With what, *your* cell phone?"

"These are your fans, sir?" the man asked. "What is it that you do to have such fine young examples of manhood following you into my store?"

"I'm writing a book."

"Ah, you'll want something that can stand up to a pounding," the man said. The boys laughed at that.

"I want a scoop," said the white kid, his phone still out, as he trotted over to Karras to stand next to him. "Logan Dark, here"—he turned the camera on himself and leaned a bit to get Karras in the frame—"with Michael Karras, so-called writer."

"I'm not a *so-called* writer; I've been published!"

"My first question is, Mister Karras, how could you? Why do you use your platform to spread politically correct propaganda for the terminally woke?"

"Sir, if you'd like a typewriter, there's another store on San Pablo…" The old man had a landline receiver in his hand now, the coiled wire leading under the display case. Everything here was old-fashioned.

"The real question is, 'Why are you doing the bidding of my very good friend Chris Bennett, who frequently sends me emails positively begging me to be on his show?'" Karras said. It was a risk to mention, but the only way to deal with a loaded question is to change the subject to something not *too* far afield from the original query. Question the premises—*What do you mean by politically correct, eh, smart guy?*—and you sound argumentative; answer it truthfully—*My propaganda isn't politically correct, uh, I mean...*—and you simply won't be believed. So ask another question, then answer it.

"My guess is that Chris Bennett appeals to your sense of rebellion, somehow. You're interfering with a place of business, and you've decided to show how brave you are by following me, an unarmed journalist, around. You wish you had a book deal, you wish you knew how to get people to talk, isn't that right, Logan Dark? Nice innuendo-laden pseudonym, by the way. Shouldn't you be an anon with a frog avatar? This is LARPing transgressiveness, not anything real. Just like Chris, who sells idiocy to low-T kids, some of whom have slightly above average IQs.

"By which I mean your friend there," Karras finished, nodding toward the other kid. "Not you, Omega Male."

"We're gonna go viral," that kid said.

"You're welcome."

"I... have no follow-up questions," said Logan

Dark. "Thank you for your time," he said, but to the store employee.

The bell on the door jangled as they left, and Karras turned to the typewriter man. "I'm trying to spend less time online," he said.

The typewriter man nodded. "I have a portable you might like. A Smith-Corona from the early 70s. A Coronet Electric, with a case. Powder blue."

"If it works, I'll take it."

"You're on a budget."

"Well, sure."

"You're a writer," the typewriter man said.

"You work in a typewriter store," Karras said.

"Supply and demand," the typewriter man said. "It's not like there are thousands of people clamoring to fill my slot, ready to work for free just for the chance to be noticed."

"Economics major, were you?"

"Yup," the typewriter man said, with a sigh. He found the typewriter he had in mind and put it on the counter and opened the case. "You going to watch that video?"

"I'm going offline," Karras said, definitively. He nodded at the typewriter. It would do. He pointed at a ream of paper, and a couple boxes of ribbon.

"Want carbon paper to go with?"

"I'm going offline, not forsaking electricity," Karras said, though Viktor Surge, the ancient radical who owned Little Round Bombs, would probably be happy to print copies of *Rumors of a Second Shooter* via hand-cracked mimeograph. Karras paid in cash.

Back at the Alazar house, as he sat in the small back yard at a small wrought iron table, Karras's cell phone started vibrating, signaling that he was being @ed on Twitter, texted, group texted, DMed via FB, and even called. Would answering the phone be violating the principle of getting offline? What if he checked his phone just to see who was calling, so he could call them back later on some landline, or even better, on the payphone he passed on the way back from Classic Typewriter?

What if he just started typing? His impressions of Rahel, and the church service. Her revelations about the police. Would that be the better hook? Did he even have enough to start writing her chapter? He was the little man living in his own skull, the fire sputtering and sending light flickering along the bone walls, a piece of charcoal in his hand, unsure of what he could write, what he could live with.

This second shooter might have been Eritrean.

No.

~~*This second shooter might have been Eritrean.*~~

There was something shockingly soothing about striking a hated sentence through.

He reached for his cell, remembered his vow, and put it back on the desk.

He reached for his cell, then made a secondary promise not to look at social media, but only to play a casual dot-connecting game full of quick, easy decisions, then realized the temptation implicit in even handling the phone, then put it down.

It buzzed, just as he put it down. He looked at the number being displayed on the screen.

It was Bennett.

9.

"WHAT ARE YOU doing in Berkeley? Joining a pansexual polycule intentional family anti-virus pod?" Bennett said. "Or just digging up some fake news?"

"If it were fake news, I wouldn't have to dig it up, Chris."

"The news is fake, the travel vouchers are real, Karras. But I'm glad you're there. I'm pretty big on campus these days—students are sick of political correctness and SJWs measuring people's armpit hair. Thanks to your little outburst, I'm viral."

"You're a virus, anyway," Karras said. "Why shouldn't I hang up right now?" *People want to talk.*

"I have a lot of listeners. Including a certain truck driver that may have given you a ride a few days ago," Bennett said.

"Yeah?"

"Garn. That's the name, right?"

A syllogism came to mind.

People want to talk.

Michael Karras is a person.

Ergo, Michael Karras wants to talk.

He'd have to be careful. For all his lunacy, Bennett wasn't bad at what he did. Congresspeople would make unguarded comments about everything from BLM (against) to UFOs (for) on his show. Bennett's emails were taunts, tests, but on the phone his radio-friendly voice and self-effacing tone had a way of impelling people to say things they'd later regret.

"Okay." He let it hang.

Karras knew that Bennett, like all broadcasters, hated dead air.

"He had some interesting insights," Bennett said. "Self-driving truck, maybe? He said that you got pretty... close to him."

"Sure."

"I think I'll have him on the show. Do you want to be on the show with him too? A little reunion, you know?"

"I'll pass."

Bennett definitely wanted to talk. "Pass? You want to pass on the show? You're working on a book; you need to build your author's platform. These conspiracy titles are basically a license to print money—"

"I thought you were against printing money." That

was a test. Bennett passed it by not firing off a canned rant about the evil of fiat currency and the Rothschild-controlled Federal Reserve system.

"You know the old journalistic saw, 'We're writing the story anyway. If you don't want to comment, we'll have a one-sided story.' Do you want a one-sided story, Karras?"

"What side would that be?"

"There's no such thing as a *self*-driving car, Karras. Ever take a philosophy course, or a physics course? There are no uncaused actions. Even if the truck had AI, someone other than Bilal Salhab likely programmed it. Your friend Garn was pretty struck by how it worked out, meeting you and giving you a ride, just as a major attack of the sort you're researching happened to occur. It was even a truck attack, not a shooting—and there he is, a trucker."

It was hard to tell over the phone, without myriad tells and twitches, but Karras knew that Bennett was lying about Garn. It was a lie embedded in truths. Garn almost certainly contacted Bennett; he was probably keen to be on the show. Might even have done it just to come back to Karras's attention. But no, Garn didn't claim that Karras was the man behind the truck attack.

For one thing, Garn was transparently an Islamophobe. All terrorists are either Muslims or nerds, but Karras didn't quite qualify as a nerd in Garn's eyes. Or he figured not, anyway.

For another, Garn wouldn't have contacted Bennett had he thought Karras was to blame. He would have simply beaten the shit out of Karras, and then handed him over to the police, or perhaps the local militia. It was a cop-show gambit—*Your friend already sold you out. Just confess, and we'll go easy on you too.*

And that bit of nonsense at the end. So what if it were a truck attack? That was just bait, to get Karras to start arguing about how little sense Bennett's story made.

"Are you recording this call?"

"We both know that California is a two-party consent state for telephonic recordings, Karras."

That didn't answer the question. Another fact that obscured a deeper deceit.

"So, are you in California now?" Karras asked.

"Yes—I mean, no," Bennett said too quickly. Karras chuckled.

"I'll tune in when Garn's on. Text me, okay?"

"Nobody says 'tune in' anymore, grandma."

Karras hung up. There was no other tactical alternative. He held the phone in his hand, eager to contact someone, or to check Bennett's social media feeds, but knowing that the conversation had been streaming online wouldn't help him anyway. There was still a mostly blank page positioned on his typewriter roller. That was his mission.

Typing was slow, but satisfying. Karras developed an okay lede—he started with Rahel under the sink, a knife in each hand, guessing that her calves had started to cramp, that she could smell mold or cleaning fluids. He'd have to ask her what was on her mind at that moment in a follow-up interview: her dead friends, the eyes of the killer she saw on the altar, the rantings of Lee Nam-jin on the subject of miaphysitism echoing from the narthex of the church, nothing but her own prayers? He'd provide the list, and she would almost certainly choose from among them, even if she had been thinking something else, or nothing at all. Manipulation—no, not really. Karras liked Rahel Alazar; he wanted to give her the chance to preserve the sanctity of the hermit who lived inside her skeleton. He didn't need to know the whole truth, just whatever approximation of it she wanted to give him.

That wasn't quite right, actually. Karras did need to know Rahel, inside and out. He wanted her to want to actually talk. His readers could get the sanitized version, if it suited her. He left notes in brackets for himself—[emotional reaction], [summary of Oriental Orthodox Christology—maybe?]—as he typed. Maybe Sharon would spring for some high-quality scans, so he could edit in Scrivener like a normal person after he finished a first draft. If not, there was always an intern to exploit.

The cell phone buzzed, signaling an incoming text rather than a social media notification, and nearly vibrating off the corner of the desk where it was charging. Karras was off the grid, and not doing too poorly on his new typewriter—he had nearly a whole page done, anyway—but he picked up the phone.

It was Sharon.

BOOKED YOU ON YEAR ZERO.

GREAT IDEA I THINK.

BENNETT A TOOL, IN BOTH SENSES OF THE WORD.

FORGET THIS OFF-THE-GRID STUFF. IS STUPID ROMANTICISM.

BETTER TO HIDE IN PLAIN SIGHT.

Karras held his thumb high, ready to text back a string of eyebrow-scorching curses. But why would Sharon text rather than call? She actually preferred to vox, unlike most people in her demographic, because she could keep her eyes on her computer monitor while talking. He flipped through prior texts; there were only about a dozen and they were all along the lines of DOWNSTAIRS IN LOBBY and CALL ME BACK IMMEDIATELY.

It wasn't Sharon. She never sent substantive texts, and wouldn't now. Someone had either hacked her phone, or at least gotten their hands on it, or had hacked his. Could spyware spoof texts from contacts? Probably. If he called Sharon, he'd either be calling a hacked phone, or calling from one. But not responding to the texts would be suspicious. Karras texted back:

ALL RIGHT SOUNDS GOOD

SKYPE IN I PRESUME

LET ME KNOW WHEN

Karras handwrote a quick letter on typing paper, folded it into an envelope, and decided that he'd find an open UPS store that would overnight it. He didn't check his phone again, though it vibrated like an angry animal on the table until Tony popped his head out the back door. "Hey," he said.

"Hey," Karras said.

"Don't writers like to write in cafes? Rahel and I are going. Want to come?"

"If I bring a mechanical keyboard to a café, I'll be beaten to death by all the grad students and their laptops."

"So just come for coffee. It's not Ethiopian coffee, but it's still pretty good."

Karras looked at the mostly empty page wrapped around the typewriter platen. "I don't want to write anymore anyway."

A quick and confusing walk later, seated in the café, Tony smiled especially nervously. "This place isn't great."

It wasn't. A couple couches, photos of Obama and some riot from the 1960s on the wall, a couple of display cases of soda cans and cake slices, a pair of toasters and a panini press behind them, and a few trays of baklava and Turkish delight. The owner had light eyes and olive skin; he flouted the law by lighting a cigarette and smoking it. Karras decided that he must be Turkish and made a note to pay in cash. He wasn't a bigot, but hiding his surname around people who might be Turkish was a habit his old papou had inculcated into him as a child.

They might just pull out a sword and cut your neck open, Papou would say, drawing his hand against young Mikey's throat.

"We'll meet here from now on, if that's all right," Rahel said.

Karras was spooked again. What had her parents said; what missteps had he made at church, or in their home? Was he not supposed to sit in the backyard?

"We should meet in different places all the time," Karras said. "I'm definitely being closely scrutinized." He unlocked his phone and slid it over to Tony, then told them both about his encounter with the college kids, his conversation with Bennett, and even the texts he'd been receiving.

"You're really going to go on *Zero Hour*? When?" Tony asked.

"I don't understand," Rahel said. "I thought your goal was to interview me for your book."

"I'm definitely going to. I…" He glanced at Tony. "You could accompany Rahel, as we agreed to earlier. I don't mind."

"I don't mind that either, but I don't understand what the rest of all this is about," said Rahel. "Why are you being targeted? Why are you telling us this?"

Rahel was afraid. A lot of persistent believers, especially civilians, were afraid. At first the authorities would take their claims seriously, write down descriptions and even sketch out a face, but too soon they'd move on to embracing and reinforcing the official story, stop returning calls, let their voicemail fill up. It's why they wanted to talk to Karras.

She must think I'm a nut now, Karras thought. *What if I told her that God did send me, or that I felt He did? Then she'd think I was "normal."*

He couldn't bring himself to lie so severely. "I'm a public figure, in a way. A small weird way," he said, which was true. "In a way, I'm inserting myself into the story, and that means encouraging others to try to insert themselves into my story too. Bennett wants me to take him seriously."

"I hope sempai will notice me," Tony said. Rahel giggled at that.

Karras said, "Exactly."

"So you're going to go on the show?" Rahel said. "Isn't the book more important?"

"Well..." he said. "The texts. I dunno, they may not even be from Bennett, after all. It could have been some college kid, going into business for himself, to prank me and Bennett both. But I do have an open invitation to be a guest."

"And what about my story? The second shooter?"

Tony was still going through Karras's phone. "Who is Sharon?"

"My boss," Karras said. "Just my boss." He was grateful for the moment's distraction; he could tell he was losing Rahel and needed to get her back in his confidence.

"I think," he said, developing the thought even as it spilled out of his mouth, "that all of this is connected somehow. Why am I being targeted now? The book in general has something to do with it, but things have gotten really bad recently. Even when I was down in Texas, I had already contacted you; any hackers must have known that I was coming here."

"This is beginning to sound dangerous," Tony said. He handed Karras back his phone.

"I've not been threatened, just, I don't know... teased, I suppose."

"I don't like it," Tony said.

"I've been through worse, Tony," Rahel said. "I want my story out there. I believe you were sent, Mister Karras"—she was formal again, hard—"even if you do not, not yet. God will protect you, the way he protected me, but I think only insofar as you are dedicated to telling the truth of what happened to me will you be so shielded."

"Thank you," Karras said. "I'll try to live up to that."

"I am very tired of hearing the name Lee Nam-jin on the news, while my brothers and sisters are hardly mentioned at all. You'll put their names in your book too."

"I will, I promise." Karras was already mentally composing a footnote. Lee Nam-jin had already been the subject of a lurid true crime paperback and a pair of breathless YouTube documentaries. He wouldn't have to spend too many words on the shooter.

Rahel looked expectant, not relieved. Tony arched an eyebrow.

"Well... start," Tony said.

"Oh, of course," Karras said. He got his pad and pen from his bag. He gave the pen a couple of rev-up clicks.

"What I want to know is," Tony said, "were you fired upon in Oklahoma?"

"Uh... yeah, I was," said Karras.

The siblings nodded and exchanged foreign words.

"News says you weren't," Rahel said. "Early false reports of snipers."

"Might have been noise from inside the truck; something bursting in the engine," Tony said.

"The news isn't even giving that explanation—it's just Tony's theory."

"I was definitely fired upon..." Karras started clicking his pen. "Heh, this is how it feels."

"Yah," Rahel said, quietly.

"All right. We'll begin."

The interview was long. Karras was especially interested in Rahel's momentary belief that the second shooter might have been an Eritrean national, with a grudge against Ethiopians. Was there a community in the Bay Area? Of course, but it hardly mattered; a real zealot would drive for hours if he wanted to.

Did he come from the Muslim lowlands, or was he Catholic? "Don't be ridiculous," she answered. "All Eritreans look alike." Then she caught herself, and muttered something about internalized chauvinism. But the shooter couldn't have been Ethiopian…

The possibility of an Orthodox shooter turned Rahel around completely—perhaps the man wasn't even African.

Maybe he wasn't even a person. He was a devil.

Lee Nam-jin was a devil as well. Had been a devil. No, was a devil, as he now existed in the metaphysical realm beyond the material, even as his corpse was moldering in a box in Colma. Rahel and the other members of the congregation were praying to find the strength to forgive him, when, in a flash, one of the deacons had the veil torn from his eyes—the man had been not merely fallen, but a devil in the flesh. Forgiveness was impossible, praying for his redemption was itself a sin. Tony interjected—"I think Deacon Abebe was speaking metaphorically; he was just trying to ease the pain of the living souls. And don't you pray for him, sister?"—but Rahel was adamant now. The demonic theory also explained the second shooter; clearly he too was a devil, and the more intently evil of the pair, as he manifested on the altar. But God intervened to keep his gun from firing.

The theological implications were staggering. The siblings attempted to work them all out, live, in front of Karras, as the sun dipped behind the Berkeley hills.

He ordered a round of red velvet cake slices for the table, as the Turk behind the counter was seemingly growing impatient. Why did Rahel live while the others died? Is that even a question one can ask God, who has already wiped the tears and healed the wounds of those who had passed, in the afterlife?

"Lee Nam-jin left behind a note, sketches, a Bible with a lot of scribbles and notes," Karras said. "But he never mentioned a confederate; he didn't appear to text or coordinate with anyone…"

"Maybe his phone was hacked," Tony said.

"Maybe devils manifest at the same time, but not in concert," Rahel said.

"When I interviewed a survivor in Texas, she had been shot. The evidence had disappeared, except for her wound," Karras said.

"Was she a Christian?" Rahel asked.

"I didn't ask, but she was an older white woman in Texas; a former police officer with a German surname. Grutzmacher. It's all but inevitable," Karras said. "How seriously are you considering a supernatural explanation?"

"We live in a fallen world," was her response.

Karras found that frustratingly gnomic, but it was also a great possible chapter title. He made a note. He clicked his pen a quick half dozen times, and then another half dozen.

"What's amazing," he said, more to himself than anyone else, "is that once high-quality digital video became ubiquitous, sightings of all the classic fringe stuff—UFOs and cryptids—dried up. But once digital video became ubiquitous, so too did rampage shootings. Correlation is not causation, but people need devils, don't they? If we can't believe in the old monsters anymore, maybe some of us decide we need to fulfill that role." Karras wrote that down. It was speculative, glib, and bordered on irresponsible, but there was a ring to it, so he wrote it down, nearly giggling.

The pen clicking was unconscious, but the giggle was purposeful. Designed to alienate the Alazars, and offer some space for them to reconsider everything, including Karras himself and the story they were telling him.

"There were no traces of the second shooter—no footprints, nobody made a video of him entering the church, or running from it. Nobody else saw him, or heard him," Tony said.

"I'm an eyewitness," Rahel said.

"Eyewitnesses aren't always reliable," Tony said.

Karras didn't even look up from his pad; he didn't want to see their mutual glares. They might remember that he existed, unite against him.

"Eyewitnesses aren't reliable when it comes to picking someone out of a line-up," Rahel snapped. "I know whether someone was standing in front of me with a gun pointed at my face or not!" She turned to Karras. "Why would anyone hear footsteps when there were guns going off? Why would anyone leave footprints? It's been dry in Berkeley for years, thanks to the big drought. No mud."

"Especially if the shooter was a devil," said Tony. He attempted to modulate his tone so as to suggest sympathetic neutrality, but he choked a bit on the final word.

"It's odd," Karras said. "We're all constantly under surveillance, and coveillance, but still, sometimes crimes occur and there's no evidence that it happened. Not *enough* evidence, anyway. There's a socio-cognitive tipping point where the incredible becomes fact…" He trailed off.

"The opposite of 'fake news,'" Rahel said.

"Sure," Karras said. He wasn't sure.

"The internet means we're all spying on one another," Tony said.

"I think the internet should just be for cat pictures."

"Oh, ninety percent of cute animal pictures are steganography—messages, encoded by how many times the kitten swipes at the flower, or the number of teeth when the baby hippo yawns. If you ever share one, you're probably helping Ukrainian Nazis communicate with their counterparts across the former Eastern Bloc, and even in the US," Karras said offhandedly.

"I'm not going to stop sharing them," Rahel said.

"Ninety percent?" asked Tony.

"At least," said Karras.

The café owner made a move with something in his hand. Karras winced, but it was just a remote control for the wall-mounted television that had been silently showing a soccer game on some channel. The man turned up the volume, and held his finger to his lips. Karras knew before the newscaster's voice filled the room that it would be another mass shooting.

But what kind of mass shooting—jihadi terrorism or domestic far-right, gay panic or domestic dispute, fragile masculinity or the return of the repressed? He couldn't help but contemplate taxonomy, the possibility of a two-page spread for a Venn diagram of his own design.

"Tragedy struck today."

Karras never liked that phrase. Sharon Toynbee once sent him to the Merriam-Webster during an argument, and made him read aloud the definition: *a disastrous event. Calamity* and *misfortune* were listed as close synonyms. But there was still something that nagged at Karras—the motor of a tragedy should be something accidental, or at least fateful. Tragedy fed into the narrative. So many shooters saw themselves as instruments of fate, the angel of death commanded by God to dish out tragedy. But the cable news was just interested in selling sentimentality. For them, *tragedy* just meant *something sadder than the water-skiing squirrel we were going to show at the end of the hour.*

Tragedy struck today had a certain utility, though.

It told Karras that the shooting was over, the bodies had been counted, next of kin alerted, and police forces had debriefed one another. *Reports are coming in* would have meant something different—a camera crew had been dispatched. *Possible multiple* means that a managing editor is contemplating whether to bother sending out that camera crew; perhaps footage from an enterprising stringer, or the local channel, would be sufficient.

In the moments it took him to think all of this, the news had repeated the bit of footage it had—an aerial view of the scene—and the broadcaster read off a slightly different version of the story. Seven dead in an industrial park in Indiana. No terrorism suspected as of yet.

"Bullshit," said the owner.

Karras couldn't help himself. "Probably someone 'going postal,' like they used to say. Either it was an older heavyweight white man who had just been laid off, or a younger guy, of any race, who was reprimanded by a female supervisor."

"This man is an expert, Yunus," said Rahel. "He's writing a book." Ah, she knew the owner's name. She and Tony were regulars.

"I've been hearing all about it," said Yunus, but his gaze was fixed on the television. After a moment, he added, "I'm very sorry about what happened at your church."

Karras's attention, or much of it, was on the

television as well. He was eager to hear if there were survivors, and if so, would any report a second shooter. Some bit of his mind was doing accountancy. Could he afford another flight, another motel stay? Would the East Coast, with its centrist Democratic voters and working-class immigrants, insulate him from Chris Bennett's increasingly rabid audience? Then there was the social psychologist, an emergent property of the corpus callosum, wondering if Rahel and Tony would take a sudden exit as a betrayal.

"Is this yours?" Yunus said, abruptly. He gestured with the remote, not at the television, but instead out the window. There, in the middle of the sidewalk, just about seven feet in the air, hovered a small drone of the sort a hobbyist might own. A camera was mounted on it, aimed at the table where Karras sat with Rahel and Tony. "You making a documentary about yourself?"

"No..." said Karras. He got up and walked to the café window. He thought for a moment about rushing outside and trying to grab the thing, or maybe taking a chair with him and knocking the drone out of the sky as it fled. But that wouldn't help. Nor would making his own video, with his phone, which he had left on the table—he was supposed to be off the grid, damn it—of the drone. The drone operator knew Karras; Karras wasn't even sure he even knew himself. That's why people became journalists, to find out what made people tick.

He heard his name, but not from anyone in the small café. The newscaster on television had just read it off his script. No, not quite off the script; it was new information being fed into his headpiece.

"We are getting word…"

At least it wasn't *We are getting confirmation…*

"There are multiple shooters, one of whom is still alive, still at large. He is asking to speak to a media figure, someone by the name of Michael Karras."

The drone rose slowly out of sight.

"This is highly unusual…" the newscaster said.

"It is," Karras said to himself.

"Usually when the police receive demands—and they get them all the time—people want to address the President, get a message to the Pope or to some celebrity like Lady Gaga…"

"She's in the Illuminati, you know," Karras said, still to himself.

"…they ignore the demands…"

She probably wasn't really in the Illuminati, but back when Gaga was at the peak of her fame, it was the sort of thing people in Karras's social circle would say whenever she came up.

"This case is different for some reason, perhaps because Michael Karras, some sort of obscure conspiracy theorist-cum-journalist, actually isn't famous."

It was just another tic for Karras now.

"Law enforcement are asking for help in locating

Michael Karras, who I suppose is on the verge of fame now…"

"This is a lot of detail for 'getting word' rather than 'getting confirmation,' isn't it!" Karras snapped, finally turning from the window. To Yunus he asked, "Will you change the channel, and see what MSNBC is reporting? Please!"

"Of course, of course," said Yunus, aiming the remote. "Anything for the famous Michalis Karras." He performed a perfect voiceless velar fricative on the *ch* and ostentatiously rolled his *r*.

There was nothing good. Just more saber-rattling against the North Koreans, who had claimed, with photos and video, to be building a nuclear-capable submarine.

"Are we going to Indiana, Karras?" asked Rahel.

"We?"

"Yes, we," Rahel said.

"No," said Tony.

"We're not," said Karras. "But we'll… hell, give me my phone." He had to make a call, and then he definitely had to turn his phone off, and keep it off.

10.

"You asked for this," Rahel said. She had a pebble tucked in the crook of her forefinger, her thumb behind it. They were standing in a small backyard belonging to an aging Folk Victorian, among dried-out grasses and skeletal brown weeds. She flicked the pebble at a second story window. It clattered satisfactorily, but nothing happened, so she selected a slightly larger one from the ground between her feet.

"Do you really know nobody else whose computer we can borrow?" Karras asked, looking at Tony.

"Nobody who doesn't watch the news or follow social media," Tony said.

Rahel hmphed at not being addressed, and flicked the larger pebble against the window. It bounced off with a loud snapping sound and she cringed, squinting, to see if she had cracked the glass. The curtains, pink and childish, swayed, and Yayu pressed her nose and lips on the pane. Rahel already had her finger to her lips, and shushed the child, to no avail.

"What are you doing?" Yayu demanded, her loud voice distorted by her insistence on keeping her mouth smooshed up against the glass.

"Mister Karras needs to use your computer," Rahel said in a harsh stage-whisper. "He has to get on the internet!"

"Why my computer? I'm using it now. I have homework."

Rahel just glared up at the girl.

"My Barbie dress homework. I'm going to be a fashion designer!" Yayu said. She was fogging up the window with her breath.

"Just how pink is Yayu's room, exactly?" Karras asked.

"We'll throw a blanket behind you or something," said Tony.

"We have to be quiet," Rahel snapped at them both. Then, to Yayu. "Open the window. We're climbing up."

"Really?" Yayu jumped up and down, presumably on her bed, excited. She struggled with the window—it was off-sized and its frame had been painted a dozen times at least—but managed to push it open. Tony stepped forward, squatted, and laced his fingers together for Rahel to place her foot. She put her hands on his shoulders, and with a simultaneous grunt, he boosted her up to the sill. Yayu slapped a hand over her mouth and scuttled out of sight as Rahel muscled her way up and slithered through the open window.

"You're next. You and Rahel can pull me up after you," Tony said. With a shrug, Karras put a foot on Tony's hand, and pumped his leg. He pulled himself up and sloppily rolled not onto Yayu's bed, but onto a fairly hard wooden bench. Yayu laughed heartily at that, then clamped her hand over her mouth a second time. He scrambled to his feet and leaned out the window, extending both arms. Tony jumped, then ran his feet against the outer wall to gain some purchase as Karras put his own foot against the bench and pulled. Rahel slipped her arms around Karras's waist and helped. Karras did his best to keep from shivering, inhaling deeply to catch her scent as he dragged Tony into the room.

"Auntie and uncle don't know about this, do they?" said Yayu.

"Depends—do they listen to the news? Talk radio?" Karras said.

Yayu shrugged.

Tony quickly set up a new Skype account via multiple proxies while Rahel mounted Yayu's garish *My Little Pony*-themed blanket behind him by hanging the sides off the posts of Yayu's canopy bed. It took only a few minutes to set up everything, and for Tony and Karras to switch shirts.

"We're all going to hide behind here and be quiet while Mister Karras speaks to a man," Rahel said. "He's going to save some lives."

"Whose?"

"The man's, probably," said Tony.

"Lots of other people's too," Rahel said.

"We have to be quiet," Yayu said.

The first Skype call was to Sharon, who had played liaison with the media and the Fort Wayne, Indiana ,police department. The shooter had holed up in a warehouse, and the police had commandeered a small security robot from a Best Buy a few miles from the park to allow for direct video communication.

"Nice blanket," Sharon said. "The shooter is pretty cagey. Not only hasn't he committed suicide yet, when the cops sent in the bomb-squad robot he shot its tires and fuel cell out before it could even get close to him."

"Ah, yeah," said Karras. "He didn't want to go out like Micah Xavier Johnson in Dallas, I guess."

"Looks like he's really worried about being bombed. He's staying away from the exterior walls, has planted himself on a swivel chair to see out all the windows— he has food and extra ammunition, too. He'd been planning on using the warehouse as a bolthole all along."

"What do the cops say about that?" Karras said.

"They told me to mind my own fucking business and get you hooked up to the fucking computer or they'd call some friends he knows in Ann Arbor and have them bust my ass for something something, fuck you, cunt," Sharon deadpanned. From behind the blanket, Yayu giggled. Sharon knew better than to ask, or even to respond in any way. She could play poker for a living if she wanted to. Karras wondered why she didn't, instead of working for Little Round Bombs.

"Fragile masculinity."

"Among the many things cops and criminals have in common," said Karras.

"The point is that he really wants to talk to you, Karras," Sharon said. "He's not a rampage shooter. You should know he's a..." For a moment, Sharon was at an uncharacteristic loss for words. "An intellectual," she decided to say. It wasn't a lie, but was clearly oversimplified to the point of deliberate inaccuracy. "I hope your computer guy is using something better than a VPN from hidemyass dot com," she said before Karras could ask a follow-up question. Karras heard Tony suck his teeth.

"Anyway," said Karras. He looked around for earbuds and found them. He didn't need the Alazars reacting to every little thing the shooter was going to tell him.

"Anyway," said Sharon. "Here we go." She ended the session. A few moments later, a video call came in, and Karras quickly accepted.

Robert Wayne Rasnic didn't bother obscuring his

Skype ID. Perhaps tonight was going to be a one-way trip for him after all. He was breathing heavily; Karras wondered if he had been shot before making it to his bolthole. He perched atop the office chair, butt on the headrest, feet on the seat, like an insouciant CEO posing for a glossy magazine, except he wore a camouflage vest and a black T-shirt stretched over his belly. He peered down at the camera, which was nearly floor-level. The security bot was probably a glorified Roomba with a smartphone taped to it.

"Michael Karras," he said. "Is that you? Your author photo must be ten years old if you are. Well, it doesn't matter if it's you, because even if it isn't, I know you are watching somewhere else, either live now, or in the future." He held up one finger. "I have a comment, and then I have a question."

Karras didn't have Sharon's poker face. He tried to look placid, but the image in the corner of Yayu's computer monitor was nervous, unshaven, jowly—a bit of a wreck all around.

"Here is my comment," Robert Wayne Rasnic said. He sounded as though he'd been rehearsing for this moment for a long time. "One cannot help but notice that my middle name is Wayne. You're familiar with Wayne theory; that men with the name, whether it's their first or middle name, are more likely to end up murderers. Convicted murderers, anyway. There was one analysis I read that claimed that point four one percent of convicted murderers carry the middle name Wayne. I found this factoid so interesting, so compelling, that I began my own study of murderers. You and I are much alike, you see. We have a lot in common. Some mutual friends."

"... I see," said Karras.

"And now, here I am, a murderer."

"Is this still the comment phase?" asked Karras.

"Yes," Rasnic said, a bit sharp. "It was the jokes, at first. Late-night TV. Comedians. I am not insane, I know they weren't addressing me personally, but as a young man I took my share of ribbing from classmates and casual acquaintances as well: Three-Named Wayne would just have to grow up to be a psycho killer of some sort. So I started reading true-crime stories, watching all the shows about serial killers. You know the kind, with dramatic reenactments and such."

"Sure I do," said Karras.

"I bet you have a similar background, Karras. Where'd you get your start again? Watching *X-Files* as a kid, getting involved in movement politics. Blogging live from the Battle of Seattle, but simple anti-corporatism wasn't enough for—" He stopped suddenly and peered off-screen. He brought up his rifle, an AR-15, and looked through the scope. Karras waited silently for nearly a minute. On the other side of the blanket behind him, Rahel, Tony, and Yayu breathed.

Finally Rasnic lowered his rifle, and turned back to

the camera. "I became highly interested in the various phenomena—serial killers, mass murderers, rampage shooters. And all because my father liked John Wayne, the actor. You know, my mother called me Robin when I was a young boy? My father thought it sounded too girly, but I liked it. I was like Batman's sidekick. My father told me Batman and Robin were gay, and pointed to the fact that Batman dressed Robin in little green panties as proof."

"What's your question?" Karras said. "Listen, I'm not a psychologist. You know what's going on here, don't you? The police are hoping that this conversation will distract you, or somehow defuse you. I'm hoping for some material. And you're hoping... for what? What do you want to know? What do you want from me?"

"I've read all your books and enjoyed them. I've read all the books you've ever read, too."

"No," said Karras, "I don't think you have."

"We have a favorite book in common," Rasnic said. "You know, the idea of the Spectacle, and terrorism."

"Ah," Karras said. *Comments on Society of the Spectacle*, Guy Debord. No need to say it out loud. The only thing that would come of that would be some loud suit on Fox News waving it around as an antifa manual. "But look, why does it matter? Knowing about the Spectacle is the first step; it's a political discussion. It's not like the internet, where some cartoon frog hands you a red pill from *The*

Matrix and you suddenly get a thousand new idiot friends. It's not supposed to lead to this…"

Rasnic ignored him. He had a script he was acting out. "You know the bit I mean? Where the author says that all culture and nature is tainted by the Spectacle, and that society only justifies itself by pointing to its great foe: terrorism?"

"Yeah, go on," Karras said. "What's the line: *Society's wish is to be judged by its enemies rather than its results*? I remember it. Despite the glamour of the Spectacle, despite its ubiquity, society still needs a bête noire outside of itself to justify itself."

Rasnic laid his rifle down across his lap. He pulled a pistol—looked to Karras like a S&W .357 with a long barrel—from a side holster and held it under his chin. "So here's my question."

Karras lurched toward the screen, as if he could do anything. "Don't!" He practically choked on the word to keep from shouting it.

"Now we've already discussed how my name, Wayne, inspired by a film star and a father without much in the way of deep cultural connections to his own ethno-social past, in turn informed my own interest in, well, mayhem. Let's put it that way.

"So, am I a terrorist? Do I exist outside the Spectacle? I'll tell you one thing; when I rolled in to work today, I collected all my usual hellos, and distributed my regular how-ya-doin's." He affected a thicker Jersey accent for those last three words.

"Everything was normal. I was dressed like this, and everything was normal. I had my rifle in a soft carry case. Some guy asked if I played a trombone, like he was authentically interested. But when I pulled out the rifle and started shooting, and those motherfuckers started begging for their lives like I was the Lord Jesus Christ"—if Rasnic heard the gasp from behind the blanket, he didn't show it—"and it was all just like you'd expect, from the movies. On their knees, hands clasped together, telling me that *they* had kids. Saying 'fuck, fuck, fuck' over and over like a skipping record. And even me, here. A guy with a grudge and some firepower. What have I done any differently other than arranging to talk to you, other than reading your books and your old blog, and watching footage of you from your soul patch days, protesting the WTO Ministerial Conference of 1999?"

"Is that the—?"

"No," Rasnic interrupted. "That one was rhetorical. Here's the real question: did I do it? Did I break out of the Spectacle? Tell me." He nudged his chin with the barrel of the gun. "This will hurt someone!"

Karras wanted to give the answer that would save his life.

Karras wanted to give an accurate answer, maybe even if it meant Rasnic would shoot himself.

Karras realized something. This was a test. A specific test. The gun, the pose.

This will hurt someone!

Budd Dwyer.

The state treasurer of Pennsylvania, back in the 1980s. He had been convicted of racketeering and conspiracy—something to do about kickbacks for a contract with a computer company. He called a press conference to discuss the issue, and his future. Everyone understood that he was going to resign. Then from a puffy yellow envelope he withdrew a long-barred .357. Journalists, politicians, hangers-on, cried and screamed.

Holy shit!

Don't! Don't!

Why?

It had been the journalists who screamed out *Why*, Karras was sure of it. They were the ones who sussed out in an instant that he had planned a public suicide rather than a murder spree, and they wanted one last quote.

Dwyer warned them back. He was worried. "This will hurt someone!"

Not much of a quote as far as last words go, but memorable last words weren't necessary. The cameras kept rolling. Dwyer put the gun in his mouth and shot the top of his head off. It got on TV across the state—Philadelphia, Pittsburgh, Harrisburg—both for the midday and the evening news. Some stations froze the video at the moment Dwyer pulled the trigger. A couple let the whole thing air.

Dwyer's crown leaving the top of his head like a bad toupee.

The blood fountain.

Dwyer slumping to the floor.

It's on the Internet now.

Karras had watched it a few times.

He formulated a response.

"Why?"

Rasnic broke script. "Uh... why what?"

Karras smiled to himself. *People want to talk*.

"Why are you re-enacting Budd Dwyer's suicide?" Karras asked.

Rasnic giggled. "I..." He couldn't help himself. "I didn't want to end up a vegetable..." *Hee-hee-hee*. "So I found the video, to make sure I could do it... correctly. Even bought the same gun, to make sure it would be powerful enough."

Karras hmmed.

"I watched it a lot. Dozens of times." More giggling. "To psych myself up. That's the funny part..." He sniffed and wiped his nose and cheek. "I'm a Wayne, but I didn't even have to think about killing my coworkers... *me*, I'll miss...

"But only if I don't miss!"

He put the barrel of the gun in his mouth. Karras shouted "No!" the word leaping from his throat as Yayu and Rahel spilled out from behind the blanket.

"Mister, please! God loves you!" Rahel cried out as she saw the monitor.

Yayu shouted, "What's going on?!" and then shrieked as Tony slapped his big palm over her eyes.

"It's a sin!" Rahel shouted at the monitor, elbowing Karras out of the way. She grabbed it and shook it as though it were a hysterical person. "You can be forgiven if you live, but never if you die unrepentant!" Something in that worked. Rasnic took the gun from his mouth. "I killed eight people," he said.

"Five!" said Tony.

"A few are still hanging on; you must hang on too!" Rahel said.

Rasnic sniffled again, giggled again, then burst into tears. "Oh, man, what a fucking day!" He straightened up for a moment, and added, "I'm sorry to curse. Your girl is too young. I can't do this while you're all watching."

Karras saw something move in the corner of the screen. "Turn around!" he told Rasnic. "Who's there?!"

"Huh?" said Rasnic.

The security bot started retreating. Rasnic slid out of frame. The bot turned, focusing its camera on the door it was headed toward. Karras thought he might have heard a bang, and a kind of strangled noise, and a thump, but the mic atop the bot mostly just picked up the sound of its own six wheels.

"They're going to say it was a suicide," said Karras.

"What did you see?" said Rahel.

"Maybe they'll even be right."

Yayu started crying in Tony's arms. There was a knock on the bedroom door.

11.

Nothing is worse than a loose tooth. There's a certain finality to it. It's not going to heal, it's not going to grow back, there aren't many home remedies. Karras had a loose tooth now, thanks to Yayu's parents. The father, who had not been at the dinner the other night, had tackled him; Gelila kicked him repeatedly in the face. *Ah, so* that's *how they're all related,* Karras thought as he hit the pink carpeting. The girl screamed and threw herself into Rahel's arms, and after maybe two painful, awkward minutes, Tony finally said, "That's enough, uncle," and it was enough. Yayu's father picked himself up and reached out for his wife, who was breathing raggedly, but gesturing to convey she had a couple of more kicks in her.

"Just get him out," Gelila said. "You've all upset

Yayu very much. I'll be calling your mother presently."

"Auntie…"

"Would you like me to call her while you're still here, and hand you the phone?"

Karras felt himself being jerked to his knees by his armpits. Tony propped him up and walked him out to the second-story landing where Rahel sat on the top step, Yayu on her lap.

"Uh-oh," Yayu said. "But we saved that man, right?"

"Yes, we did!" Rahel said, half-hissing. She rubbed Yayu's little back and glared up at Karras, or Karras decided she was glaring, anyway. His contact lenses were all messed up from the kicking, and his eyes tearing.

Rasnic might still be alive. The noise and the sudden jerk as the camera was overturned weren't definitive, not as definitive as the jiggle of two incisors and a canine against his tongue. Yayu rushed past, a blur, and called to her parents.

"We should leave, Rahel, auntie is calling our mother," Tony said.

"We should leave, the media will be here soon," Karras said. His voice sounded funny, like he was chewing peanuts.

"How would they know where to come? I'm more concerned about the police!" Tony said, and Rahel turned her glare on him as she slapped her palms over Yayu's ears.

"And mama!" Rahel said.

Karras shrugged. "We're all agreed on leaving, aren't we? Let's just go." Rahel put Yayu on the landing and stormed down the steps, Tony right after her. Karras was slower to move; he felt the need to say something to the girl, to soothe her, to have it all make sense. And her parents were watching from the doorway to her bedroom now, waiting for something, perhaps Karras tripping and falling all the way down the steps. That would satisfy.

"Yayu," Karras said, "When you get big, there's a book you should check out. It's French, its title translates to *Treatise on Good Manners for the Younger Generations*. It'll explain a lot of what happened here tonight."

"What's a treatise?"

"Another word for a book." The parents moved out of the doorway and into the hallway, father shooing Karras with his fingers, as if Karras were an annoying gadfly. "Anyway, it's about not being treated like an object."

"Tell me your favorite part!"

"Sir, it is time for you to go, my wife has tired of you," said Yayu's father.

People want to talk, and Karras is one of them. It's just that nobody wants to listen except the child he just traumatized, who is looking for something, anything, to make sense of what she just experienced. Yayu looked up at him, hopeful but teary.

"'The boat of love breaks up in the current of everyday life,'" Karras said. "That's from the book. Okay, good-bye, excuse me!" He danced past Yayu and took to the steps two at a time just as her parents made it to where he had been standing.

By the time Karras got outside, Tony and Rahel had already left. There would be no comfortable futon tonight, no traces of turmeric and fenugreek that reminded him, after a fashion, of sleeping over at his own grandparents' house. Every ethnicity had their own spicy scents, but the homes of assimilated whites only smelled of whatever cleaning supplies were available at CVS.

Berkeley—or was he in Oakland now?—was okay, though. The street was quiet and the front yard gardens full of flowers in bloom and Jurassic succulents. The walk to wherever he would go would be pleasant enough. But where? Karras didn't have a car, didn't want to use his phone to summon one, or find a room, for fear that he would be found by…

Well, who knew? The cops, podcasters, a phantom shooter?

"Get out! Walk!" That was Gelila, leaning out a window and hollering.

"Uhm… which way to hotels?" Karras called back. He wasn't near the Alazars, wasn't sure where downtown or even the café was.

She calmed for a moment, considered. "What's your budget?"

"I'm a writer, ma'am."

"Five blocks that way to Telegraph, then walk down to the 40s. You'll see where you belong," the woman said with a wave of her hand. The slamming shut of the window punctuated the sentence.

Karras had nothing better to do than walk that way, and until he got to Telegraph the traffic was so minimal that he could, and did, stroll down the middle of the road. Telegraph Avenue itself was college-town busy for a few blocks, with strolling knots of college kids self-segregating by race, innumerable bad restaurants and dingy-looking headshops and 'Tibetan stores,' which brought to mind the old joke *Free Tibet! With the purchase of another Tibet of equal or greater value*. But after a few blocks, that all dropped away. Karras stopped, wondering if he'd made some mistake. He reached for his phone, a reflex that Apple had built into his nervous system after years of positive reinforcement via vibrations and pleasant tones. The phone was directions, money, companionship, power. The phone moved the center of the universe from some distant and black point seven billion light-years away and into the frontal lobes of one Michael Karras, every single time he looked at the screen and scraped his thumb across it.

But dare he? The thing about being the center of the universe is that everyone in the universe can point right at you and say, "Ah, there's the asshole!"

Of course, that was surely already happening. A

drone had found him, his phone had been hacked, and his laptop too. He'd been on the news, the real news of the sort even grandparents consume, not just the internet. Karras was just blind and deaf to it all—wasn't there a black hole at the center of the universe anyway, or at least the center of the galaxy? Michael Karras was on the wrong side of the event horizon.

"Fuck it," he said aloud, and turned the phone back on. In the seconds it took for the screen to appear and Karras to type his code, he was already impatient. No 5G in Berkeley yet, where half the population was sure it caused everything from brain cancer to deadly viruses. A zillion notifications nearly shook the phone out of his hand.

Karras called Rahel. He knew a text wouldn't do, though he desperately wanted that second layer of estrangement. Maybe she wouldn't pick up. Generation Z never picked up—

"Mister Karras!" she answered immediately. "Where are you?"

"Where are you?"

"Home!" she said. "You think I could wait around for you? Be seen with you? I managed to fish your typewriter and papers out of the trash. Your computer too. I can meet you and give them to you. My father doesn't want you to starve to death for whatever reason, and he's decided that your work tools are like a gravedigger's shovel; you need them to live. I daresay he's righter than he knows."

"Where do you want to meet?"

"Where are you?"

"Uhm…" Karras looked around the darkening street. "Telegraph and… I dunno. There are a lot of medical offices around? Maybe ten minutes from Yayu's house? Let me look on my—"

"No no, I know where you are. There's a grocery nearby, Whole Foods. Just find it." She stopped talking, but the phone was still so active from notifications that Karras couldn't tell if she disconnected or just got quiet.

"Hello?" Karras said into the phone. "Hello, are you there?"

"Yes, yes, what?"

"Well, okay, just seeing if you're there."

"Don't you have anything else to say to me?"

His throat zipped shut. Karras had to push the words out of his belly, out his mouth. "I'm sorry. Thank you so much. I'm sorry for everything."

"Exactly. Good-bye."

Rahel arrived quickly, and she had walked. Karras must have been *severely* turned around without access to GPS.

"Do you want to go inside and get a—?"

"You are cursed, Mister Karras," Rahel said, shoving his bag, laptop case, and awkward plastic typewriter case into his hands. She was perspiring from the weather and exertion and, likely, her temper. Karras wanted to lick her face clean. "You need prayer. I am praying for you, and even Tony is, but most of all you need to pray for yourself. Get on your knees."

"You mean literally?" he asked. It wasn't impossible. The parking lot of the Whole Foods wasn't so crowded, and it was Berkeley. He'd only be the third oddest person milling around, after the bearded old man playing a pair of rubber bands in the exterior seating section, and the armed security guard boredly running through a qigong routine.

"Yes, literally," Rahel said. She grabbed his arm as he started to lower himself, "But not here; what's wrong with you?"

"Look, I'm just sorry, okay?" Karras said.

"You don't need to make a spectacle of yourself just because you're sorry," Rahel said. "Spectacle, yes, like that murderer was talking about. What is it with men, that they have to turn everything from rage to sorrow into some kind of public display—anywhere *but* church, of course?"

Karras couldn't look at her anymore. The security guard was pretty interesting, but he was making a spectacle of himself too. "I guess so; men do that. We're the peacocks of the species, not the peahens," he said. And then he muttered, "Or is that bioessentialist...?"

"And you can actually have a conversation with someone, in private, without worrying about what an invisible audience of politically annoying people are going to jump on you about," Rahel said.

"Yeah."

"What's the difference between you and that madman—he thought he was putting on a show, and he was trapped in a show at the same time too," Rahel said. "You're not violent. It just follows you around. But violence doesn't just follow people around, Mister Karras. You're not violent *yet*, maybe."

"You reached out to *me*, Rahel," Karras said. "I'm not even religious, and if I were religious, I'd be—I don't know—arguing some fine point of theology with you."

"You would be, for show. Everything is for show, for spectacle."

The argument just seemed pointless, like trying to force a loose tooth back into place with one's tongue. Of course Karras didn't care about the fine points of theology, because he wasn't religious. If he were religious, then he would care, by definition. It's not just about Spectacle, though clearly the kidases Rahel sat through every week were Spectacle, designed to short-circuit rationality through sensory overload, so who was she to even…?

He was arguing with himself about not being intrinsically argumentative.

"You're right," he said. "I'm sorry for everything. I don't have any answers for you. Thank you for bringing my things."

"Yes, I am right. It's all my fault as I was the one who wrote to you in the first place, but I am right.

Also, that Rasnic fellow is dead," Rahel said.

"May his memory be eternal..." Karras mumbled. That's what his grandparents would say whenever anyone died, on the news, in their family, or back in Greece after the letter confirming it had finally reached them.

"Do you even know what that means?"

"That we should keep the dead in our th—"

"No." Her voice sounded like Karras's mechanical keyboard. A hard fourth finger on the return key. "It's a prayer, a request that the soul of the dead be kept in *God's* memory, not ours. At any rate, as Mister Rasnic took his own life—"

"How do you know he took his own life?" Karras risked snapping at Rahel, despite her being on edge, despite him being burdened with all his stuff in hand, despite the two of them standing in public, in a grocery store parking lot. "How do you know he's even dead?"

"I saw it, just like you did!"

"And I don't know he's dead. And you don't know he's dead. And maybe he is dead, but maybe he didn't kill himself," said Karras. "Do you actually know?"

Rahel threw up her hands and took a step backward. That looked bad enough that the security guard stopped his butterfly stroke-looking qigong move mid-pose and took a step closer to the curb.

"Don't make a scene!" Karras hissed.

Rahel glanced over at the guard, smiled, and waved.

"Fine," she said.

"That's what it's all about. Who knows what happened, with him, in Oklahoma, with you? Why did the cop shoot Lee Nam-jin when he was already down? Was he even down? Some people can shrug off a Taser like it was nothing."

"I don't know… I didn't see…"

"Exactly. And what you did see, you believe."

"The second shooter."

"And nobody else did, and nobody else believes you, but—"

"My family does," Rahel said. "They know me. I don't lie."

"But you've been mistaken," Karras said. "Reaching out to me was a mistake, wasn't it? I don't blame you for saying so, for thinking so. It's been weird, dangerous even. So I'm not saying you're lying, I'm saying we don't know what's going on. But you're right; I shouldn't be a part of the Spectacle. I'm trying! I got the typewriter, but the drone came, I was trending…"

Rahel snorted. "You were trending. I was trending once. I don't want to repeat the experience. You're a writer, but for someone like me, there's only one way to get trending."

"Yeah," Karras said. "I'm sorry. I have no answers for you. I'll leave you alone if you want."

"You need to leave everyone else alone," Rahel said. "I have to think about whether I can trust you with my story, with myself."

"I was dragged into the Rasnic thing, though…" Karras said.

"You weren't dragged into Yayu's bedroom," Rahel said. "Next time, just go to the police. I know, ay-cab and all that, but you have to make a choice, Mister Karras. You're one of those 'the truth is out there' people—I get it. I'm one too. But when you're looking for the truth, someone is going to get hurt.

"And you have a choice: it could be you getting hurt, or it could be someone else. Don't *always* pick the someone else. I have no respect for someone like that."

"Okay."

"Good night," Rahel said. "I'll pray for you tonight, and contact you tomorrow. Maybe."

And with that, she jogged off, emphatically uninterested in how Karras might wish her a good night. It would have just been a woebegone *Well, have a good evening*, so she wasn't missing much.

Now Karras had a decision to make. His phone's battery was running low on juice, and the Whole Foods was closing. Rahel was right—when he put himself out there, in public, people got hurt. He was taking risks too, but it was always someone else so far who had suffered the consequences. Even a motel room or an Airbnb could be dangerous.

As the cashiers shooed the last few customers into the parking lot, the security guard made his way over to the fellow strumming the rubber bands and initiated what was clearly a nightly conversation. The strummer hung his head, and muttered something that made the guard laugh. They exchanged exaggerated shrugs. Then the strummer got up, slowly, and reached for a folding shopping wagon full past bursting with black plastic garbage bags. The security guard pointed at the man, who had a pretty severe limp and held the wagon before himself to use as a walker, and made a shooing motion. Then he turned to Karras and pointed.

"You too!" he said. "No loitering after hours. Or even during hours."

"Where can I—?"

"Don't *where can I* me. You go!"

Karras sighed and shuffled over with his stuff to the guard. He wanted the guard to get a good look at him. Karras had read a study—no, that wasn't quite right, he had been told about a study that someone else had read once—that people with homes do not register the unhoused on the streets as fellow human beings, but as some type of urban obstacle, along the lines of a boarded-up storefront or a stripped car.

The other guy, who was more fundamentally unhoused than Karras, stopped and stretched his rubber band between his thumb and forefinger, then started plucking it. *Bum-ba-bum-ba-bum*! The guard laughed.

"On November 13, Felix Unger was asked to remove himself from his place of residence…" the guard said. The unhoused guy, playing the tune, smiled like a jack o'lantern.

"Look, I need some help. Where's the nearest motel?" Karras asked.

"Couple miles thataway," the unhoused guy said, pointing with his chin. "Gonna call an Uber, hot shot? Maybe a ladybug, and have it drive you around all night? Little cheaper that way, if you don't mind pissing in a water bottle."

"Felix and Oscar, take this conversation elsewhere," the guard said. "I want to go home." He casually placed his hands on his belt. The Berkeley Whole Foods kept armed guards on salary.

"We gotta leave him to pour bleach over all the vegetables and bagels in the dumpster, you know," said the man as he put his hands back on his wagon. "Follow me."

"I don't care if you follow him or not, but you can't stay here."

"I wasn't planning on staying here," Karras said.

"Let's go, Felix. You can call me Oscar," said the man as he pushed his cart before him. Karras could feel his own spinal fluid starting to bubble.

Oscar led Karras off Telegraph Avenue and onto a very nice-looking side street filled with tiny blooming front gardens, night bees flitting back and forth, and tasteful detached homes with large bay windows and the occasional sign for Black Lives Matter and local Green Party political candidates on display.

Just two blocks from the grocery store stood a small triangular park—really, an overgrown traffic island that had been improved with some fencing, a bench, and a small swing set. "We have privacy here," Oscar said. "See—no streetlamps. It's a rich block. That's the way the world works. In the ghettos, no streetlamps because the city won't bother to maintain or repair them. In fancy areas, it's dark because a Homeowners' Association can put an end to light pollution with a snap of their fingers." Oscar snapped his now, and the sound echoed across the tiny park. "Only upon the middle does the light shine. They want to see, and be seen.

"We'll be safe here," Oscar concluded. He sat himself down not on but by the park bench, nestling between a pair of bushes, and positioned his wagon to make a little nook in the dark.

"Nobody to bother you, eh?" Karras said. He could find his way back to the Whole Foods easily. There was a bus stop on the corner of that block, a gas station across the street in the direction opposite from here. He'd find someone helpful to point him the right way. He should have gone to the gas station immediately and waited for a taxi to come by looking for a refill. His damn teeth were driving him to distraction, and he could feel a little mouse forming on his left brow too. Was he concussed? *Am I concussed?* Karras thought. *Are you concussed?* Karras asked himself.

"Nobody to bother us," Oscar said.

The little talent Karras possessed kicked in, almost. He didn't quite know what Oscar was going to say, not exactly. His vision was a little wobbly; he was almost seeing double. Two possibilities:

A knife, and a threat. In the dark, where it's safe. The wealthy have great bay windows so that others may look in; they're not for looking out.

Or, "So, are you a fag? Do you like to suck dick? Get your dick sucked?"

There were two surprises. The first is that Oscar produced both his half-hard cock and a knife. "You suck dick?" he asked, conversationally. "If you do, you can, okay? I'll do you after." The knife didn't even seem like a threat, but rather something Oscar liked to hold whenever inviting someone to get close to him.

The second surprise was that Karras's phone rang. The phone he'd turned off, and that was barely even holding a charge.

"Pick it up, man!" Oscar said between the second and third rings. "Someone's gonna hear!" He didn't put the knife away, though.

Karras dug for his phone and glanced at the screen. There was no call to receive; someone had logged on to his Google account, located the phone, and requested that it start ringing, as though he'd lost it somewhere in his apartment.

Had to be Little Round Bombs.

"One sec, one sec…" Karras pretended to mutter to himself as he unlocked his phone, started it up, and quickly called Sharon. Oscar gestured with his knife, first to the phone, then to his other hand, which was holding his half-hard dick, and then broadly at the phone and at Karras, who certainly noticed that one of the sweeping curves of the blade drew the point right across his neck.

"Good evening, Michael," said Sharon. "What's going on? You've been incommunicado and it's been a bit of a madhouse around here, as you can imagine."

"Oh, hello, darling," said Karras. Oscar hissed again, and Karras lifted a finger and shushed him like a librarian might warn a child in a television commercial for some extreme form of bubblegum. Oscar stopped waving the knife.

"Is that your wi—?"

Karras shushed him again, more forcefully.

"Am I interrupting something?" Sharon's voice was louder than Karras expected. He pulled his ear from the phone. Back when Karras first went on the road, Little Round Bombs' one-person IT department downloaded some software onto it to make checking work emails easy and secure. Karras hadn't realized at the time that this gave Sharon complete control over the damned thing. "Who is there? Who are you shushing?"

"Hello, ma'am," said Oscar from across the brief park, but too quietly.

"I'm almost out of juice, honey-bunny," Karras said, "and I suppose I was entertaining someone new.

He's very into enthusiastic consent. You might say it's like my life depends on it."

"Are you two"—Sharon both projected and somehow raised the volume of Karras's phone; he pulled it away from his ear—"doing all right?"

"Just having a conversation, ma'am!" Oscar called out. "A casual conversation."

"I'd call it a rather pointed conversation," Karras said into the phone.

"We're just sittin' on the grass, ma'am," said Oscar.

"I see," said Sharon. "Well, Agent K, I think we both know what this calls for. How much do you think the target knows?"

It took all of Karras's will to keep his face from twitching into a smile. The loose teeth, an annoying distraction all evening, helped a bit. He jammed his tongue at them.

"Aw, bullshit," Oscar said. "I saw you getting dressed down by that girl. You're no cop."

"A girl, eh?" Sharon said, more quietly, but the phone was still loud enough, and the balance of the night still enough that Oscar could hear.

"Yup, black girl sent him packing," Oscar told Sharon. "I guess if he's your man, he really has no home to get back to."

She was going to play, Karras realized. Sharon put herself on speaker—she had much more control over the phone than just being able to locate it and make it ring.

"Oh, he's coming back all right, and I want him back in one piece, mister," Sharon said. "If anyone is going to smack my man around, it's gonna be me!"

Gonna is the sort of thing Sharon never said. Karras was nearly smiling again. Good thing his teeth hurt; he could still feel the warmth of Gelila's sole on his cheek.

Oscar laughed. "Yes, ma'am!" he said. "Yes, ma'am!"

"Well, uh, bright-eyes, thanks for checking in," Karras said.

"We can talk about that girl later," Sharon said. Oscar snorted at that and put away his knife. "Sweet dreams."

"Yeah, sweet dreams." He wondered for a moment if he should say *I love you*, or would that be laying it on too thick. Oscar's knife was already away, and the man's erection was well in-hand, so no need for Karras to participate. It didn't matter; Sharon disconnected before Karras could take a breath.

"'Sweet dreams,'" Oscar said. "So, what are you?"

"What am I?"

"Like, are you an Arab? Spanish? You gotta nose on you, eyebrows," Oscar said.

"I'm Greek. Both my parents are Greek. My mother was born in Greece."

"Oh, yeah," Oscar said. "The land of souvlaki and spanakopita! I love that shit, man. Does your wife cook Greek food for you?"

Karras wished the knife and the cock were back. But he said yes, because that's what Oscar wanted to hear. Karras said yes to many, many things, about Greek food, some Italian dishes Oscar thought were Greek, and how his wife liked to be fucked, and was Chicago really that dangerous like they say on the radio, and did Karras suck dick in college and only stop after he got married, yes, yes, yes to an entire imaginary life, until Oscar finally took his leave to piss—not in the little park, as the neighbors would forget their community-minded liberalism if even a single blade of grass was turned yellow by uric acid and have Oscar arrested, beaten, and driven past the county line, but against the wall of the Whole Foods—and did not return.

12.

THE ASIAN KID'S name was Jerry, and the white kid was still calling himself Logan Dark. That's how they introduced themselves the next morning when they woke Karras up.

"What's your name really?" Karras asked. "You obviously just gave yourself that name because you like Wolverine and want to be cool and tough."

Jerry smiled, wide. Imperfect teeth. Immigrant parents, Karras knew. At least one, anyway. Neither was part of the upper class of their old countries— Jerry was probably Filipino, or mixed. Maybe half-Chinese. Logan was a mush of ruddiness and big bones; his parents probably referred to themselves as 'Heinz 57' or 'mutts,' or in their moments of self-awareness 'white bread,' and had no idea what their surnames meant or even came from.

"It's Dennis!" Jerry said. Logan—Dennis—stayed stoic, like a young man who had just read part of a book on Stoicism after hearing about the philosophy on the Internet.

"Everyone's looking for you. All the fans, here, in the city, in Oakland."

"Contra Costa County," Jerry added. "Everywhere."

"You're the lucky ones," Karras said. He hadn't slept well, but he had slept hard. The Berkeley sun was rising rapidly, steaming the sweat off his limbs. He gulped and spit out a mouthful of blood and phlegm. "You found me."

"No, you're the lucky one. The police are looking for you too," said Jerry.

Dennis pulled a smartphone, a very nice one, from the pocket of his duster. He was a chubby kid with a scraggly beard. He already smelled like sweat socks and mother's lavender soap. Jerry at least dressed somewhat sensibly for the weather—basketball shorts and flip-flops, a white T-shirt—but Karras had the sense that Jerry dressed like that for Christmas and forest fires too.

"I got a police scanner app on this bad boy," said Dennis.

"Don't say bad boy," said Jerry.

"Why do the police want me?" Karras asked. It sounded stupid and heavy leaving his mouth, like he was spitting up something he had eaten on a bet. It was obvious that they'd want to talk to him about Rasnic, in case he'd seen something.

Something along the lines of one of the cops killing Rasnic.

"We can help you," said Dennis. "We can get you to Bennett's show. You'll be safe there."

"It's like, if you're so obvious and public, nobody will try anything," Jerry added.

Karras picked himself up, and stretched. "You know, dissidents are poisoned with nerve agents, journalists gunned down in the street…"

"Pedophiles hanged in prison!" said Jerry. Dennis smacked him on the shoulder with his fat fingers. "Dude! The neighborhood."

"You found me because you live here?"

"I was watching you all night," Jerry said, "but it was Logan's idea to help you."

"We can drive you to Nevada. I want to meet Chris Bennett!"

"You guys can drive?" It was an easier question to ask than *Why on Earth would I want to go on Bennett's show? What's wrong with you incels? Can I manipulate you into driving me anywhere else on Earth? Do you know any cheap dentists?* But there was no need to wait for the answer. He had nowhere to go, and the police would probably put him in lock-up, at least, for vagrancy and impersonating an unhomed individual (a protected class).

He'd truly beefed it with Rahel. The thought

manifested as an instant migraine. Better to contemplate anything else.

"Of course you can drive," Karras said. "Provisional licenses, so you need an adult to go anywhere, and your parents aren't going to chaperone a hajj to Bennett's girlfriend's father's mansion." He pointed his chin at Dennis. "You're the one with the car. A make-up present for living in a mediocre part of town while all your friends live in this fancy joint. That's why you're nervous and hiding it."

"Not bad," said Dennis.

"And you," Karras said to Jerry. "No car, because you have bad grades. GPA perhaps even below 3.8. If only you were white, those would have been great grades."

"That's pretty racist thinking," said Jerry.

"Thoughts you've probably had nonetheless. And no hardcore Bennett fan gets to complain about racism. The only shootings the guy believes ever happens are cops shooting black kids, and he's all for them. He used to sound a vuvuzela and shout 'Goal!' when a report came over the wires," said Karras.

"One rule in my car: no political talk," said Dennis.

"I have some bad news for you about the trip," Karras said. "We're not going to Nevada."

On the way to Los Angeles, Dennis declared a number of other rules. Karras would sit up front. No touching the radio—Dennis had prepared a two-hour

'Best Of Bennett' mix, with looping breakbeats as bed music, which they'd now need to listen to twice in a row since LA was twice as far as Reno. He would choose two of the rest stops or restaurants to stop at, and Jerry was allowed to select a third stop. Karras wasn't to complain about lunch, and had to pony up, cash, for filling the tank of the 2018 Honda Civic. Jerry wasn't allowed to stretch out in the backseat, nor fall asleep.

"I'll put this mother in cruise control, climb back there, and kick your ass," Dennis said, as they merged onto 580.

"I'll choke your ass out, son," Jerry said, though he was careful to only take up three-quarters of the back seat, arranging himself as though on a chaise lounge.

"What do you kids plan on doing once we get to Bennett's?" Karras asked.

"We'll get a hotel room and stay the night," Dennis said. He glanced at Jerry in the rearview mirror. "I brought my Nintendo."

Karras allowed himself a smile. "How are you going to get a hotel room? Do either of you have a credit card—I mean one that your parents don't control? You don't think a charge made three hundred and fifty miles away from home won't trip some sort of fraud algorithm?"

The kids didn't say anything. Karras hmmed, and then hmmmed a second time, with an interrogative inflection. Dennis peered straight ahead, his grip at

10 and 2 and turning his knuckles white; Jerry twisted uncomfortably in the back.

"Were you thinking Bennett would give you a bag full of cash, maybe one with a dollar-sign stamped on the side?" Karras asked. "And that any hotel without meth pipe burns on the toilet seats and bullet holes in the walls is going to take cash and let you stay?"

"Well," said Dennis, "how about I make a rule that you secure the hotel room in exchange for the ride? Or you can get out right now."

"Okay, pull over," said Karras. "I'll walk back to town, call Bennett's people. They'll have me on a plane in two hours."

"Let's don't fight, everyone," Jerry said. Karras had a sense of what the next sentence would be, and smiled because it was something his mother used to say. "Let's play a car game to pass the time." But then Karras sensed something darker than I Spy was about to bubble forth from Jerry's lips.

He wouldn't, Karras thought, but then Jerry did. "What would you put in your kid's comfort kit?"

"To survive or to win?" Dennis asked. "And what grade?"

"We didn't have comfort kits when I was in school," Karras said.

"They're good for earthquakes too, if the kids get stuck at school because the parents can't come pick them up," Jerry said.

"Survive or win, what grade?" Dennis said again. "I'm thinking some blasting caps."

"A kindergartener with explosives?" Jerry asked. Karras contemplated a nap, but Jerry's voice, an enthusiastic door on rusty hinges, was just the wrong tone to sleep through. He closed his eyes.

"Wedge caps under the classroom door, so when the shooter kicks it open, it goes off," Dennis said. "A second-grader could manage that. Maybe use it to escape too; blow a window open."

"Remember when you were in second grade, Logan?" Jerry stretched out across the entire back seat, violating one of the rules. Would Dennis put the car in cruise control? Karras slitted his eyelids to see. "You would have blown your fingers off with a blasting cap—heck, you used to love 'smoking' your pencil. You would have blasted your jaw to pieces."

"I'm not talking about my comfort kit. I'm talking about what I would pack in my kid's comfort kit," Dennis said.

"Get laid first before you start having hypothetical kids," Jerry said.

"I only need to get hypothetically laid to have hypothetical kids," Dennis said. "I'll never be a Proud Boy." The boys giggled at themselves. Karras chuckled too, a mistake.

"I could smell that you were awake," Dennis said.

"I saw that movie when I was a kid," Karras said. "On VHS."

"So what would you recommend for a comfort kit, Mister Karras?" asked Jerry, politely.

Karras yawned, thought about it. It was sufficiently horrifying to contemplate that his brain wouldn't work properly. Having a kid, having even a spouse, being a dad. Jeans gone, inexplicably replaced with khakis. A baseball cap to cover his thinning hair. Karras didn't even like the game. If he had a boy, Karras would have to call him 'buddy' or something, and if it were a girl? 'Princess'? Do people with no money call their daughters 'princess'? He supposed he could use *koukla*, the Greek word for 'doll,' which his aunts and uncles had used liberally to refer to all young children. And what if he had more than one kid, or his partner did? A woman who wanted to breed, to be bred like some kind of racehorse, but then why bother with Karras's obviously mediocre genes—

"Mike?" Jerry prodded tentatively.

"Sorry," Karras muttered. "Uhm... what, are we talking about anything at all that fits in a comfort pack, or something practically accessible?"

"Just tell us a story, Mister Karras," Jerry said.

"Okay—practical, a burner phone with a drone app on it," Karras said. "On the night before the first day of school, just pilot the drone onto the roof of the school and leave it there. Train the kid over the summer in its use; anything from video to just sending it into the face of the shooter."

"Not bad," said Dennis with a single nod.

"Not bad at all," said Karras.

"That's the practically accessible choice," said Jerry, "but you clearly had another, more extreme idea."

Karras decided that he liked Jerry, a little. He had some discernment to him. Probably why Dennis liked him too. That and Jerry indulged Dennis on his choice of name, which likely nobody else did. Jerry was a good kid—how did he get wrapped up in Bennett, and garbage boy culture?

Karras suddenly had an answer for the boys, one they wouldn't like. One he didn't like either. He didn't even know from where in his brain it had come. "A couple drops of batrachotoxin. *Baah*-tra-xhos is the Greek word for 'frog.'"

"Whoa," said Jerry.

"Of course, the frogs, various species of poison dart frog in Colombia, get the toxin from their environment—the beetles they eat. So it's not like you can start a little batrachotoxin factory with a coffee can full of tadpoles, and wild frogs are both rare and hard to catch anyway. But a couple drops would be all it would take," Karras said. "Works quick, no antidote."

"How would you deliver it to the shooter?" Jerry asked.

"A dart?" Karras said with a shrug. "A little spray bottle. It doesn't matter. All the kids in all the classes would have it in this scenario, and we'd publicize it. Mutually assured destruction. Any shooter tries it, he doesn't get to kill anyone; he just witnesses some of the kids dying. No 'high score' for them. He doesn't get to off himself in some 'blaze of glory'"—Karras cringed inwardly as he found himself speaking in cliché and participating in the insane logic of the imperial state, which was also a cliché—"and so there's no reason to shoot up a school, well, no reason to shoot up an elementary school if you're a teenager. Defending high schools is another matter entirely. Those attacks are usually personal on some level. But then again, young men such as you two are too old for comfort kits. What do you keep in your lockers, or on your persons, as self-defense?"

Neither answered. "Yeah, it's scary to think about, so you focus on the fact that it might happen to other people, vulnerable kindergarteners. But it's even more frightening to think about your own situation, and then actually *do* something about it," Karras said. That shut the kids up. Karras even reached over and clicked off the speakers without any objection from Dennis, then settled back in the passenger-side seat and fell asleep for most of the rest of the ride south. He could feel the curve of the Earth under him as they drove, as though the car's tires were always on the verge of riding off the ground and straight into space.

"Mister Karras," Dennis said. Karras wasn't quite sure how long later, but the voice was nervous enough to draw Karras from his pleasant torpor. "Uhm… we're here."

Here was a small cinder-block pillbox of a warehouse amidst a not-great smear of concrete and soot-stained palm trees that passed as a neighborhood. The smog was heavy in the air, and it was unusually humid for LA, like the grayness of the air was a lid over a slow-simmering pot.

"Year Zero Worldwide," said Karras. Dennis was on the verge of tears, it was obvious. Jerry looked up from his phone, his mouth an aggrieved line across his face. "Yeah, this is it."

"This is it," said Dennis. "Where's the infinity pool? The big lawn? Hell, where's the blue sky? I thought the weather was always supposed to be nice in LA. Are we even *in* LA proper?"

"Ah, the pathetic fallacy," said Karras. Both boys started in their seats, the air in the car vanished. "Google it later, boys. I'm not calling either of *you* pathetic."

"Don't blame us," Jerry said. "California public schools are poorly funded. We're practically illiterate." He laughed at his own joke.

They parked in the lot and got buzzed in. Year Zero was one of several operations renting space in the building, which disappointed the boys even further. They followed Karras down the hall, around two corners, and to the significant metal door of Bennett's office with their shoulders slumped, and in silence.

"That looks promising, at least," Dennis said, eyeing the door. Then it opened and Bennett himself answered. The reality was obvious: a handsome enough guy who knew his way around barbells, but his hair a tangled mess and matted, barely five-foot-five, wearing a ratty T-shirt he'd once done some house-painting in and jean shorts. In the hand not on the doorhandle was a Glock. Dennis smiled a little, Jerry gulped, and Karras could almost feel the emesis of flop sweat from him. Bennett's face was screwed up too, eyes wide and wiggling in their sockets. A very different guy when not behind the mic.

"Hello, Chris," Karras said. "I'm here to be on the show. These two young men are great fans of yours. Jerry and... Logan."

"I'm Logan," said Dennis. Jerry practically vibrated, but said nothing. His gaze didn't, couldn't, leave the gun.

"Karras," Bennett said. "Where have you been? Offline, for real? Haven't you heard the news? This is not a good day to begin Operation Fuss-Up."

Karras knew what was coming next, so skipped ahead. "Bad, eh?"

"Come inside."

"What's Operation Fuss-Up?" Jerry asked. Bennet put the pistol to his own lips and shushed.

Year Zero Worldwide did employ a receptionist, but she was peering at her computer monitor, earbuds in, mouth agape, exhaling noisily. She didn't look up when Bennett said, "Thanks for answering the door, Suzanne." Suzanne could have been Bennett's mother, given her age and casual resemblance—she, too, was somewhat disheveled, and had Bennett's sandy hair and lemur eyes. She ignored Bennett, and the rest of them.

"We'll watch in the studio before going live. You two"—he gestured lazily with the gun to the teens—"you need to stay here."

"What the fuck is going on?" Dennis asked.

Karras knew because the words were about to leave the receptionist's lips. "School shooting. Big one. Thirty kids, maybe thirty-five. Rooftop sniping, right as some kind of field day was wrapping up. Pretty rare timing—near the end of the school day instead of the beginning. A junior high school in Central Jersey."

"There's no way a kid can kill thirty-five classmates from a roof," said Bennett. "False flag."

"We don't even know who the shooter is yet," said Suzanne. "Or what he wanted. Could have been he was after the parents come to pick up their kids? Could have been a parent."

"We know enough," Bennet said. "C'mon, Karras, let's see what we can see."

"We're coming too," Jerry said. "We drove a long way."

"Are you even anybody?" Bennet asked. He turned to Karras. "Who are these guys?"

"Your biggest fans," said Karras, who was walking away to position himself behind the receptionist to look at the news streaming from her monitor.

"My biggest fans are in the Senate and the NSA," said Bennett. "Believe it. Are you two anybody?"

"My name is Logan—"

"Are you on YouTube? How many Chit-Chat followers do you have?"

"He has a DeviantArt page," Jerry offered.

On the screen, it was typical news cycle stuff. The same forty seconds of footage airing again and again—a parent's cell phone footage of some kids doing a pep flag routine, then a group in the bleachers start running into the field. There's a general scrum, with teens crashing into one another, falling, tripping. The camera goes wild as the parent starts to stumble backward. Then a thin twig of a silhouette on the corner of the low school building and too much movement for the phone's chip to deal with, and nothing. Karras doubted the voiceover would have added anything; the receptionist was watching CNN—Bennet would likely screen another channel in his studio—and CNN didn't ever speculate overmuch until the police told them they could.

"We're live in five, Mike," Bennett said. "We're not going to run the show I just taped this morning—it's all stuff about H7N9; it's gonna kill us all if we allow it, you know, but god damn if nobody cares. This is money, though. Let's go."

"We promise not to talk if we can come too," Jerry said to Bennett, who shrugged and said, "I'm not going to put you people on my YouTube channel so your parents can sue my ass. Audio only."

"This is really happening, do you understand?" Karras said. It wasn't really a question.

"It's a false flag."

"How do you know?" asked Dennis.

"It's always a false flag," Bennett and Karras said at once.

"Four minutes," said Suzanne. "I'm going to go and turn on the mics, and the feed."

In those four minutes, something else happened. As Bennett and Karras took their seats, put on their headphones, went through the mic check, and while Karras sat wondering who it could have been that had tried to book him on the show, who was erasing his research, and was there anything at all he could say or do—admit everything he was suspected of and leave it to Bennett to explain it all to his listeners, reach out and strangle him?—a young girl from Middlesex Middle had seized a local news camera whose operator had been slain and was shouting into it:

"They killed us! We kept trying to tell the teachers, tell the counselors, but nobody listened!" The girl immediately attracted the attention of both boys, who were sitting—she had wing eyeliner, now smeared, and was bald save for a long blue braid down the middle of her head. A septum piercing and a nose ring. "The guns, they had so many guns!" More shots rang out and she ran off. The boys pulled out their phones.

"And we're live," said Chris Bennett. "Welcome, kamerads—and that's with a k—to *Year Zero*. You just heard live footage from a New 12 New Jersey camera, piped in through the satellite system. Not sure if that went on over the air in Jersey, but you, kamerads, heard it here first. 'They killed us.' And in a remarkable coincidence—but you know by now there are no coincidences—we have with us one Michael Karras. We've spoken about him before."

Karras really did want to strangle Bennett now, organically, with the man's own headphone cord. He was good, though, riffing on the tiniest data, drawing connections between concepts more like a Dadaist than a broadcast journalist, and without a single hesitation, stammer, or quaver in that black hole voice.

"And now we are speaking to him—yes, the same Michael Karras who was at the site of the Islamicist Stillwater Truck Massacre, who was more recently discovered in Berkeley, yes *that* Berkeley, California, supposedly researching the massacre carried out last year by Korean Lee Nam-jin—"

"He was born in Cupertino," Karras interjected.

"We'll get to that if we get to that, Mike," Bennett shot back. "But today we are talking about the ongoing situation at Middlesex Middle School—Middle Middle, is that a glitch in the Matrix?—and what we just heard. '*They* killed us,' said a crisis actor who apparently forgot her lines in the excitement. At least she looked alive, if a bit undead with her vampire make-up. So, *they*. Who is *they*, Mike?"

Karras reminded himself of the single most important thing to keep in mind when on talk radio: listeners are immune to irony. In fact, they invariably invert it, claiming irony only when declaiming their most heartfelt beliefs.

"*They* refers to the shooter we can see on other footage," said Karras, "and a second shooter. It's almost inevitable—echoes, confusion, shock, the fact that eyewitnesses are generally fairly unreliable. People see more shooters than there are in these events. Of course, some mass shootings *are* carried out by pairs: Columbine and San Bernadino come immediately to mind."

"So why didn't this witness just name the shooters? Middlesex Middle doesn't look like a huge school, and she claims that she and other students have been 'warning' the faculty and counselors. Something doesn't fit," Bennett said. He mashed a button on the console in front of him and a digital peal of thunder flooded the room, followed by a vocodered voice intoning the words "*Anomalous activity*."

The boys giggled at that. Bennett shot them a look.

"'They' is clearly just a memetic gambit," Bennett continued. "We all know who *they* are, they are the elites who organize these false flag operations. I'm not just talking about the government, or the so-called CEOs who are really as red as Mao when you get right down to it. The occult they, the Illuminati; *they* gain spiritual power by hiding in plain sight, by claiming responsibility in exoteric ways! You see it in music videos, you see it on dollar bills, you see it on certain dates—it's not just preparations for taking our guns, it's preparations for a Satanic New World Order."

"Maybe the shooter was non-binary," Dennis said, leaning forward and projecting.

Bennett clicked a switch on the console. "Shut up."

"Maybe the shooter was non-binary," Karras said into his mic. He glanced down at the board. The peak meter lights bounced pleasingly; he had gotten through to the audience. "So, *they* was used in the singular, as in Shakespeare." He winked and nodded, pointed a little finger-gun at Dennis, who did the same thing back. "'There's not a man I meet but doth salute me/ As if I were their well-acquainted friend,' that's from *The Comedy of Errors*, Act IV, Scene 3." There was blood in his mouth from all the talking, and the loose tooth. He swallowed the blood, then smiled, hoping his incisors and canines were painted red.

"'They,' eh?" Bennett said. "So we have an agenda here—the undermining of sexuality, of gender, of personhood, of language itself. You think the shooter is a 'non-binary' now? A hermaphrodite? We've talked about them on the show before—"

"Bet it was tasteful and thoughtful," Karras interjected.

"The Rebis; the Divine hermaphrodite of alchemy,

the Great Work of the occult elite. See, they're trying to create this, to manifest this, now"—Bennett took a swig from a bottled water—"and that girl was pretty androgynous too. Total *Fury Road* thing going on. It all makes sense now. A Satanic rite to create a goat-headed girl-titted Baphomet idol, with 'they' as the singular magical trigger word."

"Maybe she was just nervous."

"Stage fright, Michael?"

"She was almost killed. She saw her friends die. She could *still* be killed—that footage you just ran could be her last words," said Karras. "What the hell are you doing? There are a bunch of kids dying on the grass in their junior high school, right now. Some other kid in school got their hands on an assault rifle, and—"

"Here we go!" said Bennett. He pressed another button, and a staccato burst of gunfire played, followed by high-pitched female voice keening "*Assaaaault Riiiifle.*"

"Is this the time to debate gun-grabbing, Michael? I guess you think it is, but you're not on my show to spread play-pretend politics over the bodies of young boys and girls. It's not the time!"

"When is the time?"

"Not right after a mass shooting."

"It's *always* right after a shooting, Chris," Karras said. "And always right before FEMA starts herding everyone into camps."

"This one's a false flag operation," said Bennett. "It's what I've been saying…"

Karras let Bennett go on. Despite the violent worldview Bennett propounded, with its manipulative elites and malefic supernatural influences, the man was a true Pollyanna. There were no gripping social problems associated with the easy ownership of guns, or a crisis of masculinity among the youth, or paranoid schizophrenia, or even an Islamicist threat. They were all papier-mâché and chicken wire that he and his listeners could tear right down. And they didn't have to fight the elites, since secretly, Bennett and his followers—including both Jerry and Dennis, who were huddling over their phones and excitedly pointing at one another's screens—were the true ubermenschen. Their enemies, the weak liberal "social justice warriors" (for the feminine) and "snowflakes" (for the masculine), would be as easy to defeat as their genders were to invert, if only there were not *just so many of them*.

This also explained, Karras realized, why there were so few women in the political underground. Women can experience this sort of omnidirectional cosmic humiliation any time they want without having to sign up explicitly for it, without having to keep up with every podcaster and YouTuber with an unkempt beard. In a flash, Karras understood it all. He just needed to create a sentence in his mind, a simple utterance that could encapsulate his enlightenment, pronounce the words into his microphone, and shut down *Year Zero* forever. He had it now, he thought. He could see it in the chalkboard of his mind.

Then Jerry was up, taking two long strides from the bench, then shoving his head in front of Karras's mic. "We got her. We got Katrina Chu-Ramirez on Chit-Chat. She wants to talk."

Bennett flashed Karras a thumbs-up sign and mouthed the words *thank you*. Karras thought about scrambling over the desk and going for Bennett's gun, but he wasn't sure whom he wanted to shoot more: Bennett, the kids or himself.

Bennett handed Jerry one end of a USB cable to plug into and spoke into his mic. "This is *Year Zero* and it looks like our friend and yours, Michael Karras, had his many interns hard at work. We have on the line with us—live, I remind you all—one Katrinachew Rrrrameeerez."

"I was told I could talk to Michael Karras," said Katrina.

"I'm here," said Karras. "Where are you? Are you safe?"

"Of course she's safe," said Bennett. "Are you in your trailer now? Did the production assistant bring you a bottle of Evian, sweetie?"

"There's a drone, it's big, like a giant mosquito; they're firing at it now. I got across the street and kept running. I'm out of line of sight from the campus and they're not snipers. You're not supposed to leave campus—I'm gonna get suspended for breaking the rules," Katrina said, her voice wavering.

Jerry helped himself to Karras's mic: "It's true. That's how they train us: run and hide, even fight if you have to, but don't leave the school because otherwise you'll be reported missing and the school might get into trouble. They'd rather count fifty corpses than have one kid going truant."

"That's Mike Karras's intern we're hearing from now," Bennett explained. "Karras likes to surround himself with high-school boys."

"Glad you're okay, Katrina, and keep moving if you can safely," Karras said. "Can you tell us how many shooters you saw, and if you know who it is—is it a student? Some troubled boy or girl, or a group?"

"The ol' 'trenchcoat mafia,'" said Bennett.

"Is that Michael Karras? I want to talk to Mister Karras," Katrina said, louder now. She sounded a bit out of breath, there were background noises, close footfalls and distant sirens. "My stepmother has one of your books!"

"How can we help you, Katrina?" Karras asked. He didn't know how to feel. Questioning the kid further would only distract her from running away, but there was nothing he could do that would make her hang up her phone. "Do you want us to contact your parents?"

"Oh, I bet my stepmother is listening!" said Katrina. "Mocha is their name—Mocha, tell biomom I'm safe.

I don't want to come home right away, but I'm okay and I'm going to be okay."

Then she added, "Mocha keeps track of you, Christopher Bennett."

"Ah, sociveillance," said Bennett. "Middle Sister is watching me, hmm? Well, princess, unless you have something more interesting than shout-outs to moms, we're going to move on."

"Yes, I do have something to say! This can't go on! We're going to rise up, you understand?" Katrina said. "A whole generation is sick of being terrorized, sick of adults and their BS about their precious rights—rights they're ready to risk *our* lives for but not their own! We're going to end gun culture, toxic masculinity, cisheteropatriarchy, and your fucking conspiracy-mongering racism! And—"

"And there we have it, from Ms—or it Mix?— Rrramerrrez," said Bennett, as he yanked the cord from Jerry's phone. "A confession. Not only has her family been monitoring my broadcasts, not only did she, with the help of Michael Karras, hijack this platform to threaten all of us, to threaten America, and indeed, Western civilization itself... Do you understand what these false flags attacks are for? It's to take away our guns"—he reached over to pet his pistol, though the small cameras on the console pointing to him and to Karras were both off, but performative reflexes die hard—"but also all of what we hold dear. Our culture, our ability to behave and even identify as men, the nuclear family, your marriages, the free market, your right simply to live as you're used to. The entire world is on the verge of being rewritten, reprogrammed from the source code on up, like a hologram that can depict anything, but without anything at all being real.

"And so, Michael Karras, why have you decided that all of human civilization needs to be painted over, thrown into a shredder, glued back together randomly, placed before a funhouse mirror in the corner of some sort of BDSM dungeon, photographed, Photoshopped, and sold back to us for hyperinflated and thus worthless government fiat, and how long have you wanted this for all mankind?"

Nothing is more terrifying to a radio personality than dead air, so Karras gave it a second. When Bennett opened his mouth to speak again, to fill the space, Karras held up a single finger and glared. That shut Bennett, whose throat was dry anyway, right up for the long moment Karras wanted to savor.

"That's a good question," Karras said. "A good pair of questions. I guess I'll answer the second first. How about... always, or at least so far back as I can remember?"

"Yeah, how about that?" Bennett said.

"And as far as the first—all the destruction and funhouse mirror stuff, I'm not *doing* anything. And you know what, Chris, neither are you. We're both just watching it all happen, or watching *something* happening, and making up some story that we think fits the facts, and what we already know. Hell, if the family and the free market and your guns are so weak that my books nobody reads can hurt them, how strong were they ever, really?"

Karras folded his arms across his chest and waited. Bennett lifted his hands and gestured with a flick of his fingers: *more, more.* He smiled widely, nodded, and even pointed to his chin, then mimed a fist coming his way.

"Oh... yes, and furthermore," Karras said, "why am *I* public enemy number one? There are four companies that decide everything we see and hear, six that dictate all that we eat, one that mails it all to us— and all of them work together to drive down wages and get us hooked on usurious credit."

"The Jew—"

"*Don't,*" snapped Karras. "What I am saying is, Chris Bennett, your selection of targets is pretty telling. What have I ever done, really? You ever read one of my books—I mean, all the way through?"

"I have," snapped Bennett, "I have, I have. You know I have. I've gone through them, line by line, here on the show, highlighting the passages, doing close readings. And you don't even write them, that's clear. You don't; you're an actor. Katrina Chu-whoever and all those Degrassi Junior High kids now crying on CNN because squibs sting when they go off are crisis actors, but you're a *culture* actor. You exist as a face and as a name that people have heard of and that's all. When the elites need some kind of controlled opposition, there you are with a copy-paste communist screed, complete with perverted cover art of mangled girls you try to pass off as 'postmodern collage' or whatnot. You wonder why you're a target—you applied for the job, and have a very nice salary and 401k. Anyone can Google your name and 'net worth' and see the truth."

"One point two million dollars!" shouted Dennis from the bench. "Yah, right!"

"Don't believe everything you Google," said Jerry.

Karras smiled. The boys were coming around at least. But they'd interrupted the conversational table tennis match he was winning against Bennett. He'd have to let Bennett, who was smiling again as he had come to the same realization, serve again.

"I wish we had video of this, ladies and gentlemen," Bennet said into his microphone, his voice softer now. "You need to see the look on this smug... and I apologize in advance for the sensitive souls out there... asshole's face. He's laughing. Michael Karras is smiling like a jack o'lantern, his shoulders are bobbing up and down. He doesn't even have the decency to stop now as I stare at him, not to even cover his mouth with his hand. But he's not laughing at me, ladies and gentlemen. He drove all the way from San Francisco with two underage boys to come on my show. He came on my show, *my show*, to laugh at *you*. He doesn't care—he doesn't care about America, or your rights, or your freedom. He doesn't even care when he throws you down into the mud and plants his boot heel between your shoulder blades. This man hates you; he is a bag of hate and filth and garbage and mockery."

"Well, I know what you are," Karras said, pushing the sentence through his nose, "but what am I?" Jerry hooted at that.

Then the power went off, first at the console, then the lights overhead. Even the industrial thrum of the building itself seemed to stop.

"We're off-air. Fuck," said Bennett. "And it was going really well! Didn't you think, Mike?"

Dennis cleared his throat, ostentatious. He had several power strips in his hand, dead snakes. "Everything about the two of you is disgusting. Kids are dead. Kids the age of my siblings are dead. You can't just make a show about it, and then make that show all about yourselves. I was wrong about you, Christopher Bennett."

"The Second Amend—"

"Shut the fuck up."

"This is my show—"

"*Shut* the fuck up."

"It's entertainment, it's like pro wrest—"

"Shut the *fuck* up."

Suzanne entered the room, muttering, "The feed's totally—oh!" and stopping short as she took in the scene. "What are you supposed to be, a Wobbly?" she asked, waving a hand at Dennis. "Plug that stuff back in right now."

"Shut the fuck—"

Suzanne was reasonably large, the *Year Zero* production studio small. She took half a step forward, and her hand smacked the words out of Dennis's mouth.

"*You* shut the fuck up! Who the hell do you think you're talking to? Your mother?" Dennis glared, and Suzanne raised her hand again. "You want another one, you fucking fat little brat-turd? I don't get paid for this bullshit, you couldn't pay me enough!"

Dennis slowly put the power strips down, his free hand high, like he was a hero on a TV show placing a pistol on the floor and preparing to kick it over to the villain who had gotten the drop on him.

"Anyway, two calls for you," Suzanne called over her shoulder to Karras.

"How do the phones work if the power's out?" asked Jerry.

"Landlines don't need—oh, never mind," said Suzanne. She rolled her eyes. "Children." Then to Dennis, with a wave of a finger: "Plug all this back in, now."

"Thank you, Suzanne," said Bennett.

Karras was already in the small vestibule office, saying hello to Sharon Toynbee.

"Hello, my love," Sharon said. "I had a dream

about you last night; I just had to call you to tell you how much I crave you."

More security talk. Sharon never dreamed, or at least she always claimed to never dream, mentioning her 'neurological peculiarity' whenever the topic would come up, which—given the themes of the books she published—was often. Something was happening at the office, and Karras was to come back, and as quickly as possible.

"Oh, darling," Karras asked, "was it your recurring dream?"

"No, a new one," said Sharon. "Quite saucy." Karras hadn't been expecting that response, which shook him.

One of the other lights on the phone was still blinking. "I have someone on the other line," Karras said, wincing as he spoke. He would have slurped the words out of the air like spaghetti through his pursed lips if he could. Whoever was listening in was probably chuckling right now. He hit the button.

"Hello, this is Mike Karras."

"Michael Karras!" said a lilting baritone. "I've been trying to call in, and then something happened to the program."

"Is this...?" The voice on the other end was familiar enough.

"Samuel—"

"Rahel's father!" Karras said, just as Samuel finished: "—Tony's father."

"Oh, hello."

"Yes, hello, indeed hello," said Samuel. "What happened to the show? Was it an electromagnetic pulse? The NSA?"

"No, just some crazy kid," Karras said. "Everything's fine. Listen, thanks for calling—"

"I had to call the office number once before when I thought my palladium coins went missing in the mail," Samuel said. "Luckily, I retained the Post-It Note on which I had written the number, so I was able to call this line."

"Palladium coin...?"

"Yes, a very valuable metal—sound money, not government fiat currency. In the future, we'll all be using them... at least those of us who thought ahead and invested in Mister Bennett's currency scheme will," Samuel said. *Scheme* with its British connotation, not the American.

"I've got someone on the other line"—Damn, he did it again!—"how can I help you, Mister Alazar?"

"I spoke with my children. I'm disappointed that they abandoned you. You see, though you have brought some chaos with you, upset members of my family, and have disparaged Mister Bennett—"

"The other line," Karras said. "Please! And I believe we'll be back on air in a minute or two."

"Oh, good! Stay there, continue with the program. I am enjoying it. Tony and Rahel will be there soon."

"It's a four-hour drive—"

"They left nearly ninety minutes ago," said Samuel. "Good-bye." And he hung up.

Karras reconnected to Sharon, who said, "Get back on the mic, you idiot!" and hung up without saying good-bye. No secret code there.

Jerry had taken the guest chair, but hadn't put on Karras's headphones. The on-air lights were active. Dennis and Suzanne were plugging the last few items back in—there went the reading light by Bennett's console—and Bennett was talking.

"There's no way. Katrinachu was remarkably self-possessed for a tween. She must have been classically trained at the Yale School of Drama or NYU. What grade is that girl supposed to be in? Eighth grade? How old is an eighth-grader? Ten?"

"Thirteen," said Jerry, "fourteen. Plenty are fifteen if they have transitional kindergarten."

Karras smiled, sensing an opening.

"Fifteen? She was nineteen years old if she was a day," said Bennett.

"You sound like you're planning a trip to Thailand with that line, Chris," Karras said, leaning over Jerry's shoulder and speaking into the mic. He spotted the right button on Bennett's control panel and pressed it. A squeaky helium-addled voice sounded "*Peee-dough-fiiile.*"

On the floor, Dennis yawped. Even Suzanne snorted, then picked herself up, shook her head at Bennett and slid out of the room.

"When we have a live show, folks," Bennett said, reaching for his pistol, "with guests, I try to give them a fair shake. There isn't one radio host, one television broadcaster, one podcaster who is fairer than I am. I've had everyone on, from far-left liberal anarchists to Atilla the Hun, via psychic reconstruction through a spirit-medium. And my guests always know, and always should know, that there's only one rule on *Year Zero*: this is my show. It's not their show; it's my show."

A switch clicked. The small home video cameras around the desk buzzed to life. Bennett waited a moment; livestreams are never quite live. Then he pointed the gun at Michael Karras. "Michael Karras, who is working on a book now called *Rumors of a Second Shooter*. Not even out yet, no cover image available, but already seven five-star reviews on Goodreads. Pretty impressive. So I haven't read it yet, since it doesn't even exist yet—but I bet it's at least a four-star book—but my understanding is that it's basically you going around the country, interviewing survivors of mass shooting events. Is that right?"

"That's right," said Karras. He could smell the sweat evacuating Jerry's body. Dennis was up, his hands just a bit elevated, not quite a fighting stance. Bennett wasn't paying either of the boys any mind. His gaze was locked, not on Karras, but slightly overhead, as if he were addressing an audience packing a great amphitheater.

How long till the Alazars arrived? Probably another hour. Way too late.

"And what is the definition of 'mass shooting,' Michael Karras?"

"It depends. There's not a single definition," said Karras.

"I could have sworn it was something like 'four people being killed.' Am I wrong? Tell me if I'm wrong," Bennett said. "Tell me that I'm wrong."

"Uhm, uh..." Karras hated himself for the hesitation. "Not wrong, but incomplete. The FBI says four victims, whether they're killed or not. Congress says three, so the US attorney general says three. Some criminologists make a point of excluding the shooter themselves."

"Here we go again—non-binary, right, folks?" Bennett asked the air. Karras ignored that line. "So, three."

"Yes."

"So if I shot you, and, uh..."—Bennett spun on his chair and swung his gun to point it at Dennis's chest—"and this guy here, who was responsible for an act of sabotage against this program, against all the supporters of *Year Zero*, and then I decided to, oh, shoot myself, that wouldn't be a mass shooting."

"Not according to most sources, no," said Karras.

"So, I would certainly have to shoot all three of you," Bennett said. "At least."

"At least," said Karras. Karras was a being piloting

a body—he was inside his skeleton, his skeleton was not within him. In his dome of bone, he was calmly assessing the situation, Bennett's personality, the fact that only now, for this confrontation, the video cameras were live. His body, though, was terrified. The body was cold, its blood sluggish even as the heart squeezed nearly shut twice per second. The hair on its limbs stood up straight, as though attempting a mass evacuation. The organs within rumbled, squeaked, and tensed.

"And if I do shoot all three of you, perhaps one of you will see a second shooter. Maybe it'll be my assistant and producer, Suzanne, rushing in to see what the matter is, and one of you three will see a gun in her hand, or one of the bullets I fire will ricochet off a wall in such a way that you might take it in the back, and that would be 'proof' of a second shooter to credulous weirdoes, is that right?" asked Bennett.

"One thing to consider," Karras said, "for those interested in exploring the mindset of a mass shooter, is women. Maybe even women like Suzanne." He tried to keep his voice steady, disinterested, but his tongue and lungs were hard to control; they wanted him to whimper. There was a gun pointed at them. Karras might have felt safe inside his thick skull, but he was propped up atop a great veiny root system of the rest of his body, and it was wanting just to run away.

"Shooters often experience a profound feeling of humiliation. They blame women. Nearly all of them at first find a woman—their mother, their wife, some random girl who they believed spurned them—and kill her first. Thus blooded, they begin their pathetic little hero's journey to shoot up their school, or workplace, or whatever public gathering of more successful heterosexual couplings they've targeted."

Dennis inhaled sharply, about to say something. Karras stopped him with a glance. It didn't matter. If Suzanne was monitoring the program from her computer monitor in the reception area, she wasn't about to bust in again and disarm Bennett, or take the first bullet and give the boys a chance to run.

But she did do something. A light on Bennett's console went on. He ignored it. Jerry didn't. "We have a caller," he said, and reached over the small table to hit the button. Bennett sighed loudly. Jerry said, "Uhm, you're on the air, I guess."

"Hello?" It was Rahel. "This is *Year Zero*, live?" Her voice echoed, was tinny, a little distant. She must have been driving down, just as her father had said, and pulled over to make the call while also watching the show on her smartphone.

"Hold your phone a little further away from you, or at least hit mute on whatever app you're watching us on, please, ma'am," said Bennett, all business again, except for the gun he was pointing at Karras.

"Yes, is this better?"

"It is, dear—"

"My name is Rahel Alazar," Rahel said. "I know you know that name. I survived a mass shooting event, thanks to the intercession of the Lord my God Jesus Christ."

"Oh, yes," Bennett said. "Where was that shooting—Oakland, California? Rough place, isn't it? Lots of animosity between Asians and blacks in Oakland, California, isn't there? Just like in Los Angeles back in the Rodney King era."

"Berkeley," Rahel said. "But I understand what you mean, Mister Chris Bennett. My father listens to your show. He's a fan. I listen to it too, sometimes. I would be remiss if I didn't say 'Hello, Dad!' There, that's his Father's Day present."

"You called in to say hello to your father?"

"I called in because I encountered a second shooter, and Mister Karras has been kind enough to take me seriously," said Rahel. "You can imagine how I felt to see you aiming a pistol at him."

"It's just a thought experiment—"

"And I called in to see how long it would take for you to sound any racist dog whistles. Not very long, I'm afraid to report," said Rahel. "Well, I happen to have a dog whistle to sound as well."

The sound hit Bennett hard. Karras winced, and Jerry did too, but neither of them were wearing headphones. Bennett clawed at his and yowled. Dennis scrambled for the biggest power strip, swung it by its wire, and smacked Bennett right in the teeth. Karras scrambled over Jerry, securing the pistol. Suzanne charged in, and Dennis managed to swing the power strip over his head and hit her in the ear.

"Go, go, now!" Karras grabbed a fistful of Jerry's hair and ran past a stunned Suzanne. Dennis was right behind them; he donkey-kicked the studio door shut, then pushed Suzanne's desk in front of it. Karras took the clip from Bennett's gun, threw the piece in the wastebasket, and pocketed the ammo. "Go, go, go!" The three were in the car seconds later. Dennis's face was a sweaty cranberry.

"Oh, God, oh, God, I just now forgot how to drive!" He stared at the keys in his hand, dumbfounded. Karras grabbed his wrist and led Dennis to put the key in the ignition and turn it. Jerry was quiet, stooped over, in the back, looking at his hands in his lap.

Karras shifted the car into reverse and said to Dennis, calmly, "Logan. You know how to drive. Look behind you, check the mirror, light on the accelerator. You're doing well, you're all right. Just drive to a McDonald's or something. We passed a million of them."

"I want In-N-Out," said Dennis, and he looked behind him, checked his mirror, and pressed the accelerator lightly.

"Well done, Logan," Karras said, hoping he sounded a bit like Patrick Stewart; that calling Dennis Logan in a specific way would calm the lad. *Calm the lad*! God, even his own semi-panicked thinking was completely hypermediated. "You did well too, Jerry," he said. "You were so calm the entire time; you saved us by staying cool and connecting that call."

"I, uh, if we go to McDonald's," Jerry said, "I want to do drive-through only. I, I'm sorry, Logan. I pissed myself. Not here, back in the studio when the cameras went on. But my pants are wet; I messed up the seat back here."

"Don't worry, dude," said Dennis. "It's cool. Well, it's not *cool*, but it's all right. And we're going to In-N-Out. Maybe we shouldn't, though; I feel like I'm about to have a heart attack. I knocked out Chris Bennett's teeth. I hit a girl; I mean, she hit me first. Woman. Oh, man, girl! Katrina and all those kids, they're all fucking dead—we have to know what happened to her!"

"It'll be okay, it'll be okay," Karras said, once for them and once for himself. Nobody was persuaded. A distraction would be better. "Pretty interesting trick back there Rahel Alazar pulled for us. Do you know what happened?"

"I don't know; it sounded like a tea kettle, if a tea kettle was tuned to a dead channel," said Jerry. "Old-fashioned TV static and screaming."

"It was the sound of a real dog whistle; the tone is too high for people to hear, of course, but when transmitted over a phone, it comes out at the high end of audible, bound by the highest frequency the receiver can generate. Bennett took it in both ears, full force. That also tells us where she might be. I know she doesn't have a dog, and I know she's about an hour south of the Bay. When Chris pulled the gu— uh, when *Year Zero* started broadcasting video and not just audio, she probably saw what was happening and Googled for a pet shop that sold dog whistles."

"Or she found the frequency online and just played it?" Jerry suggested. "Maybe she was calling from an old-fashioned pay phone and held her phone up to it."

"There are probably fewer working payphones on I-5 than there are pet stores that sell dog whistles," said Dennis. "We can definitely find her for you. I bet there's some autist online who keeps track of working payphones."

"You think everyone interested in something obscure is autistic, Logan," said Jerry. Dennis took offense at Jerry taking offense. Karras settled back in the passenger seat, closed his eyes and let them bicker with one another. Like the hat-wearing dog drinking coffee in his flaming living room, this was fine.

13.

SOMETHING CHANGED IN the thirty-six hours after the Middlesex shooting. The perpetrator, Aram Sargsyan, was brought in alive after a drone hosed him with OC spray rated for bears, but the headlines weren't about him, the viral messages not about his haircut or which psychiatric medication he was on or the bone structure of his chin. The fact that he chose to begin his shooting campaign at the end of the day because he wanted to take a geometry test in his after-lunch math class was only remarked upon once or twice— his mother had promised him an expensive video-game if he scored higher than 90 percent on it.

Nor even was the news about the fourteen dead. The world's attention turned to Katrina Chu-Ramirez, to a seventh-grader named Aidan Johnson, and to a number of other surviving Middlesex kids. It wasn't Katrina's brief interview on *Year Zero*, but a video she shot in her parents' living room that night, with Aidan, that did the trick. The two of them, Katrina with her unusual hair and blustery confidence, and Aidan, portly and with a deep bass voice made for opera or selling used cars, looked into the camera and made a vow.

Our generation will put an end to this.

To this settler-nation's gun addition.

To this patriarchy's demand for blooding as a rite of passage.

To cishetero anxieties over masculinity.

To racism, ethnic chauvinism, and the privileges of whiteness offered up like a prize to white-adjacent communities willing to perform anti-blackness.

To the abuse and trauma inflicted upon black bodies.

To the scapegoating and abuse of the neuroatypical.

It went on for a bit. They alternated, the two of them, with a call-response cadence not dissimilar from what people of Karras's generation would have called spoken-word poetry, but which the kids watching the video on Chit-Chat referred to as slow-flow hip-hop. Four hours after the video went live, other kids were doing it. At first, they were just repeating Katrina and Aidan, but some added their own demands for a world free of child abuse, climate change, Islamophobia, pernicious copyright rules.

Then came the demands for more Latinx superhero films, better cheese powder in Kraft dinner, for the Prime Minister of Japan to apologize to the world's most popular K-Pop boy band for underdescribed but horrible imperial crimes. It got silly fast, as combustive fashions do, but every goofy version of the video just led back to Katrina and Aidan's original.

Then they marched on the hospital, nearly all the Middlesex kids who could get away from their parents, with those two on point, to visit their wounded and dying classmates. It wasn't like the news, where the cameras are set up in advance at a destination and the broadcaster lets you see them coming. The footage was from their cell phones, the target on the screen, like you were among them, one of them, marching toward the hospital, stomping over the grass of the traffic islands, filling the parking lot despite the warnings—some of which you, your collective self, were articulating—about blocking emergency vehicles. Seeing through their eyes, hearing with their ears, and speaking with their mouths.

This is the emergency! someone said, and it sounded like you were saying it. An hour later, everyone was saying it. What about the budget crisis, or the latest square foot of celebrity skin, Christopher Bennett pulling a gun on Michael Karras on a livestream, the fate of the golden-cheeked warbler? No, *this is the emergency*—children shooting children, and the great rhetorical shrug that always followed.

The Middlesex kids shouted over the shrug. This is not the ti—*this is the emergency!*

The Second Amen—*emergency!*

"Oh, but what about the children?!" say the paren—*THIS IS*

An emergency siren in a hundred howling voices. There was nothing to negotiate, or parse, or ironize, or counter-read into irrelevance. *This is the emergency* entered the noösphere like an icicle falling into an eye. Sudden, painful, blinding, slippery to hold on to, soon to melt into nothingness, but the gash it made remained, open and bleeding. You don't talk about it when one of your eyes goes red and fails, you just clutch your face and howl.

The Middlesex kids had done it!

THE NEXT DAY they tried it again. But instead of the hospital where a dozen teens were convalescing, and where one, Marcello Decoco, succumbed to his injuries overnight, the target of their *manifestation*—said in an attempt at a Haitian accent by Aidan while Katrina rolled her eyes behind him—was American Riflery, a gun shop in a strip mall three small towns away from the school. Aram Sargsyan had stolen his uncle's AR-15, and two handguns, for his rooftop rampage (that was the *Jersey Journal*'s choice of headline—"Rooftop Rampage!") and the uncle had originally bought the guns from American Riflery.

Also, a local bus stopped on the corner at the mall, so it was easy enough for the kids to fill a few of them and get there before the local authorities were any the wiser.

Stretched across the top of the store's doors, under its sign and over its transom, was a banner reading NOT TODAY ANTIFA. (Somewhere, Sharon Toynbee was annoyed by the absence of a comma.) The chant went up quickly enough: "Yes, today! Yes, today!" The crowd of children filled the strip-mall parking lot quickly and easily.

It was crowded enough that the kids' phones mostly caught the backs of one another's heads, their shoulders, the backs of their picket signs on which some of them were clever enough to write secondary slogans. Seventh-graders who wanted to help from the safety of their own bedroom picked and chose what feeds to broadcast across a few streams, getting one angle, then another, usually favoring their friends' phones. The chanting quieted, then stopped and then one of the cameraphones pushed through and showed why—three large men, their arms unseasonably bare to show off their muscles, their 'patriot' tattoos, holding AR-15s in a low ready position.

"What the fuck?" Aidan's voice came from the crowd, but it was Katrina who lowered her phone, pushed her way to the front of the crowd, and then raised her phone again. The men were wearing polarizing lenses, and the image of Katrina's face and phone, stretched out like taffy, were reflected in them.

"We're kids! We don't want to die anymore, we don't want to live in fear anymore," she said to them. The world got to see her features, the wide eyes, the flat nose, the glint of her piercings, as she spoke. The world saw the lips of the man in the center split into a clenched-tooth smile.

"We don't either," he said. "And we *don't* live in fear."

"You don't?" Katrina said. "You're not confronting a bunch of kids with your guns? You don't work out, do steroids, practice shooting, carry guns, carry knives, all of that, because you're not afraid?"

"That's right. And if you had one of these," the man said, nodding down at her but carefully not shifting the position of his rifle from low ready, aimed down and away and coincidentally at Katrina's shins, "you wouldn't be afraid anymore either."

"You are afraid! You're afraid of *us!* You wouldn't be out here if you weren't!"

The man in the middle didn't speak, but the one on his right did. "Maybe we just want to be on television." He laughed at his own joke. "You're kids. We're not afraid of a bunch of kids. Maybe the governor or the state assembly is, or the UN is, like they're afraid of that climate girl, but we don't need these guns. It's just our right, and we're exercising it. And you're exercising your rights too. And we're letting you."

For what seemed like a long time, nobody said anything. Unusual for middle school students in a crowd, after a long bus ride, after several nightmare-filled sleeps, after so much media. Maybe the seventh-grade support teams had lowered the volume on the outgoing feeds for purposes of melodrama.

"You're *letting* us?" said Aidan, finally, from behind his cameraphone. Katrina, in his frame, was just speechless, bemused.

"Second Amendment protects the First," said the man in the middle. "You know why the police ain't here, ready to bust your heads?"

"Because we're white!" a kiddie in the back shouted, to some cheers and a smattering of boos, and a quick turn and sneer from Katrina.

"Because we're right," said Aidan, still invisible in all the feeds.

"Because we're *kids*," said Katrina, in Aidan's feed. "And because we're streaming this. And yeah, most of us are white, cis, middle-class, and despite those privileges we're all still victims of gun violence."

"The police bust heads in Portland all the time," said the central man. "That town's full of white middle-class soy boys and demigirls and whatnot, and some normies too. The police aren't here, now, because we're armed and we're defending our property and your right to speak at the same time, thanks to these guns you came here to grab." He stroked his AR-15, somewhat less professionally than he probably should have before so many cameras and critical viewers.

"Oh, do you want our *thanks?* Well, thanks for all my dead classmates! Thanks for scaring the rest of us for life!" said Katrina, the feed showing her reflection in the blue lens of the gunmen again.

"I want a hug," said the third gunman, who had until now been silent. He removed the magazine from his AR-15, put it in a holster, then shrugged the firearm around his shoulder to his back. "I want to thank you with a hug. You're a tough girl."

"I am not a girl," Katrina said. Most of the streams shifted to a two shot of her holding her phone up in the face of the man, and the man himself, his arms wide. "And I'm not going to give *you* a hug, or anyone a hug. What the hell is wrong with you? This isn't some media op, I'm not going to take some picture with you so that you can have a viral moment. This is the emergency!"

They raised a fist and started the chant, but there was something wrong. The kids sounded just a little less enthusiastic, as though the phrase *This is the emergency!* had already lost its memetic power, just as the old standbys of prior movements—*This is what democracy looks like!* and *Whose streets? Our streets!* and *The people united/will never be divided!*—had been reduced to cliché through bellowing, pepper spray, and the police baton.

"This is the emergency…" Katrina kept their fist

high, but after a dozen recitations their voice trailed off. Two of the three men before the door to the gun shop stood, stoic, and the third still held his arms open for the hug he'd requested. The shot shifted as the person holding that phone pushed their way forward. The camera turned in the person's hand—it was one of the kids, a boy, slight and tow-headed with eyes red from tears, but none of the many who had been featured on the news or on any social media platforms before. "I want a hug," he told the world, his voice a seventh-grade hormonal squeak, and he slid between Katrina and the man with open arms and inserted himself into an embrace.

"Bullshit!" At first it didn't sound like Katrina, as their voice broke into a shriek, but it was them. "Bullshit! Bullshit!"

Now that was a chant the Middlesex kids could get behind, though a few of the streams blinked out thanks to anti-swear algorithms and parental controls embedded in their phones.

"Let them hug!" bubbled up as a counterchant, mostly from afar, or least far from the mics on the cameraphones near the front line of the demonstration. The kids sounded younger—other seventh graders?

"Bullshit! Bullshit!" roared the children at the blond-haired boy who had nestled his cheek into the chest of the men. "Let them hug! Let them hug!" came in from the back. The hug was a long one, unnaturally so, and when the boy finally took a step back from the man and they slapped palms and bumped fists as a mystic ward against perceived homosexuality other children starting to step forward for their hugs. Two other men repositioned their rifles and hugged and hugged one Middlesex survivor after another, while other sympathizers repositioned themselves to get close-ups.

"Oh my effin' God," said Katrina. It was their stream again, mostly. The kids at home were selecting cell-phone feeds for maximum drama, like they had years of experiencing directing NFL games from a production truck. Katrina had found Aidan in a queue four deep, waiting for his hug. Their phone went flying, spinning, the image clipping white, then the streams cut to chaotic shots from one phone, then another, a third, and fifth and ninth. A close-up of Aidan, bleeding from his brow, a flash of the blond kid running off with something in his hand, a trio of girls yelling and hugging one another, then sneakers everywhere, someone belly-flopping onto another phone, the sky again, the sun a white smear, and then a single solid scream of "Gun!"

Most streams dropped away instantly, but a few captured the kids running out onto the highway or trying the locked or held-shut doors of the other stores—the Laundromat, the Hunan #1 Chinese Restaurant, a small fitness dance school called Bootyshakers—on the strip.

Katrina found their phone, collected it in their hands

like it were a wounded bird that could be nursed back to health, and spoke into a now-shattered lens that made the scene look as though it were draped in a heavy fog. Only the wail of police sirens and the roar of two dozen children crying and tripping and shoving made it obvious that the day was still a sunny one.

"They're back!" they cried, tears and snot heavy on their face. "Oh, God, they're shooting at the police—"

TONY HIT A button on the VCR, which made a loud twentieth-century *thunk,* to turn off the video, which was nearly over anyway. He looked over at Michael Karras, who was hiding his eyes with his knees, curled up in a ball, on the tiny couch in Tony's overstuffed bungalow studio.

"You know how hard it was to find a VHS tape, and a computer with a DVD player, to record that stream onto first a disc and then the tape, and show it to you, because you don't want to be anywhere that might have wireless?" he said.

"Please…" Karras said, his voice weak and reedy. "I know what you're going to say and the answer is that yes, I know, I understand."

"So you're gonna get up today?" asked Tony.

"No," said Karras.

"Katrina's back up. So's that white boy, Adam."

"Aidan," Karras said. "I guess I lack the vigor and flexibility of youth. I had a knife pointed at me, and a gun pointed at me. I'm not going back out there. I'll just turn my chapters into blog posts, maybe start a podcast. That's where all the money is, anyway, not in writing a whole book that most people are just going to download from some edgy torrent anyway."

"And not even read it," said Tony. "I feel you, man, but here's the thing—you can't stay here."

Karras knew what was going on. Tony's place was a tiny little box, and he spent next to no time here, that much was obvious. Gutted computers and yellowed copies of free weekly newspapers littered the coffee table and spilled onto the floor, but the sink was bereft of dishes. The fridge was mini, with a microwave atop it and a hot plate atop that, but there was no oven. The place reeked of pot and ozone. Tony just came here to relax and do projects and probably occasionally get laid, but mostly subsisted on his parents' food and companionship.

"I know, I know," Karras said. "I owe you and your family everything, really. I can't keep mooching off your hospitality. But, I dunno, the book's not finished, but it is *done*. I quit."

"You quit, huh? That girl Katrina didn't just have a gun pointed at her, she was shot at, and dragged over the coals for it. You know how much porn Internet lowlifes have screwed that teenager's head onto? How many threats she gets a day. And how about my sister? She and I, we saved your ass. She had a gun pointed at her too."

Had she, though? Ultimately, Karras didn't believe it. Nor did he believe Grutzmacher's story or those of any of the other people he interviewed. People believe in all sorts of crazy things—some of them inspire the believer to drive a truck into a crowd, others to stick with horse and buggy and eschew the electric light bulb.

"Yeah, well. She has faith and she has family, and that helps. You're a strong group," Karras said. "My father spent most of his time and money playing poker, doing nothing much, and my mother... well, she showed me the best techniques for shoplifting comic books and chocolate bars so I'd have something to do after school. No siblings, no extended family. I'm the only Greek-American I know who doesn't have a million screaming cousins."

Tony rubbed his fingers together and grimaced in a faux ecstatic concentration—the world's tiniest violin, played just for Michael Karras. "Whatever, man. If you're done writing about Rahel, I'm done helping you out. Even Samuel doesn't care about you anymore; he got to tell his friends down at the coffee shop that he met you, and then he saved your ass. Anyway, you ain't writing, you gotta get a real job. In your home town, I mean. What else are you good at? Where do you even live?"

"Writers aren't good at anything; not even writing, most of the time," Karras said. "I've been living out of Airbnbs for three years—have laptop, will travel. My books and stuff are in a storage unit in Chicago.

You know how it is; when you're online all the time, you always feel at home. It's your job, it's your social life, it's your activism, it's your hobbies and entertainment."

"I know, it's part of why I keep this little pied-à-terre," Tony said, stretching his arms and nearly brushing his fingers against opposing walls. "All hardware, no software. A place to decompress, but not a place to *de*press. So you need to liven up, sahib. Sounds like you need an offline job. Why don't you get a job in a diner?" He laughed at his own joke, but Karras took it seriously enough to say:

"Greek diners are almost always family affairs—no screaming cousins, no busboy jobs."

"Gigolo it is, then," Tony said.

"Gotta be online for that these days," Karras said. "Also…"

Tony gave Karras an appraising look. "Yeah, also. Maybe Yunus will hire you to wipe down tables for a couple of weeks, and you can get a bus ticket back to Ohio."

Karras shifted, turning his face into the threadbare couch cushion. It smelled of sweat and weed and berbere. "Chicago," he said. "And I have money. A few grand, anyway. I can fly anywhere I want, I just have no place to land."

Tony heard it first. Karras thought it must have been some neighbor using a weed whacker or garden trimmer, but Tony knew better. All the lawns in this patch of dirt on the Oakland-Berkeley border were either overgrown with weeds, or barren except for broken glass and dead plastic toys. It didn't even take two steps to get to the front door, and on his tiptoes he was able to see through the smudged glass of the transom.

"Yo, Mike, reach under the couch," he said. "There's a badminton racket under there. Give it to me."

"Badminton, huh?" That was something Karras had never expected Tony to say. "Is it popular in Ethiopia?"

"It's an Olympic sport. Bring me the racket!"

Karras snaked his hand under the couch and felt around. Everything was cobwebby and moldy-moist, but the racket was easy enough to find. Karras didn't need to get up, he stretched his arm and passed the racket to Tony's own outstretched arm. Tony slipped out the door, racket behind his back.

There was a slicing of the air, the crack of an impact, and then several others each sharper than the last, then a yawp of victory. Tony re-entered a few moments later, a drone in his hand as if he had just brought down a ring-necked pheasant.

"Too easy," he said, tossing it onto one of the small piles of electronics on the floor.

"Absolutely too easy," Karras said, turning to sit upright. "Unless you're a master of whacking shuttlecocks—"

"I can see why you're giving up writing."

"You can't just knock a drone out of the air. Whoever was controlling it just let it hover so you could bring it in. Easiest way to confirm my presence here," Karras said.

"This thing," Tony said, nudging the drone with his foot, "is officially confirming nothing." The plastic casing was cracked, one of the rotors smashed, the lens bent.

"Maybe it's wired. Mics, a small bomb, gas, a few particles of plutonium—" Karras couldn't help himself.

Tony bent down and put his finger on Karras's lips. "It'll be okay," he told Karras. "My sister's praying for you."

Karras didn't say anything—it would be weird with Tony's thick finger on his lips—but he did raise his eyebrows hopefully.

"It means the opposite of what you think it means," Tony said. Then he dug into a pocket of his jean jacket and pulled out a handkerchief. With that in hand, he picked up the drone again and brought it over to the slop sink against the wall, put it in, and turned on the taps.

"See, you used a hanky. You're worried as well, about contact poisons," Karras said. "And submerging may mess up the electronics, but what if they thought of that and there's a core alkali metal in the drone, or something even worse."

Tony turned and spoke over his shoulder. "You have to stop talking now. That's it. You can be anxious and worried, but you have to be anxious and worried in silence," he said.

"I'm not paranoid. This drone located us, just like it did at the coffee shop. You mentioned Yunus and it appeared," Karras said.

"I'm not calling you paranoid—a lot of heavy shit has gone down this past week. I'm saying shut the fuck up," Tony said. He peered into the sink. "Ah, here's something."

"Uhm..."

Tony reached into the sink and from the innards of the drone withdrew a small plastic tube. He dried it off with his handkerchief, and then dried his hands on the legs of his jeans, and turned the cap.

"Tony."

"Shu-uuht uu-hup," Tony sang. "If they wanted to kill us, they could have set the whole house on fire, or just rolled up and fired shots through the walls. Nobody would even call 911. This is a shitty block; that's why it's so affordable. No need to 'send a message' with a drone, unless they actually want to send a message." He popped the cap off the tube and said, "Aha! And so they did," as he pulled out a coil of paper. "Addressed to you. Should I lick it first to show you that it's not coated with weaponized anthrax?"

"No, don't do that. Anthrax would be obvious, but it might be coated in batrachotoxin," Karras said plainly.

Tony just stared at him for a few seconds.

"How do you feel?" prompted Karras.

"Well, fine," Tony said. "What's batrachotoxin?"

"If you feel fine, it doesn't matter."

"I'll Google it later. Here." Tony threw the small rolled-up piece of paper. Karras caught it. His name was on it. He slipped off the rubber band around the paper, unrolled it, and read the note aloud.

"'At a certain speed, the speed of light, you lose even your shadow,'" Karras said. The next line was on the paper too, but he knew it by heart already. "'At a certain speed, the speed of information, things lose their sense.'"

"I think I read that on a bumper sticker once," said Tony.

"It's from an essay by Jean Baudrillard."

"'The Gulf War Did Not Take Place,' I heard of it," Tony said, a bit of a curl to his lip.

"The title of this essay is 'The Gulf War: Is It Taking Place?' actually," said Karras. "It was published in English in a book named *The Gulf War Did Not Take Place*, though."

"Don't 'actually' me," said Tony. "So, you're still alive. Not an assassination attempt. Some 'riddle me this' bullshit. Your arch-enemy is a guy who buys all his books and all his toys from Amazon."

"Why do I even have enemies? It has to be Bennett," Karras said.

"Could be a random crazy person," Tony said.

"What makes you say that?" Karras was sitting up straight now, squeezing the paper in his hand.

Tony shrugged. "Just making conversation."

"Could be one of Bennett's listeners," said Karras. "Stochastic terror. Or a number of them working together. They have listener forums, fan discords…"

"Or it could be a number of them not working together, but just getting the same idea," said Tony, his tone contemplative. Still just making conversation. "What's that, lone wolf, leaderless resistance?"

"Yeah," said Karras.

"So what's the graduate student who is after your ass even trying to tell you, and how did they find you here?"

"As to the latter, any number of ways. I guess they might have your family under surveillance. Could just be someone driving by your mom's house once in a while, and they got lucky seeing you leave with a suspicious item—a VHS tape. As to the former, hmm…" Karras spread the paper over his thigh and smoothed it out. "Hmm. It needn't be a threat or a self-conscious clue. Could be a warning."

"About what? What does it even mean—in context, what did it mean?" Tony asked. "Also, you owe me sixty dollars for a new badminton racket." He sighed and kicked the broken racket back under the couch.

"That thing was sixty bucks?" Karras said. "Well, anyway, it just means, or it's supposed to mean, that if you're watching CNN, or if you're an embedded reporter for CNN, and showing footage of war in real time, you're eliminating historical context and creating another kind of context: does this war look enough like a war? Remember all the footage of the aerial assaults on Baghdad during Desert Storm, and how the camera operator would switch to a night vision lens to make things more dramatic-looking? As if actually bombing an apartment block full of civilians wasn't already dramatic enough?"

"Yeah, green and black—it was like the computer monitors from the old days. I guess from *those* days, pre-Web. Felt, I dunno... techie," Tony said. "Even though it's really primitive when you think about it."

"And in Bush Jr.'s war, they just put cameras on the bombs themselves."

"And now, drone strikes," said Tony. "But that footage was leaked."

"Or was it?" said Karras. "Rhetorical," he added as Tony moved his mouth to speak. "Whether it was leaked by Assange or especially prepared by some psyops division of the Pentagon to *appear* to be leaked, the point was to distribute murder-as-first-person-shooter footage, with the viewer as the shooter. How many fetishists went through it all frame by frame to determine whether or not the guys who got cut in half somehow deserved it? How many refused to watch it because they would feel somewhat implicated, morally, just by being behind the eyes of the shooter? The murder gaze."

"Lots."

"Yeah, lots," Karras said. "Most people, even, they just dip a toe into the informational stream. Other people baptize themselves in the river, and never come up for air. It's easy to drown. So, yeah, maybe just a little friendly advice, in mysterious drone form."

"Who would give you advice like that?" Tony asked. "Someone close to you, no doubt, who would know about your current location and that you'd read this book and would get what the message is."

"Well, there's my editor, but this isn't like her," Karras said. "Well, not much like her. She's into codes and burner phones and the like, but, I mean, she would sign a note. And she wouldn't let you smack a drone to pieces to deliver one. Very money-conscious editor, that Sharon Toynbee."

"Hmm," said Tony. Then he got down on his knees before the couch on which Karras sat and retrieved from under it the remains of the badminton racket. He slid the racket under one knee, and twisted, cracking it further. He didn't say a thing, so Karras was just confused, until he found a jagged wooden spike at the end of the handle poking at the flesh of his neck.

"Then it was you. Nobody else would know that you were here, and send a message you'd be sure to know, to this location. You're doing this on purpose. You do work with Bennett, and you're gaslighting me and my sister," Tony said.

"Why... why would I do that?" Karras said.

Tony's voice was calm, practiced, but his eyes were blazing. The mien and bearing of someone who had to navigate the world that automatically saw him as a threat, someone who had been tested time and again, by police, by rich kids who knew the police would always take their side, by bosses eager to express dominance while performing empathy. "I mean, Rahel contacted *me*. Your father sent you two to help me."

"So you think we're committed, because damn it, we were. If it wasn't Rahel and my family, it would have been one of the other people you interviewed. We're all traumatized, all ready to believe that someone is going to listen to us—my dad and I wanted more than anything for someone to take Rahel seriously."

"I'm taking this very seriously," said Karras, his eyes nearly crossed to keep his gaze on Tony's hand, on the stake.

"What's your goal here, man? What's your game?" Tony asked, for real. Questions he wanted answered. "Why do you even care?"

"I... really?"

Tony nodded. "Mm-hmm."

"You know how your father is, ah..." Karras felt himself swimming a narrow strait swimming between the grasping claws of condescension and the whirlpool of euphemism. "Politically engaged?"

"Yeah, you can say that." Tony snorted, almost a chuckle.

"For me, it was my mother," said Karras. "She was obsessed with the Kennedy assassinations. All three of them." He let himself wink.

"Junior too, eh?"

"Well, at first she thought he had faked his death—years before the right wing took up that idea," said Karras. "Though in her version he did it to enter Cuba for reasons and assassinate Castro for reasons. Anyway, then she settled on the assassination story. But her real favorite was JFK."

"Cubans?"

"No—"

"Nixon?"

"I *wish* Cubans or Nixon," Karras said. "It was changeable, but she was obsessed with the identity of the second shooter. She turned my action figures into her own diorama of the scene. Skeletor was Babushka Lady, an old Luke Skywalker with the telescoping lightsaber was Umbrella Man. She tore the roof off one of my model cars to make a convertible Lincoln Continental for Spider-Man and a Barbie a cousin had left at the apartment once to sit in." He exhaled deeply; Tony had let some of the pressure off the splintered wood on his Adam's apple.

"So, who was the second shooter?" Tony asked.

"It changed. Obsessives don't finally figure out the truth and call it a day. She liked the Mafia for a while, but which one? The New Orleans mob, the Bufalino crime family from Pennsylvania? And why? Because

JFK fumbled getting their casinos back from Castro, or because Hoffa called a hit on Bobby Kennedy and there was some confusion?" Karras sighed. "Oh, man. Then she got into whether or not the Kennedys killed Hoffa."

"You're pretty relaxed now, given this is the third time in recent days that someone has pulled some kind of weapon on you," Tony said.

"In the moment, all one can do is... well." Karras said. "Look, I'm sorry you got roped into this, that Rahel did. Thanks for taking me in, and showing me that video, and—"

"And burying your laptop and cell phone in the yard," Tony said.

"That too."

"It's not the only thing buried there," Tony said. Then he laughed, and finally took the point of the stick away. "I still don't know if you sent this drone here yourself, and you still can't stay here. You have to figure this all out on your own from here on in. If you write about Rahel, be kind." He twirled the racket handle like a baton and the point ended up near Karras's eye. "Just, please... be kind. She's been through a lot. More than you've been through."

"Yeah, I mean of course I will," Karras said. "I like Rahel, your whole family. And I'm on the side of the victims here. I'm not involved in anything crazy."

Tony tilted his head dubiously at that, but then lowered the racket handle in his hand. "Have a blessed day, Michael Karras. I'll pre-order your book on Amazon when it goes up." He nodded toward the door. "Trowel's out there."

Out in the small patch of weeds behind the bungalow, Karras dug into the obvious pile of disturbed dirt for his phone and his computer. Hiding from the mediasphere had done Karras no good. He was easy to find in meatspace, and as vulnerable as any scampering animal. Might as well be online, where he could fire back at his enemies with bons mots, ripostes, memes. Or where at least he'd get advance warning.

Tony had put his stuff in a metal box, and the box in an empty burlap sack, both of which had Amharic characters on them. The sack still had the whiff of coffee bean about it. Karras was going to have a cup or three after this. Not a single speck of dirt on Karras's bag. He quickly dug out his phone and battery, and turned it back on. It felt so good as the screen lit up, like he had woken up and discovered he had a new sense, better than the typical five combined, that he hadn't even known was missing. Then he cringed; notifications were already making the phone vibrate so insistently he'd nearly dropped it right back into the hole at his knees.

Then, in the hole, he saw another metal box. Like the one Tony had put his laptop bag and phone in, it seemed to be some sort of military surplus or other souvenir from Ethiopia. It was stained with dirt in a way the coffee-bean sack wasn't; Tony must have buried it a season ago, but not so long ago that the soil had settled completely and grass grown over it.

Karras edged the box out of the dirt with the trowel, and glanced over his shoulder, half-expecting Tony to be peering out at him somehow, despite the fact that the little bungalow had no rear windows. Maybe a second drone buzzing away over the roof? But there was nothing. The box was latched, but not locked. In it, a smaller box, not metal.

In that smaller box, a pistol and box magazine. A semiautomatic, heavy in Karras's hand. Five-pointed star on the grip. Probably needed a cleaning, but wasn't so bad, really. The gun felt like something from another world, and it was, a world that no longer existed. Karras knew it just from wrapping his fingers around the grip—Soviet Makarov.

Ethiopia had a communist moment of sorts in the early '70s. Military communism, complete with a war against Somalia that the Ethiopians won thanks to an influx of Soviet weaponry. The Alazars were religious, but Samuel had definitely been politicized in the arbitrary way of the autodidact at dinner, and clearly had seen himself as some sort of leader when he sent his children to rescue Karras. He was the right age to have been a conscript in the late 1970s, and perhaps of the correct temperament to walk away from the horrors of a godless battlefield soaked red with the blood of his brothers... but keep the free gun.

And a free gun was a free gun. For a moment, Karras wondered if Tony had been carrying it while driving down toward LA, or even when he had come with his sister to pick him up at SFO. Had he even placed the laptop and phone purposely atop the gun, so that Karras could discover and appropriate it? Karras had never fired a handgun, but he was sick of being an unarmed target. If he was going to gear back up and deal with the online world, he might as well do something even stupider—carry a stolen, concealed weapon manufactured in a nation that had vanished into smoke and chaos when he was a child.

It wasn't as though the Makarov was legally Tony's either, not given its provenance and the fact that Tony stored it in a hole in a yard in a secret pied-à-terre on this shit side of town. Hell, the rental probably wasn't legal, much less the gun.

14.

"Shook up, huh?" Dennis said. "We've been sitting here for ten minutes." *Here* being in Dennis's car, in the parking lot of the Diablo Valley Rifle & Gun Range. The lot was large, and half-full. A not very busy Saturday. The range building was a pair of double-wide trailers, and the range itself outside, and a bit ramshackle—if not for the sounds of gunfire and the metallic taste on Karras's tongue, he could have mistaken it for a defunct auto-mechanic's back lot, with clotheslines put up by enterprising unhoused people.

"I want to understand the clientele," Karras said.

"What's to understand?" Jerry asked from the rear seat. "Oh, I know. You're racist."

"How am I racist?" Karras said. "And it's only been five minutes."

"You're surprised that the parking lot isn't full of Ford 150s and white guys with trucker caps and beards from Moraga," said Jerry. "You're sitting there, counting the people of color, trying to figure them all out. Are the Filipino guys hardcore Catholic reactionaries, the Korean families shopkeepers here to hone their skills for the next race war against the African-Americans? Are the black guys Panthers; will they like you, have they read one of your books?"

"Sounds like *you've* read one of my books," Karras said. "Anyway, I'm more worried about the cops."

"Oh, you think there aren't any Asian cops in the Bay Area," said Dennis through a chuckle. "Man, you *are* racist."

"White ethnic types are the worst racists—'Blah blah, my grandpa was Zorba,'" Jerry said. "'Was yours a kung-fu master?'"

"My grandfather was an accountant!" said Karras.

"You're one of those coastal managerial professional class elites! MPC!" said Dennis.

"I'm a freelance writer. And it's PMC, not MPC."

"Ah, an intellectual too," said Dennis.

"A public intellectual!" Jerry said. "An NPC, reciting whatever NPR tells non-player characters to say."

"I am going to tell you a secret… Dennis," Karras said. "A secret only writers know." He leaned over, nice and close, the tip of his nose tickling Dennis's ragged curls. Dennis snorted and laughed again.

Then Karras began to speak, his lips so close to Dennis's ear.

The boy's eyes widened, the color drained from his face.

And when Karras was done, Dennis muttered *Oh, shit* to himself.

"What, what?" Jerry wanted to know.

Dennis looked in the rear view mirror and just shook his head. Karras smirked.

"What!"

"Oh, man, Jer," Dennis said after a pregnant pause. "Michael here, he told me his last year's income."

"And?"

"And you made more money than he did last year."

"I don't even have a job."

"I mean your allowance."

Jerry laughed, and blew air out his lips.

"Happy to whisper it to you too, son," Karras said. "I've also never gotten an income tax refund." Dennis shook at the sound of that, but Jerry leaned back against the cushion of his seat and folded his arms over his narrow chest. "That just means you're a class-reductionist. We gonna shoot or not?" he asked.

They were going to shoot. The boys knew their way around the range—one of Dennis's mother's boyfriends had taken them target shooting many times, once even to handle full autos and a minigun in Vegas. Karras rented them the handguns of their choice, and paid for range time, and bought the ammunition. All tax write-offs, he reminded himself. *Just finish the book.*

Karras headed to the wrong line—"You think you gonna shoot 100 yards with that, boss?" said an old guy with leathery skin, shirt open to his navel to better show off the half-dozen crucifixes hanging from his neck. Karras didn't know if the man worked at Diablo Valley or was just one of those senior citizens who informally attach themselves to a place of business.

"Twenty-five yards, Mister Karras," said Dennis. "First three firing lines. Hey, Manny."

"Hey, Logan, how's it poppin'?" said the old man. "This guy your guidance counselor, or mama's new boytoy?"

"He's my cousin," said Jerry, which got a laugh.

Once on the proper firing line, Karras fumbled, his hands sweaty, as he tried to load the Makarov's magazine. Dennis and Jerry watched him, both impassive. There was no smiling at the shooting range except for hellos, no chatting save for one or two clipped words of instruction or praise. The noise-cancelling earmuffs and the constant reports of the firearms were only partially to credit. Men only rarely have anything to say to one another in men's spaces. It was going to be difficult, Karras realized, to get the boys to talk.

Karras aimed, squeezed the trigger but jerked in anticipation of the recoil, fired, flinched as the jacket of the bullet bounced off his forehead, then fired again, too quickly. The staffer who had sold him the ammo explained that the range rule was to wait three seconds between trigger pulls. He stopped, looked around. Nobody had noticed his faux pas, or perhaps nobody cared.

He emptied the clip, not quite three seconds between shots. Some of the expelled casings hit him in the arms and chest, lightly but annoyingly, like being hit with the spray from a car rolling through a puddle. Other than that, he felt nothing, and he couldn't even see if he'd hit the target at all. As an experience, it was entirely alienating. Had he even accomplished anything?

Putting the gun down, Karras said, "Can't imagine anyone doing this!" a little too loud. Dennis tapped on the muffs, so Karras slid them down to hang around his neck.

"First time, eh?" Dennis said as he depressed the button that brought the paper target forward. Karras had missed the silhouette itself with every shot, and landed only three of his eight on the white border of the paper target. "Take *that*, grass," said Dennis.

"Nah, there's hardly any grass," said Jerry. "Take *that*, dirt."

"Now my joke is much better, thanks," said Dennis.

"Shooting just isn't for me, I guess," Karras said. "Who wants to go next?"

"You just shot one clip, you can't decide it's not for you based on that. Was the first sentence you ever wrote good?" Jerry said. "The first time you drove a car? You have to practice."

"You have very good parents, Jerry," Karras said. Dennis was pushing bullets into Karras's clip. He loaded the gun and handed it over.

Karras emptied another clip. Again, the bullets left the gun too quickly. He was just getting started when it was all over and he had to talk to the boys again, give Dennis a turn with the Glock.

Dennis was a pretty good shooter, or at least Karras thought so. Eleven of his fifteen shots hit the silhouette, the rest hit the white. Dennis was disappointed, though. "I was aiming for the head, not center mass. Dead is dead. I guess."

"You wanna keep going, Michael?" Jerry asked. "Try this one. It's a 1911, classic."

"You don't want to take a turn?" Karras asked.

"Nah, you go ahead."

"Don't mind if I do," Karras said. His cheeks burned. He was a beginner now, the child, and these two teenagers were the experts. But once he leveled the gun, which felt better than the Makarov in his hand, and opened fire, all the humiliation in his blood vanished. He exhaled correctly this time, didn't blink when an ejected casing bounced off the tip of his nose, and took his time to refocus and fire again. When the target slid forward, Karras broke into a wild grin. Three bullets had pierced the center mass of the silhouette. "Fucking yes!" he said. He even pumped his fist. There it was. That's why people kill. Instant feedback—the petrified stare, the sudden jolt in one's body followed by a far more profound one in the body of the target. Maybe a scream, or a bloom of blood, a slow collapse or sudden slam against a wall if the gun were big enough or the victim had seen enough movies to know how to act when shot. Like a baby discovering a light switch and wanting to flip it a hundred times, this was the gun in the hand of a young man. Target practice was awful at the first trigger pull, like one's introductory puff of a cigarette or swallow of black coffee, but the fatal essence of it brought you back to try again and again. Karras smiled and thought nothing but *Yeah*.

"See," said Jerry flatly. "Practice."

"Take it easy, though," said Dennis. "This isn't a Chuck E. Cheese."

Dennis shot some more. Karras shot some more, but showed no further improvement. Jerry repeatedly waved off the guns when one or another was offered to him.

"Worried about getting your prints on 'em or something?" Dennis finally asked.

Jerry didn't answer for a moment. He glanced out across the expanse at the firing line, at the target, then over his shoulder at the other parties with their pistols, their long guns. "I had a gun pointed at me two days ago. I'm just glad my parents don't pay attention to English-language news media; they would have killed me. I don't want this anymore. I just wanted to have a nice summer and work on my college applications."

"My mom saw everything; she said that I could take the week off for mental health reasons," Dennis said. "She got my shrink to write a note. I told her I was going to the movies all day."

"She didn't ask why you were packing a gun?" Karras asked.

Dennis snorted. "What, you think she's a homemaker in a frilly apron, baking cookies for me? She commutes to the city for work every morning."

"Dennis's mom texts him good night," Jerry said.

"That's how I like it," Dennis said.

"What do the kids at your school think of the Middlesex movement?" Karras asked, knowing what they would say next, which was nothing, and knowing what they'd do next, which was scowl at him for bringing up the topic at a shooting range.

"We're out of ammo," said Dennis. "More, or lunch?"

Karras knew Jerry would say lunch, and Jerry did, but Karras did walk back into the double-wide trailer to return the rentals and buy a box of ammunition for the Makarov.

Karras also knew he would be paying for lunch, despite having revealed his income. Thankfully, the boys were happy with tiny bags of potato chips and extremely mediocre boiled hot dogs from Caspar's, a fast-food restaurant of ancient vintage back in Oakland.

"Why do you want to learn how to shoot, anyway?" Jerry asked after swallowing his first hotdog in two bites. He'd been quiet, not sullen but just affectless, the entire ride back from the range. "Are you going to write yourself into your book?"

"Dude, self-defense, obviously," said Dennis.

"Well, maybe I don't want to learn how to shoot, but I needed to experience shooting a gun to properly write about shooters. I mean, I've already had a gun pointed at me, and a knife, I saw someone kill himself in front of me, I witnessed the aftermath of a vehicular mass murder, I've been arrest—" Caspar's was a small place, just three four-tops and two smaller tables, and two employees ringing customers up, but it was fairly full and now all eyes were on Karras.

"We've all had our troubles, no?" Karras asked the entire room. "We all have stories. I'm a writer." He dug into his bag and pulled out legal pad and his clickable pen. "Anyone want to talk about their experiences with gun violence? Police brutality, street crime, gangs, domestic violence, right-wingers marching through town?"

People want to talk... but not when they're eating. He clicked his pen twice for emphasis, then placed the pad on the table and the pen atop it. "If anyone changes their mind..." he said to the backs of the other Caspar's customers.

"Dude," said Dennis. "Self-defense. Obviously."

Karras hmphed, took a bite of his hot dog, masticated it nice and slow, and swallowed ostentatiously. "I need to talk to a shooter, or a potential shooter. You guys know any?"

Dennis and Jerry peered at one another, didn't say anything, looked back at Karras.

"I get it now," Karras said. "Holding a gun is like holding a smartphone. Pure power, once you get used to it. I'm already ready to go back to the range, or up into the hills to shoot cans off tree stumps—whatever it is people like to do with guns around here."

"How are we supposed to know a 'potential shooter'?" Jerry said. "You think just because we have access to guns and are very online and listened to Bennett—"

"Yes, I do," said Karras.

"Fuck you, man."

"No, fuck you, Jerry," Karras said, calm as ever. "You think you don't owe me after the whole Bennett fiasco?"

"You're the grown-up; we didn't force you to come," said Jerry. "You're just flailing around, thinking of anything to occupy your time so you won't have to finish writing your stupid book about dumbasses who can't count the number of people who are shooting at them. I procrastinate too, but just with Xbox."

"If it hadn't been you two, it would have been someone else! Bennett fans are a crazy cult, and he is obsessed with me," Karras said. "You can't just log off when you're being cyberstalked by a celebrity. I found that out the hard way; it's the ultimate suspicious act, and your enemies move against you very rapidly when you purposely and publicly blind yourself to their actions."

"I know someone," Dennis said.

"You could have called in," Jerry said to Karras, "you could have posted about how Bennett wanted you on the show just to cause controversy!"

"He clearly wanted more than that," Karras said. "He pulled a gun on us!"

"I know a shooter," Dennis said.

"Nobody expected a school shooting to happen while we were on air," Jerry said.

"According to Bennett, there has never been a school shooting, just a perennial touring production of a stage show called 'The Latest Uniquely American Tragedy.'"

"You know, he said that you arranged the false flag event to coincide with the show. Of course I don't believe it," Jerry said, "but he does have an answer for everything, and that answer is you."

Karras shrugged. "If you still listen to him after he waved a gun in your face, you're a hopeless cause. I don't care what your GPA is, Jerry, or that you're just basically a child—"

"A child you texted immediately when you needed help."

"Not immediately." That was true. Karras had had dozens of notifications to deal with when he recovered his phone and turned it back on. It had taken perhaps a half an hour to handle the most urgent non-law-enforcement messages, and then another twenty minutes of firearms research before he decided to find the boys on social media and contact them. "And thanks for all your help. Really."

"I can help, I know a shooter," said Dennis, his jaw clenching. "You asked for a shooter! I know one!" Karras raised an eyebrow, Jerry just peered. "A potential shooter, anyway. Not a wannabe, though. He doesn't go to our school or anything, I know him from online. Zombie media board."

"You're still on that?" Jerry said.

"It's not much about zombies anymore—it's a real community, we're friends."

"So who is your friend, the potential shooter, who is a part of your community, which is no longer about zombie movies?" Karras asked.

"And other media, like games and television and literature," Dennis said.

"Ah, yes, zombie literature," Karras said. "Pardon me."

"His real name is Serj," said Dennis. "He goes by Schweick online. Schweick is a character from Fulci's *The Beyond*, which is a classic of the genre. Schweick is an artist from New Orleans who—"

"What makes him a Future Special Boy of America?"

asked Karras. "I mean, what distinguishes him from any other weird kid on the internet?"

"He's on the board even I left because it was too autistic for me," said Jerry. "I think I remember Schweick, but he didn't stand out as a number-one seed for shooting."

"He knows the Middlesex shooter, Aram. I guess they're both Armenian-American," said Dennis. "I mean, you know, he spells Serj with a J, and he's from New Jersey too."

"Now who's the white ethnic chauvinist?" said Karras.

"Anyone can be named Serj. Might be Sergio, might be Serge with a gee-ee in real life, so French, and that's even if," said Jerry. "Really, Logan, you should know better."

"Yeah, Dennis," said Karras.

"I don't know why the two of you are ganging up on me—the point is that after I got home, I was catching up on social media and the boards in general last night, and I found a post by Serj that said he knew that Middlesex was going to happen before it did. And he also posted, during the shooting, 'That's my *jan*.' It means 'friend' or 'dear' or something. He wrote it in that crazy Armenian alphabet." Dennis jabbed at the screen of his phone with both thumbs.

"Since when you do know Armenian, Logan?" asked Jerry.

Karras knew how Dennis would answer. *Obviously*

Serj wrote another post explaining 'jan' at length. And Dennis did say that. "But was his first post about the shooting really posted before it started, or just when it started hitting social media but before making it onto the mainstream news channels?" Karras asked.

"I'm checking," Dennis said.

"Even if it's after, that might mean he identifies enough with shooters to be a potential shooter himself," said Jerry. "Sometimes a fan becomes a professional."

"Check his post history," said Karras. "Maybe he's one of those scam accounts that makes dozens of posts that purport to predict the future, and then deletes all the ones that don't read as though they're an accurate prediction. There are plenty of places called Middlesex in the English-speaking world. Fuckin' Saxons got around." He winked at Jerry. "*Now*, I'm a racist against white ethnics."

"Nope, nothing like that," said Dennis. "He's a normal guy… I mean, not a normie or anything."

"No shit," said Karras.

"A typical internet guy. He's real. I even called him once. Here's the post." Dennis said, holding up the phone so that both Karras and Jerry could read the screen.

The board was *Shock Waves* and its look hadn't been updated since the early 2000s—black background, red borders, white letters, and all of it poorly organized for mobile. Schweick's avatar was a deformed-seeming face that Karras guessed was taken from the same movie whence came the name—it had the grotesque but unconvincing look of spirit gum and latex haphazardly plastered onto only a mildly attractive actor.

IF YOU'RE IN JERSEY, I AM NO SHIT PRAYING FOR YOUR NORMALFAG ASSES. YOU KNOW HOW CHADS USED TO SAY, 'PLAYGROUND 3PM YOU'RE DEAD MEAT' WHEN THEY WANTED TO POUND YOUR FACE INTO MEAT SAUCE IN FRONT OF AN AUDIENCE OF STACEYS? THAT'S WHAT'S GOING TO HAPPEN THIS AFTERNOON IN CENTRAL JERSEY (YEAH YEAH THERE'S NO SUCH PLACE AS CENTRAL JERSEY I KNOW) BUT IN REVERSE. HIGH SCORE COMING AND NO THERE WON'T BE ANYONE MAKING THEMSELVES A HERO. JERSEY GIRLS AND JERKIN' TROONS? STAY HOME, PLAY VIDYA. DON'T GET IN THE MIDDLE OF ALL THE SEX!

Pretty typical semiliterate garbage from someone unable to write in anything other than the cant of the miscreant, though that last line was a compelling clue; it stood out from the rest of the post and did hint pretty directly at the location of the shooting.

"Click on his name so we can see his other posts, especially right before and right after," said Karras.

"Sure," Dennis said, and he turned the phone's screen back to himself and clicked the name SCHWEICK. "Fuck."

Jerry glanced over Dennis's shoulder. "User Not Found."

"Fuck fuck, just *now*." Dennis clicked back. "All his

posts are gone. Mods must be cleaning up—probably someone reported it to the cops."

"Just now, this second, as we're talking about it? Not three days ago, not this morning, not tomorrow?" said Karras. "Let me see that phone."

"I know how to use a ph—"

Karras snatched it from Dennis's hand.

"Should have capped that shit," Jerry said. "Probably somebody did."

"Was there a thread?" asked Karras, his forefinger pushing and poking against the screen. "Did you respond to it, or anyone else?"

"Give me back my phone!"

Karras held the phone up over his head as Dennis lunged for it, his belly flowing both over and under the edge of the small table.

"Excuse me!" the cashier called from her station. "Don't make me..." She didn't have to finish. Karras handed the phone back.

"Nothing," Dennis said after several sullen seconds of wiping his phone screen with his sleeve. "Someone erased everything. His whole posting history."

"He did it himself, then," Karras said. "Did you tell him about me?"

"No, this board is custom—too many people were flouncing and it would ruin threads and the image archive. Only the admin, Barbara, can delete," Dennis said. "Barbara isn't a woman, I don't think."

"Yeah yeah, 'They're coming to get you,'" said

Karras. He glanced out the window. Telegraph Avenue again, but much less busy in North Oakland, just south of the highway on-ramps, than it was in Berkeley. No sign of cop cars.

"So they did it because they were worried about the cops," said Jerry. "Do you know Serj from anywhere else online?"

"Yeah, I'm going now to Twi—" Dennis said, then stopped.

"No user," Jerry said.

"He's gone," Karras said. "Totally erased from the internet. Is that right?"

"The internet is forever," Jerry said.

"Not anymore. I've had this happen to me. My own profiles haven't been erased, obviously, but the people I've talked to about second-shooter experiences have been targeted. My notes have vanished, just like the video evidence of second shooters, the wire reports of them..."

"Are you blaming me?" Dennis said, suddenly a child again, red-cheeked and plaintive.

"What a coincidence that this happened just now, Logan," said Jerry. "Remarkable."

"I really didn't do anything, not like that..." Dennis said.

"Look, I've seen it before, Jerry," Karras said. "I'm sure Den—uh, Logan?—wasn't just messing with us. And you said you called him once. Call him now."

"Uhm..."

Both Dennis and Jerry stared at Karras as if he'd suggested they start kissing for his amusement.

"You called him before."

"Yes, but... can't I just text him?"

"It's kind of creepy to just randomly call someone, isn't it?" asked Jerry.

"Ah, Gen Z, afraid of dialing a number. Give me your phone."

"What if it's tapped? What if everything just got erased because someone heard us talking about Schweick and Middlesex?" Dennis asked, still nervous. Karras could see sweat on his cheeks, his fingers red where they were clenched around his phone.

"Imagine the Facebook ads you'll get after this," Jerry said.

"Then write down the number and, with luck, the payphone in the parking lot, or the one across the street, will still work," said Karras. He pulled a few singles out of his pocket, and flattened them against the tabletop before handing them to Jerry. "You're the most attractive one at our table, and the cashier didn't snap at you in particular. Go flirt with her till she makes change for these from her tip jar."

"We probably should have left her a tip in the first place if we wanted her cooperation," said Jerry, but he scooped up the bills and walked over to the counter.

"More chips," Dennis called out after Jerry.

"Not more chips," Karras said.

"This is pretty exciting," Dennis said. "I mean, the

Bennett thing was absolutely sick, but this is cooler. Like a real investigation. You know, I didn't know how to bring it up before, but I do a little writing too. I'm working on my first manga. Maybe you could take a look at the script sometime?"

"Yes, definitely," Karras said as he collected a palm of quarters from Jerry. "Let's go try the number you have for Serj. Don't worry, I'll do all the talking. Is it his personal cell phone or his family's landline?"

Both boys answered with a roll of their eyes, but they bussed their trays without being reminded to and joined Karras at the graffiti-covered payphone. There was actually a dial tone. Karras whispered his little mantra—"People want to talk, people want to talk"—as he slid coins down the slot and hit the numbers Dennis read to him. He didn't hear the pair of cars pull into the parking lot, didn't notice that they ignored the striping on the asphalt to park diagonally behind him, didn't feel the reverberations of the doors opening and closing and thought it was Jerry obnoxiously looming behind him as a telephone somewhere in New Jersey—the area code was 201, anyway—began to ring.

But the hand that reached over his shoulder and pressed the hook down wasn't Jerry's. Nor was the voice that spoke.

"You took my father's gun, Michael Karras," Rahel said. "You are a thief."

15.

"THAT WAS ALL our quarters," said Dennis to Karras, who wasn't paying attention to anyone but Rahel. She stood before him like a smoldering torch planted in the ground. He could practically feel his eyebrows frying and falling off. Tony was in the passenger seat of her car, and another car he didn't recognize, but filled with people he did—Samuel and Bruk's husband, whatever his name was.

"My brother is so angry with you, I would not let him leave the car," said Rahel. "He would strangle you with that telephone wire and the police would come and shoot him down because he is a black man!"

So much for the theory that Tony had purposely buried the Makarov where Karras would find it. Karras just sighed.

"And you're associating with children while carrying a stolen firearm," Rahel said. "Have you gone insane?"

"How did you even know where to find us?" Karras asked. The man sitting in the passenger's seat of Samuel's car stuck his head out the window and shouted, "Your fat friend has been tweeting about you all afternoon!"

"Not cool, bro!" Jerry shouted back.

Dennis shrunk into his long black coat. "Sorry," he muttered at Karras.

"Let's get out of this parking lot," Karras said to Rahel. "However you want me to solve this problem, it can't happen here in public. And Logan, don't tweet where we are going next for once."

"Can I text my mom? It's later than I was expecting."

"No."

"What about calling Serj? He's on the East Co—"

"Let's go, or I'll drag you by the roots of your thinning hair. You can sit with Tony in the backseat and explain yourself," said Rahel.

"Fine, where to?" asked Karras.

"Shut up and follow."

Quickly and without speaking, Karras and the boy loaded themselves into Dennis's car, but there was enough noise from slamming doors and three revving engines and a bit of shouting between Samuel and his children that nobody noticed that the payphone had begun to ring.

*　　*　　*

THE ETHIOPIAN CULTURAL Center wasn't very large, being the bottom floor of a small office building that also held a dentist's office and a title search company, but it was just a couple of miles up Telegraph Avenue, back into Berkeley. A few leaflets promoting musical performances were stuck to the inside of the windows. It was also directly across the street from the Lutheran church where Lee Nam-jin had shot four people, and where Rahel had encountered a second shooter. Karras briefly caught the boys up on what had happened as Dennis struggled to parallel park.

"They are going to kill us in there," said Jerry. "They're gonna take your gun back and shoot us all with it."

"I'll keep the ammo in the glove box," said Karras.

"Don't!" said Dennis. "And shut up about me being killed; I'm trying to park here."

"This is your fault," Jerry said.

"You two can leave if you're nervous," said Karras. They'd start arguing in a moment, and then one of Rahel's relatives would weigh in. "I'm not trying to shame you into coming inside! Thanks for the ride, and I don't think this'll be dangerous, but you guys should probably just get home and do your *Everquest* raid or whatever, or homework, or whatever you need or want to. It's been nothing but lunacy since I got to town. Have a normal day. I'm sorry about

245

what happened with Bennett."

They both just looked at him. Finally, Dennis said, "*Everquest*? Don't you mean *Pac-Man*, grandpa? We're totally going in, right, Jerry?"

"No way, I'm going home. I'll walk," said Jerry.

"Dude…"

"Logan, what?"

"You know…" Dennis said.

"Maybe I don't know."

"Isn't it exciting? We met Bennett, we talked to a girl who went viral, I knocked a gun out of someone's hand! We're about to have some kind of weird meeting about a stolen Soviet firearm! It's crazy!"

"That's why," Jerry said. "I've had enough crazy to have some good stories when I go off to college. But I don't care about any of this anymore; Bennett's an asshole, this guy—no offense—is also an asshole and a criminal, and you fucking tweeted about us hanging out together."

"I left you out of the tweets—"

There was a rapping at the passenger-side front window, Bruk's husband. Dennis lowered the window from the control panel. "Hello, Mister Michael Karras. I'm Djimon. We've met before." He tapped his foot meaningfully. Karras's loose tooth throbbed in sympathy. "They sent me out here to drag you inside if you are not prepared to come peacefully." He winked. "Not that I would, but come on already. Samuel is extremely angry with you."

"What about Tony?"

"Him too, probably," Djimon said.

"I was just leaving," Jerry said. He opened the curbside back door, nodded to Djimon and stalked off.

"And we were just coming," said Dennis.

"Don't talk," said Karras. "Just open the trunk."

"Leave your phone in the car," Djimon said. "Bring everything else. You know what I mean."

Except for the posters of Selassie and other figures Karras didn't recognize, and a pair of statues in opposite corners, and the faint lingering smell of incense, the cultural center could have been a Greek Cultural Center, a Finnish Brotherhood of America meeting hall, a semi-illicit mahjong parlor, or any other space for people to sit around folding tables and drink coffee and read newspapers. Once every few months, for some dance night or party, the furniture would be moved away, and the large flat screen TV covered in decorations or a banner.

There was no coffee today. The Alazar family sat at three of the seven seats surrounding a round table. Rahel was still fuming, Tony stoic but his eyes wide, blazing. Samuel smiled at Djimon at least and bade them all to sit.

Karras tried to clear his mind and think about his goals. He could still save the situation, find the right words to say that would get him out of here with the gun in his possession and Rahel on his good side. But the trick he depended on, the ability to know what someone was about to say, failed. He looked at the four faces—grim, ornery, glacial, and insincere—and he could sense nothing, the fuzz of old television static filled his ears. Karras took his seat robotically, and realized with an ice-water splash of terror that he didn't even know what *he* was going to say next—or ever again. Dennis noisily plopped into the chair next to him, his coat flapping like broken raven wings.

"So, thank you for coming," said Djimon. "I think it's best if I speak for the family. I've already had my hands on you. Personally, I'm satisfied. I should have called the police on you after I found you in my daughter's room, watching a snuff film." He raised his palm when Dennis went to say something. Karras could read him—some pedantic objection regarding the definition of the term *snuff film*. "But then I would have had to explain the antics of Tony and Rahel at the same time. So you see, while they are angry with you, and their father angry at them, I am universally and equally angry with all of you. Samuel, you should have raised your children better. Children, you are a pair of fools! Mister Karras, you are nothing but an imp. Your very presence among my family has caused nothing but grief and trauma, and now you endanger us further. So here is what I recommend. Return Tony's property and leave this place. Delete whatever notes you've taken or chapters you have written or information you have gathered about us, and not just

Rahel, but my daughter and all that happened in her room, and then you may write your book and live your life."

Dennis chuckled. "Or what?"

Djimon ignored Dennis entirely, as though he was entirely unable to perceive the boy.

"I'll do all that... but I need the gun," Karras said, surprising even himself. Never mind what Rahel or Tony would say, Karras didn't know what was about to come out of his own mouth. "It's not practical for me to return the gun, because I am being surveilled and pursued. I can't afford security and wouldn't know where to begin to even get a bodyguard. I'm no Salman Rushdie. I need the gun, and I know that nobody at this table can legally carry it, or probably even own it. It wouldn't have been buried, like you're waiting for the uprising, if it was legal. I'll do you the favor of taking it off your hands."

Rahel inhaled deeply, placed her hands on the table, spreading her fingers wide as though seeking purchase on the side of a cliff she was slowly but inexorably sliding down. "You are a sociopath," she said. "Incurable, untreatable, soulless. A monster."

"I just need the gun," Karras said. "I'm sure there are other guns among your extended family buried in their yards as well."

"There are not!" Rahel said, but Samuel and Djimon shared a knowing look that suggested the opposite.

"What are you going to do—call the police and

have me arrested for stealing your illegal gun? Beat the shit out of me in front of a witness?"

"Yes!" Tony roared, jumping to his feet, his chair tumbling behind him, his arms flashing across the table, his hands brushing against Karras's neck, and just as suddenly he was flung backward, his ass thumping hard against the floor, by Djimon's hand on his belt.

"Ow! Uncle!"

"Enough," said Djimon. "I handled you when you were a boy, and I can handle you now. No more interruptions."

From the inside breast pocket of Dennis's duster erupted a big band jazz number, swinging hard. "Ooh, sorry," he said, digging for his phone. "I forgot to turn it off. One sec." Djimon flexed his large hand, and Dennis held up a finger. "Might be my mom. She'll kill me if I don't pick up—if I don't answer texts within an hour she calls and screams at me... Oh, no."

He turned to Karras. "It's Serj."

"Answer it."

"Decline it!" said Rahel. Tony groaned and picked himself up off the floor.

"Who is Serj?" Samuel asked. Then he snapped at Djimon in Amharic. Djimon shrugged, and responded in a way that sounded to Karras like a canned aphorism, or at least something philosophical.

"Hey, Serj... yeah, I did. Wait, what? Yeah, he is,

but I shouldn't—well, okay, you asked for it," Dennis said into his phone. Then he put the phone on the table and tapped the speaker icon.

"Hello, Michael Karras?"

Rahel moved to snatch the phone, but Djimon was faster and grabbed her wrist. She tugged, he twisted more roughly than Karras ever would have thought. Samuel put his hand on Djimon's shoulder, and Djimon let go.

"Karras here," Karras said. "What is this?"

"You know what this is," Serj said. Dennis's phone was only last year's best, and the voice sounded a little tinny, but Karras could tell that Serj was trying to deepen his voice beyond what puberty had granted him. "I got a call from a 510 phone number and called it back and let it ring a dozen times. Some lady yelled at me in Spanish. I looked up the area code and saw it was Logan. I remembered seeing you both on Bennett's feed, and then I checked Logan's tweets and knew that it was probably you trying to call me."

Djimon spoke. "Young man, you should not be associating with either of these characters. Michael Karras is a dangerous man, erratic."

"What is this all about?" Samuel said. "Boy on the phone, you explain everything."

"Cops!" Serj said, and hung up. Dennis groaned, and the men—Tony was back in his chair now—exchanged perplexed glances. Rahel grabbed at the phone again, and this time nobody stopped her. She hit redial before the phone went to its lock screen and held it up to her air.

"Hello, don't hang up," she said when Serj picked up. "This is Rahel Alazar... Yes... Yes... None other... Yes, there was... My father, my uncle, my brother, Michael Karras, and Logan... I swear that I did see a second shooter, on my life. No, I will not take the Lord's name in vain to swear to you, my own life will have to do... All right... Yes, I'll put you back on speaker phone." She placed the phone back upon the table.

"Why do you fear the police?" Samuel asked the phone.

"I don't fear the police," said Serj. "They won't be able to stop what's coming."

"Can't, you mean?" asked Karras.

"No, *won't*. Have they ever? Weren't they just sitting in their cars, eating donuts and sipping coffee, watching the carnage on the fields of Middlesex, until DHS brought in a drone? One of the students was the son of a DHS bigwig."

"Cops stop a lot of mass shootings before they can become mass shootings, so the incidents don't get counted in the stats," Karras said. "And the plurality of mass shooters are stopped by the cops—they are either killed by the police, or commit suicide when the police arrive."

"This is 101 stuff," Dennis said. "What's up, Serj—how did you know about Middlesex before it happened?"

"That's a boring question. I can't believe nobody is asking me what's coming, and why the police won't stop it," said Serj.

"This is fuckin' stupid..." Tony muttered to himself. His father raised a brow and Tony looked away, like a child might. Then he turned back to the table and peered down at the phone and after a sigh, which was also childlike, said, "Can the Dr. Doom shit. What is coming, and why won't the police stop it?"

"Oh, ho, you wish to know what—"

"Yes, and you wish to tell us, or you would have hung up again," said Karras. "People want to talk, ever hear that?" Then, to the assembled, he explained, "I've tweeted that several times. It's like a slogan, or a personal mantra."

"Serj, how did you know about Middlesex, and why didn't you say anything?" asked Dennis. "I mean, why didn't you say something substantive, really warn the students, call the cops, I dunno..."

"Here's your warning. You know who carries out shootings, and why. It's always the bullied bullies. Kids who are picked on, but not so much that they just spend their whole lives cowering. Not from the richest families, but they can always afford a few guns. Same with the grown-ups: it's not the CEOs or the dishwashers who do the shooting, it's not the immigrant zillionaires or the poor illegals who smell like motor oil or cooking grease or housecleaning supplies, it's somebody right in the middle of society.

It's all the same, every time, like watching reruns on TV."

Reruns on TV. That was wrong. Not what Serj was saying but that Serj would say it. He was a teen in the second decade of the twentieth century. Netflix had started streaming when he was an infant, and DVR came out years before that. Serj wasn't a teen, or if he was, he was being fed lines by someone with a less than perfect understanding of the media ecology in which teens lived.

"… three days from now, they are going to murder America," Serj finished.

"Why are you telling us this now?" Rahel asked. That was also interesting—there wasn't a trace of disbelief in her voice. Serj had described coordinated and competing mass shooting events, squads of special boys, jihadis, and postseeking to hit new high scores. "We're just going to call the police." She looked up and swept the table with her gaze—she would brook no disagreement regarding the authorities.

"Go ahead and call them. Did they believe you last time?" Serj asked. "Did anyone believe you last time, except for Mike Karras? And he might just be looking to pad out his book by pretending. I'm a fan, but—"

"Of course you are," said Rahel.

"Mastermind or monster?" asked Karras. Most of the table looked at him, confused, but Dennis nodded. On the phone, Serj nipped off a syllable. "Well? It's a tricky one, isn't it?"

"What do you mean?" Djimon asked.

"It's how the media describe fatal attacks—if there is some political goal or terrorist design to the mass murder, the government and the news talk about the 'mastermind' of the plot. If the issue is psychological, or personal, or inexplicable, then the police simply write the attack off as the act of a 'monster,'" Samuel told Djimon. "It's from an article by Mister Karras. He can be clever, this fellow, when he isn't being a fool."

Karras shot Rahel a look and a smile, and Rahel rolled her eyes.

"So, what about it? Are you a monster, or a mastermind?" Dennis asked Serj. "I mean, I know you're a monster, Middlesex—"

"Katrina Chu-Ramirez is not going to grow up and be your dakimakura, dude. No need to white knight for her," Serj said.

"There's much I don't understand about this conversation," Djimon said. "Let us just say that we have received your warning, son. Is there anything else you want to tell us?"

"This message will self-destruct—"

Rahel stabbed the screen with her finger. "Enough of this idiot child," she said.

"Self-destruct?" asked Djimon. "Was that a direct threat?"

"It's a meme," said Dennis, which did not clear up Djimon's bemused expression.

"It's from a TV show," said Tony. "*Inspector Gadget*, a cartoon from when I was five."

"*Mission Impossible*, originally," said Karras.

"That just tells me there's no reason to take that child seriously," said Samuel. "He's telling us a tall tale, and I presume you two"—he waved a hand at Dennis and Karras—"did it purposely to distract us from the issue we're here to discuss. Why would radical Islamicists, and disaffected white boys who spend all their time playing video games and eating junk food, and countryside militiamen, and Catholic Crusaders bellowing 'Deus vult' cooperate to blanket America in mass murders?"

"I had nothing to do with that call, but I have reason to believe that 'Serj' wasn't who he claimed to be, and the threat to 'murder America' is worth taking seriously. And I suspect that if we go look for his digital trail, it will all have been erased," said Karras.

Dennis picked up his phone and checked it. "Yup. Even the number I called is off my phone now... sorry, I should have turned it off or left it in the car or something. The same hackers that have been messing with your stuff have probably been listening in on our whole conversation." The two older men groaned.

"Like you were saying, Dad, it doesn't matter. It's a bullshit story, a prank. Mike's being played by some deranged fan. There's not going to be a nationwide shooting rampage; none of those groups have anything in common."

Rahel sighed, snorted, and put her hands behind her head, then leaned back in her chair, her legs straight. "Of course they have something in common," she announced. "They all hate women."

16.

DENNIS LEFT KARRAS on the curb, still complaining about the sexism of one Rahel Alazar, and how unfair it was that she could be so terrible, and that this was why so many men become 'zetas' who go their own way and separate themselves from the socio-sexual spectacle of attracting mates. As if it weren't already obvious that Rahel was right and that both the men in her family and the supposedly clever and politically aware Michael Karras were wrong.

The Alazars kept the gun too. "Follow your foolish friend, and take the gun with you!" Djimon declared, his voice thick with disgust and loud enough to be picked up by the phone as Dennis noisily stormed out of the community center lounge, ranting about 'gender feminism' versus 'radical feminism.' Rahel bent down and retrieved the gun from Karras's bag. Tony said, "Okay, we should be all right now."

"We're keeping the gun," Djimon said. "Thanks to your friend's phone, the police may well know that you're carrying it. The gun may not be strictly legal for any of us to hold, but at least it isn't stolen property in Samuel's hands. Go now, right now."

"But the police, or whomever, still think I have the gun, thanks to you!"

"They'll think you're in your idiot apprentice's car as well…"

Karras nodded and jogged after Dennis to make sure that he could say, "Wait up, I'm coming with you!" in range of Dennis's phone. He even walked around the car to open the passenger-side door to retrieve his phone, but let Dennis pull the door shut. As a ruse, it wouldn't last for long, though Dennis was still muttering to himself, fueled by rage and shame.

Rage and shame—those were two other things the groups supposedly planning for the nationwide shooting spree had in common. Maybe too much rage and shame to cooperate with one another. Rage and shame was why Karras had wanted the Makarov in the first place. He'd been powerless to stop Rasnic's suicide, humiliated by the man in the park, and threatened by Christopher Bennett in front of an audience of God only knew how many…

How many what?

Potential mass-shooters.

"Okay, you'll drive with us," Tony said, tapping Karras's shoulder. He turned and saw Rahel waiting next to her brother, her arms crossed, her eyebrow up.

"Where are we going?" Karras asked Tony.

"Just get in the car," she said.

"I understand why you wanted the pistol, Michael," Tony said after they all loaded themselves into Tony's boatlike Cadillac. "So I am going to be your new best friend. I'll carry it and be at your side, like a bodyguard."

"Men!" Rahel said to her reflection in the mirror in her sun visor. Karras saw that he appeared to be very small, like a lonely single child back in the days before booster chairs and car seats, being brought on a long car trip by his parents.

"Where are we going?"

"Doesn't matter. They'll find you sooner than later," Tony said. "We can just bolt-hole up at the bungalow and wait for the next drone or teenage Bennett fan to show up."

"I'm not doing that," said Rahel. "One, that *shed* is disgusting and I refuse to spend any time there. I'm not going to clean it either. Even if I did there would be no space for me."

"Then go home. You can pray for me from home."

"I'm not going to go home and leave you on your own, brother," said Rahel. "Neither of you is clever enough to deal with what is coming. Turn here."

Tony obeyed, though his face was questioning and Rahel unready to explain.

"So what's the plan then, Rahel?" Karras asked.

Rahel answered by way of looking at and addressing Tony, as if Karras were just a buzzing fly that had reminded her of something.

"We need to speak with Katrina Chu-Ramirez. As I was saying: One, your shed is gross. Two, all of this, the rampages and conspiracies, are a problem caused by men. Men can't solve the problems men create. Turn again."

"They're a kid," Karras said.

"You, Mister Karras, were working with children! They saved your life!" Rahel snapped. "And don't tell me that those boys were older. Girls mature faster than boys, and your little Mutt and Jeff friends were clearly underdeveloped for their age."

"They should get part-time jobs or something," Tony said. "Give them something to do."

"A church youth group, like we had at their age!"

"It worked... for you," Tony said.

"Is the plan to fly out to New Jersey, then?" Karras asked. There was no way Sharon would pay for a last-minute plane ticket.

"Turn again."

"You're kidding," Karras said, just a little ahead of Tony, as they pulled up next to the church across the street from the community center.

"When I'm kidding, you'll know, because your sides

will be splitting with laughter. That's my promise to you, Michael," said Rahel as she tapped her brother's shoulder and then pointed to the curb, bidding him park the car. "Come."

She led them into the church via the side entrance, and into the church office where sat a pair of momentarily confused Lutherans whom she told, "I need to get something from our stores in the basement. Abun lent me the key." They nodded at her and at another door that Rahel was already on her way to.

Karras and Tony followed her through the door and down a short hallway to another. Rather than digging out a key, she withdrew a wallet from her back pocket—Karras realized for the first time that he'd only ever seen Rahel in men's denim jeans, and that she didn't carry a purse—withdrew a credit card from that, replaced the wallet, slid the card into the gap between the door and frame, squeezed the door knob, and after a practiced four seconds of jiggling, opened the door.

"We'll all be lighting some candles after this," she said. "Come on." Karras turned to Tony and shrugged, but he just followed his sister down the darkened steps without any sort of acknowledgement of Karras's existence.

The basement did contain some of the accouterments Karras saw during the kidase, and also a number of Christmas trees, clothing racks holding choir robes on wire hangers, half-empty shelving units for Sunday school workbooks and some perhaps out-of-favor hymnals, and in the corner a computer of twentieth-century vintage popped up on a folding table. Rahel sat down at it, powered it up, and then turned on the modem, which squealed in 2600 baud.

"I can't believe a building practically on top of the Hayward fault has a basement," Karras said, looking up at the low ceiling. "We're gonna die down here."

"God will provide," said Rahel between keystrokes.

"And, is that... DOS? Whoa. 'In the beginning was the command line...'" He was babbling a bit, feeling nervous and out of place. He could smell his own sweaty self, the aroma overcoming the dust in his nose, on his lips. "Black and amber monitor too. I'm amazed it still works."

"It's not DOS, it's Unix," said Tony. "Back in the day, the church tried to run a few computer classes for poor people, so they could get white-collar jobs. You can guess how well it worked, given the local competition. Half a mile away, at Cal, the smartest kids in the state are getting CS degrees like they're free vaccines."

"I bet," Karras said. He leaned in to peer over Rahel's shoulder as she typed, hoping to get *something* right. "Telnet?" She keyed in another command and Karras gasped.

"Oh my God, a MUD," he said.

"A MUSH." Rahel didn't have to be snotty about

the distinction, but in two words she managed it. "You have many questions."

Hash marks on the screen spelled out the legend BRUNCHMUSH. Multi-user Dungeon or Dimension. Shared Habitat or Hallucination. Depended on whom you asked, as if there was even anyone to ask anymore. MUDs and MUSHes were chat programs, social games with environments built of text, good for everything from killing monsters to meeting the love of your life, and once upon a time, when modems screamed in the night and computer memory was usefully measured in megabytes, they positively ruled. Then the web came and by the year 2000, most of the games were abandoned for blogging sites, chat rooms, and the beginnings of social media. How bizarre that Rahel was a member of a MUSH that had probably been built while she was in the womb, Karras thought. He glanced over at Tony, who was wearing a half-amused, half-bemused smirk. It felt familiar to Karras; his facial muscles had just organized themselves in the same way.

"Katrina Chu-Ramirez is on a MUSH?" Tony asked. "Sister, you're on a MUSH? How long have you been coming down here to log in on... *Brunch*?"

"Since I learned how to read. Twenty years. A girl in first grade showed me *Brunch MUSH* in the computer lab. Her mother was a system administrator at Vista Community College," Rahel said.

Karras knew what they'd say next. *How come you*

never show—It's for women only. But Katrina is non—

"We are going to chat with her stepmother. What on Earth would a teen be doing on a MUSH?" said Rahel. "I spoke about my experience last year on here, and when Middlesex happened last week, she spoke to me about Katrina and her concerns. We've been praying together."

"How come you don't log on at home?"

"Do you think I'd want to answer all your questions at home? I can barely tolerate them here."

Tony shut up.

"Plus, no wireless, crazy old modem, maybe the phone wires leading into the church aren't even tapped," said Karras.

"Security through obscurity," said Tony. "Better than nothing."

"Here she is," Rahel said. Karras and Tony crowded around her. "Bug off, I hate it when people read over my shoulder. Why do you think I've been breaking into this basement three times a week for the past two decades?"

"Is that why you had so many lessons but can't play the violin for crap?"

"Shut up." Rahel started typing, two finger search-and-destroy, but dexterous nonetheless.

Karras peeked at the screen from what he thought was a polite enough distance. Rahel, whose MUD name was SailorChereka, was using the page function to speak to MochaJoon one-on-one, rather than chatting in one of the virtual 'rooms' any user could enter to place a recording device into.

"You too, Michael," said Rahel. "Go wait on the other side of the room, by the icon of St. Macarius the Great."

"Uhm…"

"He's on one of the easels."

"There are lots of easels."

"He's a saint in the Greek Orthodox tradition as well, you know," Rahel said, turning around in her chair to stare daggers at Karras. She planted her palm on the monitor screen. Karras shuffled across the room to the spot where the Orthodox icons sat on their easels like a live studio audience watching a situation comedy, and placed himself next to a promising one.

"John the Baptist," said Tony. He flapped his fingers a bit, indicating the right, and Karras took a single sideways step. "There he is. The great-looking one."

"You too, Tone," Rahel said.

The clatter of the mechanical keyboard echoed throughout the small room. Karras leaned up and stretched his toes, to speak softly into Tony's ear. "Why did you change your mind about helping? Your father again?"

"No," Tony said in his normal tone of voice. He was not one for whispering. "The kid on the phone."

"I don't think he was really a kid," Karras said.

"Me neither, and that's all the more reason, then," said Tony. "If something like this ever happened to you, wouldn't you want to work to stop more bloodshed?"

"It *is* happening to me!" Karras said, his whisper a hiss. Tony winced and shot Karras a look of disgust.

"So, you helpin', or are you just taking notes while events unfold? You want to walk out of this with a book, or with the knowledge that you saved lives and made a difference? It's like Burning Man—no spectators," Tony said.

"Do you have a plan?"

"Yes. We need to lure out the mastermind. We need bait."

"They're coming," Rahel called out from across the room. "They are already on her way. Katrina ran away from home this morning, and they're coming to California."

"How does her mother know that?" Karras asked.

"She must be worried sick," said Tony.

Rahel shook her head. "No, it's a very modern style of running away. Katrina got permission from their biological mother, and left Mocha and their father a detailed itinerary and texts them from one or another burner phone every day at 5pm, and again at 5am Eastern, using a series of code words based on their childhood stuffed animals and imaginary friends. They're riding the rails like a hobo."

"Off-the-grid. Hope it works better for them than

it has for me so far," said Karras. "Brave kid, too. Teenage girl, alone, pretty dangerous. But I bet they were receiving plenty of threats at home and on the Internet. Any drone visitations?"

Rahel typed in response, and hmphed at the screen. "Yes. A drone, maybe from a news channel... triggered them?"

"That's how the police took out the shooter," Tony said.

"Maybe it was the police, or maybe it was another party," Karras said, remembering how he had described using a drone to intervene in a school shooting to Jerry and Dennis, just hours before Middlesex. And Dennis's phone had clearly been compromised at some point.

"The police said..."

"Of course they did. And it may have been a police drone, and there will be litigation and law-journal articles about the civil rights and ethical implications, maybe some hearings at the State House," said Karras. "Or maybe it was not a police drone, but the police took credit for it anyway."

"Why would they do that?" asked Rahel.

"To take credit. To cover up the fact that some private citizen or organization is building drones and flying them over schools. All sorts of reasons. I'm just saying it's a possibility—it's smart never to take any law enforcement claim at face value. You guys know that."

"One Christopher Bennett blames you for all these recent events," said Tony. "The drone that visited the bungalow…" He flashed his teeth at Karras. "Maybe it's smart to never take any journalist's claim at face value."

"That would be smart, but drones cost money and journalists don't have any money," Karras said.

"Your publisher has money."

The sound Karras made was half guffaw, half cringing swallow. "That's definitely not an accurate description of my publisher," he said after. "Rahel, where in California is Katrina supposedly headed, and why?"

"Here," said Rahel. "For you."

"Why?" asked Tony.

Karras didn't need to ask. He knew the answer.

"She wants to talk."

17.

Rahel had a plan all worked out. MochaJean would log onto *BrunchMUSH* at 2am and report the results of her next communication from Katrina to Rahel, but Rahel was going to be sleeping in her own bed, like a normal person. Nor would she dare log onto *BrunchMUSH* from her own computer, using her family's wifi, not given the events of the past week. So MochaJean had agreed to communicate with Karras instead. But there was no way Karras could simply stay in the basement all day and night, as the Lutherans had seen him go downstairs, and would expect him to leave with the Alazars; they'd already been mucking around down here for too long. But as the church grounds were a popular spot for the unhoused, Rahel would lend Karras her sleeping bag—which she hastened to add was a normal green and brown bag, nothing too feminine—and he would sleep under a bush by a basement window they'd leave open. At just before 2, he was to wake up, lower himself back into the basement, turn on the monitor, and log in. Rahel used TinyWar, a client that logged her in automatically, so Karras wouldn't need to know her password, just the octets for the MUSH. With luck, MochaJean would have good news: Katrina was fine, travel was proceeding apace, and she would arrive at the church in another day or two. Karras only had to sleep outside for two, maybe three nights. Djimon, who owned a truck route delivering bags of coffee and various North African spices and foodstuffs to groceries and restaurants around the East Bay, would drive around with Karras's phone and laptop, making it look like Karras was doing something or other during business hours. Karras could retrieve his stuff the next afternoon at one of the shops Djimon serviced.

"Why can't I stay with—?"

They both glared at him.

"Bungalow's compromised," said Tony. "Drone."

"My mother hates you now," said Rahel. "My father doesn't find you very amusing anymore either. We've not even told him we're continuing to help you."

"No motel?"

"Your cards are probably compromised, and that means ours might be too."

"Speaking of being compromised, what if Djimon gets droned by whoever has been stalking me, what with my stuff in his van?" Karras asked.

"He can handle himself," said Rahel. "A drone wouldn't be the first rotorcraft he shot out of the sky."

"Wait, what?"

They just looked at him.

"Okay, then, I guess, but…"

"Don't guess, *know*. And know this—Katrina saw something at Middlesex, and she wants to tell you and only you what it is."

Why me? Karras wanted to ask, but he knew that Rahel would say that she wasn't told, she didn't know, and that it would be all up to him to figure out what was going on. There wasn't much to do but leave the basement, the computer fan still buzzing away in darkness, and join the Alazars in Tony's car to get the sleeping bag.

"Can I come in and use the bathroom?" Karras asked after they pulled up to the curb in front of a smallish apartment building that was certainly not the Alazar home.

"No," said Rahel. "I'll be right back." She slipped out of the car, walked onto the lawn in front of the building, ducked around a large aloe vera plant, and vanished.

Tony turned, propping his elbow and forearm up along the seatback. "The post-curfew route home to get the sleeping bag," he explained.

"I'm surprised Rahel ever violated curfew," said Karras.

"Once or twice," said Tony. "Rahel, she likes girls, you know."

"Oh," said Karras. He didn't quite understand why his intestines had suddenly filled with quick-drying cement. "How did that go over with your folks?"

"It's not a topic of discussion," said Tony.

"Because of religi—"

"It is not a topic of discussion between you and I, Michael," said Tony. "I'm telling you because your mooning over her makes us both uncomfortable."

"Sorry. That wasn't my intention, and I didn't know," Karras said. "I mean, when she first contacted me, it was clear that she was really into Christianity, so…"

Tony wagged a finger, and turned back to start the engine. "Here she is." The right-side rear passenger door opened and into the back seat tumbled a sleeping bag that smelled like dirt, a quickly applied squirt of Febreze Fabric Refresher Moonlight Breeze, and Rahel herself.

Tony traded a fraction of bitcoin for some cash from a gas station ATM of the sort found only in the ever-hopefully exploitative Bay Area, and handed Karras fifty bucks. He smiled, said, "See you tomorrow," and then got back into the car without explaining where he or Rahel would be spending the night. Not the bungalow, not the home they shared with their parents, surely not Djimon and Bruk's house, but they did have a lot of relatives and a lifetime of connections to exploit. It was better if Karras didn't know. That's what he told himself anyway. Rahel wouldn't even look out the passenger-side window at him as the Cadillac pulled away and left Karras on the street corner just four blocks from the church.

Karras ducked into a hardware store to buy a hand-cranked combination radio/flashlight, and selected a ratty-looking Ruth Rendell paperback from a Little Free Library in front of a three-story Edwardian of the sort he couldn't afford even in his recurring dreams of getting a TV deal from an article about UFO cultists he'd never published anywhere but in his sleep.

Michael Karras wouldn't be having that dream tonight. There was nothing to do but read and hang out on a corner waiting for a message, like it was the twentieth century. He sat atop the rolled-up sleeping bag, placed strategically over the open window he'd have to shimmy through when the computer beeped. There was nothing stopping Karras from going down into the basement now, except that one of the church employees might pop downstairs for something— typewriter ribbon, an emergency nip of communion wine—and then they'd call the cops. After work hours, the alarm would be set, but all Karras needed was a couple of minutes to read MochaJean's message. He'd have sixty seconds to get to the computer, turn on the monitor, see what MochaJean had to say and... what?

Wait some more, this time for a teenager to whisper in his ear some terrible truth. Serj, a supposed teenager, had done that already. It didn't pay to be credulous anymore. Conspiracy had something in common with Communism: the gap between theory and practice. Even when conspiracies were real, when history and politics *were* being nudged by secret forces, that didn't mean the theory about the conspiracy was correct.

With night came the cold and the other unhoused. *Other* felt like the wrong word to Karras, though he was in fact unhoused. He had booked a cross-country itinerary, thrown most of his stuff in storage, and let his landlord back home keep his deposit in order to break his lease. He had money, though it was all being watched very carefully, and could spend months bopping around various Airbnbs and motels if he had to. But he wasn't hanging out on a patch of grass on the side of a street-corner Lutheran church that rented space to an Ethiopian Orthodox Tewahedo congregation because that was his best option, except that it was his best option, except that this option had to do with some Jurassic technology in the basement, and damn it, the Rendell paperback in his hands was not engaging at all. Karras hadn't turned a page in forty minutes. He was so distracted by himself that he didn't hear Oscar speaking to him until some spittle hit his cheek.

"Hey, man," he said. "Remember me? You high, or you reading the best paragraph ever written?"

"Hi," Karras managed. There were a few other men setting up for sleep, flattening out cardboard, withdrawing filthy blankets from two-wheeled shopping carts, pissing against the trunk of a tree in front of the church.

"Back outside, huh?"

"Yeah."

"It's all right, it's cool. This is better than the park. You know sometimes the ladies come in the morning with bagels," Oscar said. "But it gets crowded sometimes. Too crowded."

"Not trying to crowd anyone," said Karras. Where was Tony with his promises now, where was the Makarov? Not that Karras would feel much better, cowering behind Tony's legs as he interposed himself between Karras and Oscar as a result of Karras's psychic pleading.

"What you talkin' to him for?" shouted the pisser, who violently redid his fly. "He's a cop!"

"He's not a cop!" Oscar said, laughing. "This guy is not a cop."

"Get away from him; he's contagious!"

"Are you contagious?" Oscar said, not quite to Karras.

"Yeah, I'm contagious. One of those things that sneak up on you. First it feels like just a cough, then just a flu, and then next thing you know your lungs are full of pudding and broken glass."

Oscar hesitated for a moment. "What?"

Karras just shrugged and ran his thumb across the pages of the paperback in his hands. The sound was a pleasant one, to Karras at least. It was the sort of thing only the person doing it liked, but it annoyed everyone else in earshot, like revving a motorcycle engine or rapping along with the car radio. He did it again.

"You for real?" Oscar asked.

Karras pretended to cough.

"Just leave him alone!" shouted the pisser, who was moving his stuff away from the tree to set up his bedding on the church steps.

"Well... good night," said Oscar. He didn't have nearly the layout the other men had, nor Karras's relatively newish sleeping bag, just his cart full of empty bottles and a couple of towels and a coat, which he used for bedding a couple yards away. He did still have that knife, though, Karras had to assume.

The men didn't huddle close, didn't talk to one another much. Whenever he looked up from his book, one or another of them was peering at him. There were only four of them, including Oscar, and the other three looked to be much further along in the process of physiological collapse. He could take any of them if he had to, if they weren't armed like Oscar was, and if they didn't combine against him.

Karras blinked and shook the thought from his head. That thought, still simmering somewhere under this consciousness, was *not his*. Karras had never been in a fight in his life. The occasional protest—like back in Seattle in the 1990s, and during Occupy—that had been rushed by the cops, but Karras was no hero; he just ran, every time. Karras had never even been physically bullied as a kid, and took no exercise except for the occasional set of push-ups and jumping jacks when feeling guilty about eating room-service French fries. His only physical advantage against these men was having had lunch every day for the past week.

At any rate, these guys weren't mean-mugging him. Even Oscar didn't seem to care. They were just curious, seeking a way to start a conversation without offending him. Karras knew what they were going to say next, which was nothing at all, unless he said something first. When Karras focused on the half-second into the future that was about to manifest, he heard only static.

"Hey," said Karras. The cross streets were quiet, so his voice carried. "What's the sports station around here?" He pulled the radio from the brown paper bag the store had given him and turned the crank a quick dozen times. "Is there a game tonight?" Karras knew only that summer was baseball season and that the As played in Oakland, but it was a start.

"95.7 FM," one of the men immediately offered. "It sucks, but it'll sound better than AM on that thing."

"No game tonight, but Saturday—hosting the Brewers," said the pisser.

"That's really nice of you, sharing your radio like that, Felix," said Oscar.

Karras found the station and his brain immediately turned off. No game, but somehow plenty to talk about, both on the air and on the church grounds. The broadcaster was terrible, all rounded vowels and popped Ps, and had many complaints about coaches and players whose names Karras didn't recognize. Oscar and the others exchanged a remark or two, mostly agreeing with one another that it was in fact the guy on the radio who was an idiot, and not their team favorites. They took turns cranking the radio to keep it going, and were careful to place it within reach of one another so as not to make a claim on it. When the traffic died down and only the occasional low rumble of the city bus passed by, the radio signal started to fade and the chattering turned to murmuring turned to snoring.

Karras retrieved the radio, cranked it up again to look at the screen, then swallowed a groan. It was only 11pm. He turned on the flashlight, made a solid effort at reading the book, which involved a kid who tried to sell his soul to the devil, his sister who believed him to have magical powers though he had none, and his widowed father, who repaired typewriters for a living. Honestly, it all hit a bit too close to home, and Karras's ass was cold, his feet wet from the evening dew seeping into his shoes.

The next three hours didn't go well. Karras finally

had to urinate, but didn't want to piss too close to where the sleeping bag was to roll out, and he felt his feet were too wet to use Rahel's property anyway. He walked halfway down the block, found a bush in front of someone's yard, relieved himself there, and was disappointed that only five minutes had elapsed. He took off his socks and shoes and laid the socks out on the basement windowsill, which also felt like a mistake as now his little space had started to smell, but he did get in the sleeping bag and set the radio to play a Spanish-language station and hugged the speaker against his ear so he wouldn't succumb to sleep, but of course he did.

Something loud woke Karras up. He checked the time, it was 2:43 am, nearly an hour after he was supposed to drop himself into the basement and log in to *BrunchMUSH*, but it wasn't dark as it should have been. Light flooded the little patch of grass on which he had been sleeping, throwing tree shadows like creeping black fingers against the stone walls of the church.

Shit, shit, shit, Karras thought as he wiggled out of the sleeping bag and clutched at the window pane. His socks were still wet, and gross under his palms. He made the further mistake of pushing himself through the window head first. Some yards away, he heard Oscar shout something, but not at him.

The basement ceiling was low, and there was a card table under the window, so Karras was able to do an awkward handstand and lower himself onto it, then crawl off the surface and onto the floor.

He ran to the computer, turned on the monitor, and sighed with relief when the screen quickly came to life. The fan kicked up, the cursor was blinking, and the commands Rahel had scrawled on the back of a donation envelope hidden under the keyboard were a breeze to type in, thanks to the light pouring in through the open window.

BrunchMUSH, check. Login, automatic, a moment of confusion as the first room, Limbo and its brief description of a dark emptiness stretching out in all directions, was pushed up and off the screen by SailorChereka being transported to another room, this one called 'Night of 512 Stars,' the description of which was nothing but that number of asterisks in thirty-two rows of sixteen. MochaJean was in inventory, and nothing else. Rahel's client program supposedly would have spotted any 'dark' objects that could be logging conversations. So that was good. Of course, someone could just be looking over MochaJean's shoulder in her home, Karras realized, with yet another ribbitting skip of his overworked heart. Then the text on the monitor moved up one row as a new line of text materialized near the bottom of the screen.

MochaJean says, "Finally did you fall asleep lol?"

Karras's fingers were cold, but he was an expert two-fingered typist. He typed *Yes, sorry. Thank you for waiting. I'd love to hear what news you have for me.* and only after pressing return, getting an error message and typing all of that again but remembering to start with a " so the MUSH would allow SailorChereka to 'say' his message, and only then did he worry if his use of punctuation made him look uptight, which of course he was.

MochaJean sighs. "Don't you have news. She said she was on her way there."

Karras had forgotten that MUSH characters could emote as well as speak, and he didn't know how MochaJean did it, but if he could he would have puffed out his cheeks or widened his eyes and gritted his teeth as part of his question: *Where's there?*

MochaJean says, "Where you're typing from. Your usual typist's favorite place in the world."

Karras didn't bother typing a response, though he was curious. The alarm was going to go off any moment. It may have already been more than a minute—MochaJean was not a fast typist, not first thing in the morning. He planted a foot on the card table, pushed himself up. The table wobbled a bit, but he threw himself at the window, got a decent grip and picked himself up and through.

Bright lights flooded the side street. It took a moment to figure out what was going on: a semi-truck with a rack of running lights atop the cab, plus headlights, had woken Oscar and the others. The truck lacked a trailer, but was in the wrong place anyway—the side street, not Telegraph, in the middle of the street and not on a curb—and was spewing exhaust. Just short of an alien spacecraft.

One of the unhoused guys, not Oscar, was at the passenger side door, speaking loudly in Spanish and gesturing. He turned around, then gestured toward Karras. The light was such that his face was shadowed, but his posture didn't seem menacing. He wasn't turning Karras in, just pointing him out. The passenger-side door opened and awkwardly, because they were small and the truck high and the step steep, out came an oversized hooded sweatshirt with legs: one Katrina Chu-Ramirez.

Karras rushed across the lawn, scooted around the man, and made to help Katrina down, but they jerked their arm back.

"Leave me alone," they snapped.

"But I'm—"

"I know who you are," Katrina said. They didn't sound like a teenager anymore, they had grown into something hard. "I've been in a truck for fifteen hours. I need two seconds. I need a toilet."

"It's the middle of the night," said Karras.

"I know that too."

"Nothing's op—"

"Stop." Katrina sounded like the hissing of an air brake. "Talking."

"Michael!"

Karras didn't even hear the first time, or the second.

"Michael Karras! The writer!"

That he heard of course, and turned away from Katrina, who was skulking off to the curb anyway, and looked into the truck of the cab.

It was Garn.

18.

THERE WAS NOWHERE to go but Garn's semi-tractor. "What did you do to them? Turn off these lights. You're going to wake up a million Karens with smartphones and your license plates will go viral."

"I gave her a ride, a long one. I had a container to deliver to Oakland. I found her at a rail yard in Denver," said Garn. "Recognized her from the news. She's lucky I did. Catching out on the rails is no way for a young girl to behave. The FTRA would have loved to get their hands on her."

"FTRA?"

"Freight Train Riders of America—hobo gang," said Garn. "Buncha killers. They'd throw her from the cattle car as soon as look at her."

"'Hobo gang,'" said Karras. "It's the current year

and you're talking murderous hobos."

"They're big in the Pacific Northwest," Garn said. "And here." He dug into the breast pocket of his flannel and withdrew a can of tobacco, and took a pinch. "She did okay three-quarters of the way, but that little girl's a bucket of chum and she was just about to enter shark-filled waters."

"They're actually non-binary…" Karras started, but the look on Garn's face, that of a hound confused and slightly angry as to why you refuse to surrender your dinner, made him stop.

"Yeah, I heard all about that," Garn said. "Anyway, she didn't want to piss in the bucket *or* pull over at any rest stops, so…"

"All right, let me up," said Katrina Chu-Ramirez. "I need hand sanitizer. Is there a 7-Eleven nearby, or some place?"

"Go south into Oakland," Karras told Garn. "Just a few blocks. Nothing's open twenty-four hours in Berkeley." Katrina clambered up into the cab, casually bear-crawled over Karras's lap and slid into the sleeper immediately behind the seats.

"Socialism," said Garn. "Figures."

"It's not socialism," said Katrina. "Please." They stretched out in the sleeper. Katrina really was still a kid: the top of their head and the bottoms of their feet brushed either side of the sleeper, but only just.

Two grown men driving around in a semi-tractor with an ersatz runaway down streets not meant for truck traffic at three o'clock in the morning struck Karras as a bit dangerous. How much of the past couple of weeks could have been solved had Karras just owned a used car of his own, outright, something without a computer in it, and had then just driven his own stupid ass around the country interviewing people?

And Karras had two more people to interview now. "So…" he said, "what a coincidence, eh? They say that there's no such thing as a coincidence, that everything happens for a reason."

"Who is *they*, Mister Karras?" said Katrina, shooting up to a seated position, their head just missing the ceiling. "That's an absurd belief, anyway. Not everything happens for a reason. Do you think Middlesex happened for a reason?"

Of course Middlesex happened for a multitude of reasons, and just as surely Katrina knew some of them: toxic masculinity, white supremacy, the ubiquity of firearms, perhaps adverse effects of psychiatric medication. But Katrina wasn't asking, they were objecting.

Karras and Garn spoke over one another: "I'm interested in what brought us all together" and "There are no uncaused actions," but only Garn immediately repeated himself: "There are no uncaused actions. I told you that before, Katrina. There's a master plan at work here. And you know it too, which is why you got into my truck. We've been brought together as if by some occult hand." His tone was grave, but he quirked his lips at Karras and winked.

"Oh, look, there's the 7-Eleven," Karras said, thrilled. "I'll go in with you, Katrina."

"I'll join you all," said Garn.

"Wouldn't you rather stay with the truck?" Karras asked. He met Garn's sudden gaze and lied. "This is a pretty dicey neighborhood. Somebody might try something. You know, *Oakland*."

Garn relaxed, nodded.

"C'mon, kid," said Karras, and Katrina did not object.

The 7-Eleven was busy for the early morning—four customers, two employees, one behind the counter and the other cleaning up. Karras and Katrina didn't stand out, because he'd been hanging out outside all night and got sweaty doing the stunt of getting into and out of the church basement, and Katrina had been on the road for days. They grabbed a small packet of Oreo cookies, a larger bag of Frito's corn chips, some unpromising bananas, and a couple tall cans of Monster Energy drink. *Vegan*, Karras thought.

"Slow down, we can talk without having to include Garn," said Karras as he slipped into line behind them.

"How do you know him, anyway? Are you friends with him? I bet he's one of those guys who thinks the only thing Hitler did wrong was invade Poland and interfere with the 'free market,'" Katrina said, juggling the stuff in their hands to dismiss the 7-Eleven, and all consumerism and capitalism, with a single gesture.

"Oh, he's not that bad," Karras said, but then he realized that he didn't actually know how bad Garn was. "Sorry. He's bad."

"He is. I tried to tune him out," said Katrina. "Miss me with that 'well-regulated militia' shit. Are you going to buy this food for me, Mister Karras? It's a tax write-off, isn't it? I'm going to go back home, and I spent more of my budget than I thought I would getting out here."

"Sure. But Katrina, you wanted—"

They whispered, "Buy cigarettes."

It was a good idea. Karras bought the food and decided to ask for Pall Mall Gold, his mother's old brand, and Kurt Vonnegut's. "A classy way to commit suicide," he said to the unblinking man behind the counter, who didn't get it, and didn't get that it was Vonnegut's line. He bought a cheap Bic lighter too.

The pair exited the store. Karras waved the cigarettes at Garn as they passed the truck and found a corner by a dumpster to light up. The sun was coming up, it felt too warm for cigarettes already. Katrina took a proffered cigarette and Karras's new lighter, lit up, and sucked on the butt without inhaling. Karras did the same, except he actually knew how to smoke. He uselessly turned his head to exhale away from Katrina.

"Mister Karras, there were other people on the roof of my school, and in the hallways, not just Aram.

They were like holograms or something, from a movie or a VR game," Katrina said. "I'm already seeing a psychologist and a psychiatrist and a family therapist with my folks. They all want to put me on Risperdal. You know who else was on Risperdal? Aram."

"Were you friends? Do you know if he has a cousin named Serj?" Karras asked.

"We weren't friends. He wasn't the type to have friends. Not even in third grade, when everyone was friends with each other, much less in middle school, where we're always at each other's throats," said Katrina. "He liked to brag that he was on 'crazy pills,' as he called them." They played with the cigarette some more, made a noise something like a hiccup, and then began to weep. They turned to Karras, held up a palm, and then turned their head away. Karras had no idea what this gesture was supposed to mean except that Katrina did not want a hug. So he raised his own hand, pressed his palm against theirs and they both laced their fingers together.

Then Katrina pulled themself to Karras, stood on her toes, and whispered in his ear. "One of them looked just like you."

Garn flashed his lights impatiently.

BACK INSIDE THE 7-Eleven, Katrina Chu-Ramirez getting close to Michael Karras and putting her mouth to his ear was enough for the man behind the cash register, who whistled rudely for the man with the mop to take over, and then went to the tiny office behind the cooler. There, he rewound the recordings of both the exterior camera by the dumpster and the one normally pointed at his own bald spot during his shift, then pointed his phone at the split screen quad monitor, and recorded Michael Karras purchasing cigarettes while standing next to Katrina Chu-Ramirez, and then the pair of them smoking and touching. It was less than a minute of footage, but the employee didn't know how to compress the file, so it took nearly fifteen minutes for him to upload it to the Michael Karras Tip Page on Christopher Bennett's website.

By then, the sun was up in the Bay Area and the fog melting away. In LA, where there was no fog at all, Christopher Bennett's girlfriend Melinda slid her sleep mask off one eye, found Bennett's phone on her nightstand, and tossed it over to the other side of the California King-sized bed where Bennett snoozed kittenishly in a semi-fetal position. Blindly he groped for it, found it, and thumbed the screen. The phone, on most days, woke up faster than he did, but this morning the notification from the tip page sent him bolt upright in bed.

19.

"I AGREE," SAID Garn. "It is more than a little odd that none of the mass killings in your immediate proximity have been carried out by straight white males." They were in the truck, in another parking lot down in the warehouse section of West Oakland by the port, waiting for Djimon to come by with Karras's electronics. Then... nobody was quite sure, though Garn would reclaim his semi-trailer and get a new container to haul. He was losing a lot of money chauffeuring Katrina and Karras around, and was happy to let them both know it. "So, is that racism? Is *everything* racist? Am I doing it right, Katrina?" They exchanged sneers.

"Rasnic was white. Aram Sargsyan is white," said Karras. "I'm not going through the whole 'Are Armenians white?' thing again."

"It's interesting, though. Where are the white men?" Katrina said. "Aram's cousin—"

"We don't know anything about Serj as a fact yet," Karras said.

"Some *dude* told you that there would be a nationwide shooting spree in a couple of days, coordinated and organized," Katrina said. "That has to be a white dude thing. At least mostly a white boy thing."

So far Katrina hadn't said anything about the other shooter they had seen at Middlesex looking like Karras, probably due to holding Garn in such intense and reasonable suspicion. "So what do we do?"

"You go on home. We'll put you on the Amtrak," said Garn. "You completed your little mission to meet the famous Michael Karras and said what you had to say to him, didn't you?"

"Yeah, I did…"

"When I get my phone back, we can look up a schedule," Karras said. He'd offer to wait with Katrina at the station, and there get a chance to question them a bit more. Anyone overhearing him would just think him another Bay Area crackpot, and Katrina—he hoped—wasn't so famous that they couldn't blend in as just another post^2-punk street kid.

"What if it's happening now?" Katrina asked. "And we're just sitting here. If we don't believe in Serj's identity, why believe in Serj's timeline?"

"Why believe in his claims at all?" asked Karras.

"Gir...The teen is right—we believe in his claim because it's already been happening. School shootings, terror attacks, church shootings, that poor fellow who killed himself on TV. Something's building, something's cresting, like a wave," said Garn.

"We don't need another hot take on social media, or a book in two years, Mister Karras," said Katrina. "We need you to do something now."

Karras knew what was coming next. Garn asking Katrina why it would be up to Michael Karras to do something, and Katrina saying that Michael Karras knows why, and both of them simmering and waiting for him to do something. To forestall the conversation and awkwardness, Karras reached to turn on the radio, and found a local news station.

"You'll drain the battery," Garn said.

"Of a semi?" Karras said. "Anyway, maybe there will be news. If this was some sort of contrived narrative, we'd hear about a mass shooting event right now."

The next story was about a criminal case surrounding a fire at a warehouse housing an illegal nightclub. Then one about a wildfire several counties away and how imprisoned felons were being pressed into service to dig firebreaks. A story about the Tau variant of the small version of the big virus. Nothing longer than ninety seconds—the commercials, for solar power, for new Fiats, and for the station they were listening to, those were all at least seventy seconds.

Katrina's attention span collapsed on the eighth minute. "God, turn it off! Take me to the train station, Mister Nibley."

"Garn'll do," said Garn. Karras had to smile at *nibbly*. Maybe the surname was the key to opening the rusty, battered footlocker of his soul. Not very masculine, 'Mister Nibley,' so there's the reason for his performative stoicism; but also a Scots name, so Appalachian background, and maybe Garn was somehow related to the old Mormon apologist Hugh Nibley, which could explain his conservatism—

The reverie, and the revving of the semi, were both interrupted by a small truck barreling into the parking lot and blocking the exit. It was Djimon's bread route truck, of course, but the surprise was Tony and Rahel spilling out the back and rushing out with the sack of Karras's electronics and their own phones held high in their hands. Tony got to the passenger-side door first.

"You have the child with you! Bennett's all over it!" he said, presenting the screen of his iPhone to Karras.

"Well, shit."

"*Peee-dough-fiiile*," Tony said, in mimickry of Bennett's sound effects board. Rahel finally caught up with him, jumped onto the running board and started yanking on the door handle.

"Oh, God," said Katrina, slumping back into the depths of the sleeper.

"Bennett—friend of yours, as I recall," said Garn. He chuckled. "Friendly acquaintance maybe?" Rahel started banging on the window, and Garn looked past Karras with his basilisk gaze aimed at her. Karras unlocked the door and let her in before she damaged something and gave Garn a reason to perform misogyny and racism.

She muttered a 'Thank you,' then reached past Karras and grabbed Katrina by the ankle. "Come with me!"

"What? No! Who the heck are you, lady?"

"I am a lady," said Rahel. "Much better company than these two, and we need to get you somewhere safe." She clamped down on Katrina's foot. All Karras and Garn could do was look on.

"I'm going home, they're taking me to Amtrak!"

"You can't get on that train, it's run by the government. You're a missing person, a runaway, and these men are suspected of kidnapping you, of doing worse things," said Rahel.

"I have my parents' permission—"

"I know Mocha, I was the contact," Rahel said. "The permission's been rescinded. A visit from men in black suits can be very persuasive."

"But… my mom, I, I don't want to go with you…"

"This is the emergency," Rahel said, softly.

Then Katrina sighed, expelling the tension in their body, and nodded, and scooted to the edge of the thin mattress. "Where are we going?"

"Do you like Ethiopian food?"

"Probably!" said Katrina.

"And you two gotta get this truck out of here," said Tony, tossing the bag with Karras's stuff in it onto Karras's lap as Rahel and Katrina slipped past him. "Full of malware, by the way. Get your files off there and go to an Apple store and get a new computer, that's my suggestion. The phone, I'd toss under the wheels of this truck. Total lost cause."

"You went through my phone and computer?" Karras said.

"Me and half the world, from the looks of it," said Tony.

"Why don't you come with us?" Karras slid his right hand down to his thigh to keep it hidden from Garn and stuck out his forefinger and thumb to hint at the shape of a pistol.

"Us, eh? Where are you and that frog in your pocket even going?" Garn asked, "Because your ticket on this ride is about to be rescinded."

"We're going to go see Bennett," said Karras, surprising himself.

"I heard the show—did he really pull a gun on you?" Garn asked. "Was it just another fake?"

"Fake as the moon landing, Mister Nibley," Karras said.

"Okay," said Tony. "Move over. I'm coming in." He pointed up at the sky. "Time to go."

Coming in high enough and slow across the gray soup of the sky was a helicopter. Too far off to hear the rotors or see the markings upon it—news, police, tech billionaire out on a lark?—it was obviously making a beeline for the parking lot. Rahel shouted something to Tony from Djimon's van as it roared by. Tony wedged himself in the sleeper, banging his knee and then his head against the walls. "Follow them!" he barked.

"Yes, *sir*," said Garn, his finger on the great gear shift, foot on the clutch.

"Okay, where are we going?" asked Karras.

"Not to Bennett?" said Garn.

"Follow the van, please," said Tony. "Please."

Karras half-expected the helicopter to disappear, like a hacked file or a second shooter in updated wire reports, but it followed him like the moon back when he was a kid, watching the sky from the back seat of his parents' car.

"Sorry you're going to miss your next pick-up," said Karras to Garn.

"I'm an owner-operator, I don't have a boss to answer to," he said. "Or a wife. I want to know where we're going, though. If it's the I-80, we'll be sitting ducks."

"There's always a ton of truck traffic there; we could blend in," said Tony.

"There *is* always a ton of truck traffic there; average speed in the early afternoon is thirty miles per hour," he said. "Sitting ducks. Your sister better have a better idea."

"She said God will provide," Tony said.

"You believe that?" Karras said, distracted.

"She said God always has so far."

The van avoided the on-ramps and kept to the surface roads, where trucks rarely rumbled. West Oakland was a mess of decaying Victorians, squat pillbox warehouses-turned-auto mechanics-turned-trendy restaurants-turned-boarded up and vacant ruins, low overpasses, and long-abandoned streetcar tracks poking out from the asphalt like oak tree roots. Garn was a Liszt in the driver's seat, playing the gearbox, steering wheel, and clutch with a chaotic genius, taking turns like he was in a Honda Civic with a backseat full of sleeping toddlers. The van drove through Oakland and into Emeryville, the little spit of a town that was seemingly eighty percent shopping mall, all parking lots and corporate logos, and the semi-trailer followed it.

After picking past the movie theater, endless chain restaurants, and a scattering of slightly upmarket storefronts, they came upon the huge blue wave of an IKEA overwhelming the horizon. The van pulled into the adjacent multistory parking garage, and Garn turned his vehicle away and brought it to the big loading dock behind the enormous building where a few more semi-tractors were parked. "Better than nothing," Garn said, "but what's the point of stopping here?"

"They're probably going to go inside. The Bennett stans won't try anything in public," said Tony.

"That's absurd. An IKEA is an excellent place for a mass shooting. Well, a moderately appropriate one," said Karras, his voice so tired he felt the urge to repeat himself just to make sure he heard even his own words. "Not *appropriate*... just, lots of corners and turns and places to hide." He shrugged. "Helicopter won't follow us in anyway."

He opened the door, grabbed his sack, slid onto the running board, and jumped to the ground just as the helicopter swung in low over the open-air parking area, sending discarded coupon flyers and napkins that once held ice cream cones and hot dogs flying.

Garn and Tony jumped from the truck and bulled past Karras, nearly knocking him to the ground. Both were jocks gone to seed—Garn two decades earlier than Tony, but both easily outpacing Karras, who was out of breath by the time he got to the employee entrance on the far end of the loading dock. There was no need to explain anything to the security guard, who dashed past him, or the other workers that had been breaking down pallets. The helicopter landing in the parking lot did all that. It was black at moments, iridescent most of the time.

The men scowled at Karras as he ran to meet them. "Split up!" shouted Garn, and he opened the employee entrance and ran down the left side of the hallway.

"I'm going to look for Rahel and the girl," said Tony to Karras, taking the right. There was no third option except staying where he was to be murdered, or captured, or interviewed and then broadcast and cancelled by whomever was going to step out of the helicopter and find him. The copter wasn't for Katrina or Garn or the Alazars, it was for Karras.

From inside his bag, his phone chimed. Karras opened it, and saw that along with his laptop and phone was the Makarov pistol. He collected the phone, saw that the number was from the 773 area code and figured the call was from a robot targeting residents of Chicago, from where he had moved a decade ago. Karras slid it into his front pocket, and felt for the first time in weeks that everything was going to be okay.

He took the right turn; not to follow Tony, exactly, but because he knew that Tony would find Rahel.

20.

WELP, KARRAS THOUGHT. The plan was working insofar as he was sufficiently lost in this IKEA that whomever had come out of the helicopter hadn't yet found him. Nor could he find Tony, or the restroom, or his way out of the home furnishing sections. He could use his phone—IKEA had been providing internal maps of their stores worldwide via Google for more than a decade—but he didn't trust the phone at all. Nor did he trust IKEA at all, having just passed a build-out display of a clean, stylish home bathroom, in which a sign reading DISPLAY ONLY PLEASE DO NOT ATTEMPT was pasted atop the toilet lid. Someone had scribbled over the PLEASE with a ballpoint pen, perhaps fearing that the politesse undermined the imperative. There were only forced choices within an IKEA, the organization had mastered the dark trick that made compulsion seem like freedom and spread across the globe. For a moment, Karras wondered if Tony had spoofed the 773 call to compel him to open the sack and recover the Makarov.

Then the phone rang again. It was Bennett.

"Hey, Mike," said Chris Bennett. "Want to go live in five minutes? We're talking about you, and the Deep State camps, but—"

"You threatened me with a gun," Karras said. "You flooded the world with video footage of me with Katrina Chu-Ramirez and implied that I was a kidnapper and a pedophile, and that's after telling your fans for months that I was somehow personally responsible for everything that makes them afraid and angry."

"Hmm," said Chris. "Sounds like I really owe it to you to give you a platform from which you can tell your side of the story. So, four minutes?"

"Chris—I never wanted to have a fake fight with you, and I don't want to have a real fight with you. You're just trying to keep me on the phone so that your cultists can find me and take me down while you're broadcasting."

"You know there's going to be some kind of nationwide event today, don't you? You've heard the online chatter. Coordinated mass shootings—schools, churches, shopping malls," Chris said.

"Schools and churches on the same day?" Karras asked. "You know that none of your stories make sense."

"It's Wednesday. Many Protestant denominations have Wednesday evening services and Bible study," Chris said. "Or maybe you don't, Greek boy. Time zones. It's going to be a cascade: schools in the West, churches in the East, shopping malls everywhere at once."

"Aren't all mass shootings false flags? How many crisis actors are there?"

"Two minutes, Mike," said Chris. "You can ask your provocative questions on the air. Maybe you'll even change some minds. C'mon, man, don't be afraid. I can't hurt you from afar."

Something shimmered by the bin of Ullkaktus throw pillows a few yards away. Karras turned his head to look and it was gone, but it had been there. A toddler in a shopping cart was pointing and gibbered something at their mother. A middle-aged man carrying a lamp tight in both hands like a weapon was looking at the same spot.

"I'll get back to you," Karras said, and thumbed the phone. He walked up to the bin and smiled, depending on the inevitable fact that people want to talk.

"Hey, what are you?" the guy asked. He was bigger close up. The lamp rested across his protruding belly, and his forearms were thick and veiny. "One of those YouTube magicians?"

"Hi," said the toddler, pointing at Karras.

"I saw some guy here, and then—"

"It was *you!*" the man said, his voice like a

motorcycle backfiring. The woman leaned in to her shopping cart, and pushed it and her waving toddler away. "How'd you do it?"

"Aw, you know I can't tell you..." said Karras.

"I'd say mirrors, but you changed clothes so fast too," said the man. "Tearaway Velcro?"

"Something like that..."

"Do you need me to sign a release or something?"

"Relea—" Karras started. "Nothing like that. We're not recording, just rehearsing."

The man opened his mouth to say something else, but then came the echoes of gunfire, followed by a wave of screams. "Run!" the man shouted, more to himself than to Karras, and it seemed as though everyone but Karras started running.

IKEA was busy, as it always was, and Karras had no choice but to throw a leg over the top of the pillow bin and step in, to avoid the crowds rushing past him, adults dragging kids or with handfuls of merchandise, wagons spinning wildly as people pushed past them. At the edge of his vision, he saw a few other people with the same idea diving into crates of plush toys or diving under beds and desks.

This wasn't a shooting. Karras knew it, somehow. There were *only* second shooters here, phantasms driving mass panic and confusion. There would be casualties, maybe even deaths, but it wasn't a shooting. There was no smell other than those of sweat and cloth and furniture, and the shots hadn't continued.

Mass shooters don't stop. Could have been a revenge shooting, or even someone targeting Katrina, Rahel, but still, there would have been something else—a delay, then one last shot fired, into the assailant's own head, like a period at the end of a sentence.

There was a shift, subtle as a riot, in the direction of the stream of customers. They had been surging toward the bathroom section, and the large room that held the area rugs, Sporups and Kyndbys and Langsteds. Something else had happened. Helicopter people, maybe. Karras pulled the Makarov from his bag and stuck it in the waistband of his trousers, dangerously. More dangerous was what he was contemplating next: cutting through the crowd— although he'd know what they were about to do, as individuals, nearly as easily as he'd know what they were about to say, so he'd be safe—and confronting whomever or whatever was behind the gunfire.

Karras leapt from the bin and smacked hard into a knot of frantic customers. They beat him with their forearms and knees, a hand grabbed his left bicep and spun him around. He ate a faceful of a metal Bror storage solution, and he felt that already-loose tooth yank nearly free except for a thread of fiery nerve. Some tween kid, almost Katrina's height, barreled through, clipping the back of his knees and sending him staggering. The mob wasn't a collection of individuals. It was a being of its own with a radically distributed and hopelessly insane mind. No octopus, all tentacles. Some eager to grapple and sweep, others to pummel and whack. He threw his forearms around his head, hunched over, and was sucked into a stream of people heading into the room layouts.

Another hectic, kinetic, moment, Karras found himself under an Idåsen desk in a small box designed to look like a casually hip office. The desk was useless as cover; it was just a board held up by two pillars, themselves kept vertical by a pair of angled legs at the base of each, but Karras felt strangely safe for a moment. Then he recalled why—this desk was identical to the one belonging to Sharon Toynbee at Little Round Bombs. He had invited himself over to the office one day, back when his first book, *The Devolution of Everyday Strife: From the Battle of Seattle to Occupy Wall Street*, had just come in from the printers. It was hardly a book, more a saddle-stitched pamphlet than anything else, and its contents nothing but a series of aphoristic in-jokes purporting to be political strategy. And Little Round Bombs was hardly a publisher. Karras took a small scratched-up elevator to the fourth floor of a building in Ann Arbor, the first three of which were stuffed with industrial sewing machines operated by women from every country in the Americas in which the US had once overthrown a government, and when he came in, Sharon instantly shoved a screwdriver and a sheet of pictographic instructions in his hand and put him to work. After constructing a third Nominell office chair, he was allowed to shake hands with the publisher, who was known to the few people who knew him at all as Viktor Surge. He was a hopeful-seeming guy whose grandmother had died and left him a house, which he had sold and poured into 'the revolution,' i.e., Little Round Bombs.

Then Sharon had directed Karras to build her desk, which he did.

The chair by this desk under which he hid now was also a Nominell, Karras now noticed. And the flooring was at least very similar to what he remembered at the Little Round Bombs office. His phone rang again. Was it Bennett, looking to gloat or to declare Karras dead if he didn't answer?

No, it was Sharon Toynbee.

And the phone accepted the call itself, without his intervention.

"Mike!" she said. He put the phone to his ear and tried to cup it with his free hand so he could hear over the screaming, and slapping of flesh against flesh and furniture, and the conspicuous absence of reports from firearms. "There's been an accident!"

"What? Wait, listen, I'm in the middle—"

"Exactly!"

"Sharon…" She wasn't making sense, and it wasn't fair. He was the one trapped in the corner of a fake room as a riot unwound all around him, his allies missing, presumed enemies en route to his location and likely with reinforcements circling the building.

He should be the one not making any sense. Sharon Toynbee *wasn't allowed to not make sense.*

Karras saw a flash of blue streak by. "Katrina!" he shouted, and they turned, and squirmed, and wormed their way to the desk.

"You can come to the office!" Sharon shouted into his left ear as Katrina explained something he didn't catch about the location of the Alazars in his right. Something about Djimon on the roof? *You can come to the office!* Was her mind that scrambled, or did Karras just mishear the impossibly ignorant question *Can you come to the office?*

"Michael, I need you to focus on my voice, and do exactly what I am about to tell you," Sharon said. She started describing office furniture.

21.

It DIDN'T TAKE long, fewer than three minutes, to find the right IKEA bookshelf and place it next to the Idåsen. Karras was hardly the only person repeating the names of IKEA products into his phone, and rushing to grab them. He was just the only one not to try to rush past the cash registers after. Katrina helped too.

Viktor Surge hadn't been rich, and neither had his grandmother. She'd just been born at the right time and with the right genes and temperament to marry young, resist the lure of cigarette commercials on the Dumont Network, and bury a husband who could not, but only after he'd paid off the Old Town rowhouse he'd purchased for her to raise his family. You could edit and design works of underground literature as well on flatbox furniture as on anything else, so Viktor spent his money surprisingly wisely for a radical publisher. It was easy to collect facsimiles of all the stuff in Sharon Toynbee's small corner of the Little Round Bombs' office, and arrange it in the set-up just as she had it.

Karras saw a flash of blue streak by. "Katrina!" he shouted, but they didn't seem to hear.

He sat down at the desk, put his phone down upon it, then placed his fingers on the home keys of his laptop, which was just like Sharon Toynbee's laptop in the office, and thanks to a whisper of public wifi active in the riotous air the laptop was connected to the Little Round Bombs server. He was supposed to close his eyes, as Sharon instructed, and think about a certain shape, as Sharon instructed, and type a certain phrase, which Sharon was about to reveal, but then he heard Rahel call his name, so he opened his eyes again. She was just two feet away from him, within the perimeter of the office mock-up, her beautiful face nearly purple with confusion and rage, Tony breathless and bleeding from a cut above his eyebrow next to her, Katrina wide-eyed and wondering. Rahel said something about Djimon on the roof, a weapon from his days among the irregulars in his hand, the helicopter burning in the parking lot, reports of young men and more than a few women with awkward haircuts and surgical masks obscuring their faces, brandishing weapons and opening fire in San

Francisco; in Portland, Oregon; in Tulsa, Oklahoma; in Westmont, Illinois, where Michael Karras had been born and raised and it all sounded very exciting and horrifying, but he promised Sharon he would close his eyes and type the phrase she was reciting now, so he did so, and then he vanished.

22.

"HELLO," SAID SHARON Toynbee from behind Michael Karras. She reached over his shoulder and put the receiver of her desktop landline back in its cradle. "That worked—Oh. Too well."

Karras swiveled in Sharon's chair to look at her, but she was looking past him.

"Hello," said Rahel Alazar. Tony and Katrina were silent.

"Were you all in the room mock-up?" Sharon asked them. "At the IKEA?"

Rahel nodded. "Mm-hmm." She folded her arms across her chest. "So what's this place then?" She cast her gaze about the room, which was little more than three desks and chairs, just as in the IKEA model room, shelving units stuffed with dozens of identical copies of new-seeming books, and tacked to the back wall an aging banner reading LITTLE ROUND BOMBS RADICAL BOOK CLUB—WE MAKE MIND-BLOWING BOOKS. The Os in 'books' were two black circles with lit fuses protruding from them. She smiled. "Where the magic happens?" Next to her, Katrina fell to their knees and vomited. The spicy stench of whatever Ethiopian food they had been offered in the van instantly filled the small room. Tony wobbled but stayed standing. He drooled a bit.

"Yes," said Sharon. "It is, exactly, where the magic happened."

Sharon Toynbee never misspoke, Karras knew that from experience. At one point, magic happened here, in the Ann Arbor offices of Little Round Bombs, and then, at a later point, it ceased to happen.

"I've felt this before, in my church. I thought it was God at work who wished the man who wanted to kill me away, but it was the Devil who summoned him in the first place, I see…"

"That must be why you're less… disturbed than your friends," said Sharon. "I recognize Katrina Chu-Ramirez from the news. You're brave folx, kid. Who is this man? A relative? He looks dehydrated. It happens. There's a water cooler in the corner."

"Uhm…" said Tony. He licked his lips. "I don't think I can walk that far."

Rahel exhaled harshly and walked to the corner. "Me too…" Katrina called out behind her.

Karras didn't feel thirsty, or nauseated, or even confused. He didn't comprehend what had just happened in the slightest, and some part of his brain had simply decided that it hadn't, to protect the rest. He was watching television, or listening to a source describe some inexplicable and impossible incident, without judgment or concern. He reached for the mouse, clicked it, and woke up Sharon's monitor.

The Grutzmacher notes on the Dallas Library Killer incident. He minimized Word and found an extremely messy desktop display littered with Word and text files, .jpgs and .movs, all named some arbitrary string of numbers. Sharon, who normally snapped at anyone who touched her computer or read over her shoulder, said nothing as he clicked on a video file. It opened quickly, more quickly than any video file ever had on his own laptop, and he saw himself, partially obscured by a rectangle of blue light, on one side of a café window, as Rahel and Tony sat at a table and in the background, behind them a small television flickered. The drone at Yunus's place.

"Hmm," he said.

"What's going on?" Tony asked. "How did we get here?" He looked around, at his feet and the floor under them, at Katrina, who had their head practically between their knees. Rahel returned with three paper cones of water and said "Mmm," and moved her chin, and that was enough for Tony to kneel down and get Katrina back to their feet.

"Black magic," Rahel said, passing out the paper cones. "This is my fault. I never should have written to Michael Karras. I was a fool."

"Not black magic," said Sharon Toynbee. "Red magic. The reddest. Perhaps red and black magic if you're feeling whimsical."

"I am not," said Rahel. "Michael, send us back."

"I... what?" Karras said. "I was just typing something, and... I guess, uh, *the universe is a hologram?*"

Katrina groaned, and put themselves in Tony's arms and muttered something about 'white bullshit.'

"What did you type?" Tony asked. Sharon watched the conversation unfold, disinterested, even when Karras looked at her, pleading for assistance.

"*Vivez sans temps mort,*" Karras answered. "Live without dead time." He shrugged. Tony shrugged back. "It's a Situationist slogan, graffiti on some brick wall somewhere in Paris in May 1968."

"Oh," said Tony.

"There was a general strike, and it was both more and less than a full-blown workers' revolution," Karras said, saying true things but not actually explaining anything. "Lots of... uhm... things happened, but then not much, in the end."

"Okay, you explain," Tony said. The water had helped, or the gently weeping middle-schooler in his arms did. His voice had steel in it. "First explain, then send us back."

"Send you back to a scene of mass hysteria and

senseless violence?" asked Sharon. "You can just walk outside for that. It won't be exactly the same, but the world is a jazz musician's fake book. Any place you go will be good enough."

"Is Michael telling the truth?" Rahel asked.

"About almost everything, except for every detail. Yes I did tell him to type *Vivez sans temps mort*—but no, the actual slogan from the days of May was '*Vivre* sans temps mort.' It wasn't an imperative in the original, but it became one when recontextualized as a slogan. Memetic evolution.

"Further, it wasn't graffiti on a brick wall, but rather on a set of exterior wooden double-doors. You can find photos online if you look, but nobody looks because everyone simply imagines and is satisfied.

"Finally, some people know exactly who coined the phrase and painted it that day, so it's not quite anonymous."

"You don't look a day over fifty, lady," said Tony.

"I don't mean me," Sharon said, touching the greyish streak in her hair. "I—" There was a sound of metal screaming and a bang and air rushing away. The office was in an old building, old enough that one wall was composed of windows the height of a grown man. One of the small transoms above them was open. Sharon rushed to the window and peered outside. "Hmm. Looks like someone drove a truck into the crowd. Not good. I've always wanted to say this—Katie, bar the door."

"I... uh," Katrina was more or less able to stand under their own power.

"I'll do it," Tony said. "Mike, help."

"What kind of truck? Self-driving? Uhm..." Karras said.

"Just move!" Rahel snapped at him, and Karras pushed himself out of the chair and walked awkwardly, like one of his legs had fallen asleep, to the door. Tony was waiting, his hands on a metal shelving unit against the wall, ready to drag it across the door.

"You get the bottom, I get the top," said Tony, and when Karras bent his knees to get a grip on the bottom of the shelf, Tony reached down, plucked the Makarov from Karras's waistband, and leveled it at Sharon. With a grunt, he yanked the shelving unit across the closed door, sending Karras sprawling to the floor. Tony planted his foot between Karras's shoulderblades.

"Gun!" Katrina screamed, and fell back into a cowering mass of limbs.

"Start talking," said Rahel.

"Look, I don't know how anything—"

"They're pointing the gun at me, Michael," said Sharon. "And I'll explain. 'Vivre sans temps mort' is a good idea, and a way to save travel time when articulating it under the right conditions. I shouldn't be surprised that Michael managed to move you all. There's another slogan you might be familiar with:

'There are decades when nothing happens, and there are weeks when decades happen.'"

"Lenin…" Katrina said from their spot on the floor.

"No," said Karras, underfoot.

"That one was mine," said Sharon. "Attributing it to Lenin was a way to spread it across the noösphere, and give it some oomph. It worked too, finally. Took more than twenty years, but it worked. Too well, maybe." She gestured out the window. Whatever was going on outside was bad. Worse than college-town bad, which the Alazars were used to, and even beyond *This is the emergency!* bad.

"What kind of operation is this?" Tony demanded. "What are you talking about, slogans and the newsphere? Is this even a real publishing company?"

"Not if you ask our authors about the advances we offer," said Sharon. Karras thought about trying to laugh at that, but Tony's foot was heavy and his tooth was bothering him and he was burning with humiliation from being so easily tricked and disarmed.

"LRB started out as a book club," Sharon said. "Viktor Surge founded it. He was my TA in school, and we got along. There were six of us to start, and we read it all—Marx and Gramsci, Bookchin, then the French theorists, the Invisible Committee."

"The Bible?" said Rahel.

"Excerpts," said Sharon. "Gnostic texts from Nag Hammadi too. 'The Thunder, Perfect Mind.'"

Rahel clucked her tongue.

Karras pressed his palms against the floor, considering his options. Sharon never liked talking about herself much, but she loved listing what she'd been reading and her thoughts on it all. Tony couldn't keep the gun pointed at her forever. The noise outside was rising and receding, like multiple protests, or riots, rolling past. But Serj had claimed that the big nationwide attack would be in a few days. The current dramas in Emeryille and right outside were clearly just episodes of mass hysteria caused by people looking too intently at their smartphones. It was happening in this room too—why this pinning predicament Tony put him in, why threaten Sharon Toynbee with a weapon? Karras was going to need an ally. He turned his head, slowly enough so Tony wouldn't notice, and peered at Katrina, focusing on them.

Scopaesthesia does not exist, at least not as a psychic phenomenon, Michael Karras knew that much. Sure, there were three shelves of copies of *Goshinbo Secrets of the Shinobi* that claimed otherwise in the opposite corner of the room, but Karras knew the truth. Katrina would not perceive his staring. However, until a few minutes prior, it was impossible to close one's eyes, touch type, and translate a room full of people from California to Michigan.

Ah, that's all he had to do.

"The reading group, all of us, as a collective, were extremely interested in putting our ideas into practice," Sharon was saying. "Did you know that every revolutionary movement since the creation of the Stanhope press began as a reading group? Our idea was a simple one: undermine the state by manipulating the Spectacle."

"I don't care about this part," said Tony.

Karras turned his head away from Katrina, and faced the wall. The floor under the shelf Tony had moved was coated in a near-perfect rectangle of dust topped with shredded cobwebs, some crumbled Post-It Notes, a thick paper bookmark celebrating the once-frontlist and now out-of-print *Hack Ur iMac: Doin' The Jobs Steve Jobs Won't Let You Do To Unlock Epic Performance* and—ah, a retractable pen. Karras slowly started snaking his left hand toward it.

"Nobody can escape Spectacle—believe me, we tried. Drugs, sex, privation, and yes, even religion. Why are the churches of your sect so beautiful, Rahel Alazar, so sensuous? And in the cosmic center of it, you have a Holiest of Holies, a reification of the contents of the Ark of the Covenant, but you can't peek inside to see it. And the real Ark of the Covenant, nobody gets to see that though your bishops and Popes all swear it exists in a monastery in Ethiopia. At the center is a void," Sharon said. "I'm not trying to be disrespectful—the semiotic void in the midst of a sensory swirl of consumption."

"That's devil talk! Devil talk and you cast spells! You're not telling us of some postmodern book club," said Rahel. "You're talking about a coven!"

"No, it was a book club," said Sharon, matter-of-factly.

Karras got his fingers around the pen, put his thumb on the plunger and clicked a half-dozen times in quick succession. Katrina noticed, raised their head.

"A book club with a goal, and one we almost achieved. Make the void more obvious, through publication and other, most esoteric practices, and undermine the Spectacle, and thus the power of the state. Think about it—do you two believe the so-called official story anymore? About anything? Forget the news, and vaccines, the wars and rumors of war—when was the last time anyone even managed to consume a film or a novel without undermining its story via interpretation?"

"You're the one with the book club, you tell us," said Tony.

"We don't undermine, we reveal," said Sharon. "We reveal the necessary implications of auctorial praxis—"

Karras switched the pen from his left hand to his right, rolled it over to Katrina, then planted both palms on the floor and tried for a push-up, sending Tony reeling. Katrina leapt across the small room, pen held like a knife in a film, and aimed for Tony's other foot. He stumbled awkwardly over them, flailing into Sharon, tackling her, sending them both into her desk. Karras was up. Rahel was too. Both went for the Makarov, to secure it; that's what Karras wanted to do, and what he couldn't imagine Rahel not wanting to do. Katrina grabbed their shin—it had been stomped on—and rolled about on their back, whimpering. Sharon grunted angrily, pushed Tony off of her, said something about Crossfit and xinyi.

Karras wrapped his hand around *not* the gun. Rahel's hand. It was warm, tense and unyielding, five fingers of rebar.

She didn't let go, but she didn't struggle to pull her hand away either. She met Karras's gaze for a moment, and then turned to Sharon. "I'm not an intellectual like you are. You probably think I'm stupid and naïve, that all Christians are stupid and naïve. So tell me if I am being stupid and naïve, but all you can do, the magic, just by reading books in a certain way and chanting the correct slogans, it depends on authors and what they 'really mean.' But"—then she flexed and the barrel of the Makarov was kissing Karras's sternum—"isn't the author dead?"

"I wouldn't do that were I you, Rahel," Sharon said.

"Me neither," Karras said. It was both a ridiculously dumb and incredibly intelligent thing to say, as it made Rahel want to respond. Every moment she was speaking was one where her brain wasn't oriented toward convincing her twitching nervous system to squeeze the trigger of the pistol in her hand.

"You may recall our interview, when I told you that at first I thought the shooter at the altar was an African," said Rahel, with a lick of her lips. She was sweating, near to stammering. "What you didn't bother to even ask me was if I had a second thought, and I did, and the man appeared to be, right before he vanished, someone who looked rather like you."

"That was also my experience," said Katrina, from the floor. Rahel tensed.

"Please don't kill me," Karras said. "It would be a sin."

"Would it? What if you just reappear at the next event? Then I would not have killed you at all; it would be more like opening a window to shoo a fly out than swatting one."

"I don't know what's going on…"

"I do," said Sharon. "And it's not Michael's fault. Mostly not. Like I told you on the telephone, there's been an accident."

"What was the accident?" asked Tony. "And Rahel, give me the gun, please. You didn't tell me you recognized Michael from the church. I wouldn't have slipped him the pistol had I known."

"I think I'll keep it," said Rahel. "And I didn't tell you because I didn't know. I just realized why Michael looked so familiar in the IKEA. Something about how he looked when he closed his eyes, just like the man who threatened me did right as he introduced the barrel of his rifle to my face"—she put the gun up against the top of Karras's nose, where a million dubious diagrams mark the location of the third eye—"before the gun jammed and he disappeared."

"That's what we need to discuss, and why you mustn't kill him," Sharon said. "Our experiments in influencing the Spectacle worked, after a fashion."

"Robert Wayne Rasnic spoke about escaping the Spectacle before he killed himself," Tony said.

"He was a member of the book club in the early days, before we incorporated," said Sharon. "He was a silent partner in the publishing company. Part of the accident isn't that we went too far, but that we didn't go far enough. We sought to undermine the Spectacle and thus the state and we did—we bred suspicion, undermined institutions and cultural mores. Phantasms and whispers. Rumors and cases of mistaken identities. We summoned that, but we got the second shooters."

Rahel took the gun from Karras's forehead and pointed it at Sharon, who raised her hands as if to surrender and then did something complicated with them and suddenly Rahel yelped and was holding her wrist against her stomach, wincing in pain, and Sharon had the Makarov in her hand. She removed the magazine and placed both it and the pistol on her desk.

"Take it easy," she said. "As I was saying, we were as surprised as anyone—*more* surprised, really, as despite our dalliances in the noösphere we are ultimately dialectical materialists. It's one thing to plant the idea of mysterious second shooters in blog posts and chit-chats and even wire reports. It's quite another when we start seeing them on video."

"Okay," said Katrina, finally getting to their feet. "Someone tell me what the no-eh-sphere is?"

"*Nous* is the Greek word—it's cogitation, basically. Using your mind to understand what is real," said Karras, shuffling two feet backward to get out of range of Rahel's reach, and Sharon's. "And sph—"

"I know what a sphere is, Mister Karras," Katrina snapped. "I'm so tired of men. Anyway, so mass brainwashing made things look real, or be real, is that what you're saying, uhm…?"

"Sharon is fine," said Sharon. "And that depends on what you mean by real, or more specifically The Real."

"Let's all move on, please," said Tony. "It's real enough because we're here and that kid is covered in puke, and ten minutes ago we were in California. So is that what's going to happen? Are crazed killers going to zap themselves all over the country?"

"Who told you that?"

"A kid named… Serj," said Tony. "Oh, like Viktor Surge."

"Hmm, like Viktor Surge," said Sharon. "Who is deceased."

"Nobody returns from the dead via black magic," said Rahel. "Though I admit that this afternoon I'd have said nobody teleports across the country by any means, and yet here we all are."

"And Serj was not a kid," said Karras. The Alazars turned their gazes to him, and he leaned over and confided in Sharon, loudly, "He used the phrase 'reruns on TV.'"

"Kids know what the word 'rerun' means," said Katrina.

"But have you ever used it in a sentence?"

"Yes!"

"Before five seconds ago?"

Katrina bowed their head in defeat.

"I'm prepared to assume that the threat is real, and that it is a result of the accident I brought Mike here to try to fix," said Sharon. "We should begin by—"

"But what was the accident?" said Karras.

Sharon screwed up her mouth before answering. "It was you."

23.

THE UNIVERSE HAS no center. The Big Bang did not occur in the center of some space, leading the universe to expand outward from that point. It was an explosion of space, and time, and void. The universe is expanding uniformly in all directions and perhaps even within dimensions we cannot perceive, nor do more than speculate about with the type of mathematics we mistakenly refer to as higher. The universe is not growing into a void—we cannot turn around and see the darkness we are traveling into— but is *growing* a void.

Humanity lives on a ball of mud somewhere in a distant corner of the universe, and it is a corner becoming ever more distant. It's all expanding, remember. But, the universe has no center; it's all distant corners. Since the universe has no center, an observer can arbitrarily assign it one. In fact, observers almost invariably do assign the universe some center, and call it God or the nation-state or the soul or the self.

Our experiments in undermining the Spectacle bore fruit right away. The void is always there, writhing and squirming, pressing against the borders of the Spectacle, leaking through in the moments between frames of a film, in the slow grind of computing power as a video game loads, in the breaths you take after the dream ends but before your eyes open.

We lost track of what we had done. There were other forces at work, but we also hit the limits of our competence. It takes scientists, fueled by either altruism or sociopathy and funded by the state, to create a deadly virus, but any dumbass can drop a test tube and then hop on the commuter rail back to the suburbs without first washing his hands. We needed someone to track down what was happening. Enter you, Michael.

You've worked with us before, and one time, long ago, you said something odd that rewired your brain in a certain way. Do you recall terrifying your schoolmates with the claim that there were no skeletons inside them, but that they were inside their skeletons? That little bit of metaphysics, the way you decided to put yourself at the center of the universe, as a void you cannot even see in the mirror, made it so that people would talk to you about void-events they experienced. The void itself would be keen to speak to you. It would seek to become you, and bring you into it. Once we saw Katrina, in that security camera footage Bennett leaked, whispering that one of the phantom shooters at Middlesex looked like you, we knew we had to call you in.

But you're still only a freelance writer, more fast than good if I'm honest, and best of all you work cheap. We didn't want a book, we just wanted notes, and we wanted to keep you on the road.

Our mistake was thinking that we could use the void without negative side effects, spark a revolution that wasn't 360 degrees. The accident was our inferior linear understanding of time. Viktor Surge died this morning, by his own hand, for your sake. Our book club practices meant that he continued to exist posthumously, as a conscious being, within the void. And you spoke to him yesterday, before his death, though the Serj you spoke to was long dead, and communicating from beyond the grave. Know that as the universe has no center and is infinite and is infinitely expanding and as we are in a distant corner of it, we cannot see much of that infinity and nothing of the many other infinities that make up the universe. Everything has already happened. Everyone is already dead, and everyone and everything that ever lived still lives. Serj communicated via a zombie-themed virtual environment—apropos!—for years before Surge died, but they are one and the same because the void that makes up most of infinity also makes up most of eternity. Imagine the universe as a balloon, galaxies painted on its surface. Blow up the balloon—the galaxies expand and separate. You're holding all of space in your hand. You're also holding all of time in your hand, Michael Karras.

You've met the boss; you received his warning. You're the center of the universe, and as a dumb void you cannot even perceive yourself, because you placed yourself inside your own skull, Michael. You already have the information we need to stop the murder of America, to stop the void from totally consuming the Spectacle, somewhere and somewhen within you.

So sit down at Viktor Surge's old keyboard, close your eyes, and type whatever comes to mind. The surrealistic game of automatic writing will allow you to articulate the ineffable, to write down the void.

24.

FOR MAYBE THIRTY seconds, nobody spoke. Then:

"Are you crazy? Is that your problem?" asked Tony.

"I was going to ask if you were going through a mental health crisis and how we could all support you, but generally I share Mister Alazar's question, Sharon," said Katrina.

"We teleported," said Rahel. "We're not all dreaming, or hallucinating, or dead and in some limbo, facing some kind of spiritual test. She's speaking the facts, if not the truth."

"How do you know that?" Katrina snapped.

"I know," said Rahel, "because I am saved." She looked not at Katrina, but at Sharon, a fiery challenge in her eyes.

Sharon shrugged. "Sure, babe." Then to Mike: "Sit

down and type. If it helps, pretend that you're getting a buck a word, like the magazines would pay in the old days." She pointed at the third desk in the room, one slightly larger than the others, but still definitely an IKEA build.

"Nothing about this all being true means you're not crazy, Miss," Tony said to Sharon.

"All right, thank you for telling me," Sharon said.

"This keyboard…" said Karras as he took his seat. "It's… what is this? Oh, I get it."

"It's big. What is it?" Katrina said. They walked across the small room and the others followed them to take a gander. Of course the desk was a large Hemnes, Surge's computer needed the space. The laptop was typical, but it had attached to it a unique keyboard. It was large, and square, and the keys were laid in a grid of 49 by 49, with five function keys on the left-hand side and five on the right. The glyphs upon the keys were—

"Enochian," said Karras. Weird twisting characters, vaguely reminiscent in shape to that of Hebrew, of Ge'ez, of Greek. Rahel and even Tony made the sign of the cross over themselves, and Rahel muttered some brief prayer or at least expression of discontent. Karras noticed that they made the sign in what he had always been told was the 'Western' manner.

"You're a touch-typist, Michael. You can't perform automatic writing on a normal qwerty keyboard, and it's hard to find a Dvorak," said Sharon.

"You found *this* easily, though?" Karras said, gesturing at it, half-astounded, half-disgusted, like his grandmother used to at take-out food set upon her kitchen table. He wished she were here now, to brandish a wooden spoon at everyone. Supposedly, in the void of infinite time and space, there was some distant set of coordinates where she was even still alive. He squeezed back a tear at the thought. Something about the keyboard, the way the silvery glyphs shimmered against the deep black of the keys, was unsettling. Of course Sharon had told him to close his eyes; his mind was already trying to escape into quotidian grief, normal spiritual agony.

"MacOS will let you switch to Dvorak pretty easily," said Tony. "Mike won't know the letters anymore than he knows this. You don't need to use this, Mike." Tony couldn't stop staring at the keyboard either.

"He's using this one," said Sharon. "It was Viktor's. It's modeled on the Dee and Kelley Enochian cells. The function keys let you switch cells. He did everything on it. Now you know why I handle all LRB's correspondence."

"Michael, I'm praying for you," Rahel said. "We all should. Tony."

"Yes," said Tony, absently. He was still looking at the keyboard, watching Karras's hands move over it, fingers like spider's legs careful in a web. He held out a hand and took Rahel's in his. Katrina said "uhm" or some similar phoneme and turned their back and put their hands over their face.

"Do I need to fetch the gun?" Sharon said. "You're on *dead*line. Type, Michael."

"Why do I need to close my eyes?"

"So you'll be surprised."

Karras closed his eyes. He didn't try to empty his mind. It was already the ever-expanding void, according to Sharon Toynbee. Were there home keys on this keyboard? Unlikely. He placed them on a row that felt ergonomically acceptable. It was true that Karras often considered himself the center of the universe, found himself tearing up at the thought of death not because of the loved ones who preceded him, or for fears of an afterlife of eternal torture, but because of the horrible unfairness of it all. The world would go on spinning, history would continue to bubble away like the seas, and he wouldn't even be there to see any of it. Even his family members would continue going to work and watching television and having more children and giving them names other than Michael. His books would be deaccessioned and forgotten, his stuff thrown out onto the street or sold for dimes and then pennies until it disintegrated and rejoined the ecosystem, except for his electronic toothbrush and his obsolete phones. That would be his legacy.

Karras typed for longer than he had planned. He opened his eyes and put his hands on his lap, sheepishly. The Enochian cells appeared on screen, and the individual glyphs flickered in the pattern Karras had already typed. The cells swapped position, characters shifting up and down columns and across rows. Karras recalled something about John Dee and Edward Kelley: Kelley was the one capable of communicating with angels; he would call out the number of the grid and the column and row of the glyph for Dee to transcribe, and Dee would then reverse the text of the message prior to translating it. A similar process was being run through via the graphic user interface, for whose benefit, Karras couldn't say and Sharon wouldn't.

The translation finally appeared on screen. Karras burst out laughing, loud enough to fill the small room. He half expected a wall to collapse to the floor and reveal a now-empty and thoroughly ravished IKEA display floor, but no. Ann Arbor remained stubbornly just outside the windows, and the ruckus on the street below continued without a break for applause or collective hooting at the marks.

Sharon read over his shoulder. "The Mall of America. Well, it's right by the airport, anyway."

25.

"Teleport us there," said Tony as he strode over to Sharon's desk and reclaimed the Makarov. "We'll hang out there all night and take care of it in the morning."

"I can't," said Karras.

"Is there a mall around here, a Disney store? Stare at Mickey Mouse and think good thoughts and bring us to the Mall of America's Disney store," Tony said. He shrugged in response to his sister's disappointed look. "What? It has to have one. It's the biggest mall. It probably has two. Or a movie theater. They're all the same in the dark. That's how it works, right—go to some place, some contrived place that looks just like where you want to go, and say the line and you're there?"

"I know. I just can't do it," said Karras. "I don't even know how I know, but I know."

"It only works once per lifetime," said Sharon. "And one needs to have that solipsistic yet ultimately empty worldview—"

"Thanks, boss," said Karras.

"Solipsistic, empty, disposable? Sounds like any cis man will do," said Katrina.

Sharon hooted at that, startling everyone. Rahel clutched her chest, and Katrina giggled nervously. "You're clever. If you ever want an internship—"

"I'm already writing a book for Harper Collins about Middlesex and the This Is The Emergency movement," said Katrina.

"Great. Anyway, once in a lifetime doesn't mean that Mike could do it once, and then someone else could do it once. It means once per lifetime. Someone else will be able to use the technique once someone else has been arbitrarily determined to be the center of the universe. Once Mike passes away. It worked for him today because Viktor Surge's lifetime ended yesterday. Viktor had used it to escape a GIA attack during the Algerian Civil War. Luckily, he was a talented street artist and had been carrying some pastels. He drew a trompe-l'œil of his home kitchen, which was luckily quite Spartan as he never cooked, on the wall of his hotel room, and walked right through."

"Oh," said Tony. The Makarov was in his hand, hanging low by his thigh. Karras sighed with relief when he didn't raise it and make some speech about shooting Karras so that he could be instantly transported to the Mall of America. "Too bad you didn't know you could do it before, Michael. You might have saved it for another time, teleporting yourself from one Starbucks to another or something. Like one across the street from the other."

Rahel helped him by giggling a little.

"This is meant to happen tomorrow," said Sharon. "It's a three-hour flight. It's midweek. It'll be expensive, but we can probably get tickets." She was very happy to loudly announce these plans. Sharon thought the room to be under surveillance, Karras realized. How much of the Viktor Surge story was true, then? "If not, it's a twelve-hour drive. We'll rent a car."

"'We'?" said Rahel, her voice a diamond on glass. "We? Do you know that among our party is a child who needs to be on a plane, heading east to New Jersey, immediately? And I've no idea what you expect me or my brother to do about all this Satanic summoning you and your Mister Surge have been doing. I reached out to Michael Karras because I wanted to understand what I saw in my church the day my brothers and sisters in Christ were murdered by a madman. Now I understand. It was *you* and your coven, dabbling with black magic."

"I want to go," Katrina said. "I'm not afraid."

"Yes, you are," said Karras. "And it's good that you're afraid. If you weren't, that would mean that you're insa—uh, experiencing a mental health crisis, and a dangerous one that was doing damage to your self-preservation instincts."

"You probably *are* experiencing PTSD symptoms from the Middlesex event," said Sharon. "Sometimes people want to relive their traumas. Rahel is correct—I wasn't talking about you when I said *we*." She slipped her smartphone from the inner breast pocket of her blazer. "There's also another issue: you're extremely famous at the moment. That could attract undue attention, and not just from the mass media or angry gun-owners. There's..." she was looking closely at the screen, "a Sears and a Hooters on-site, and Minnesota has a decent gun and hunting subculture. Who knows who might recognize you? Hmm, an Emoji Store too. Anyway." She tapped at her screen again. "The void forces manifesting tomorrow would be highly interested in you. You'll fly with us to Minnesota, but then you're getting on a flight to Trenton as an unaccompanied minor... unless you want to take charge of her, Rahel?"

"My uncle Djimon is in the middle of a riot back home, and my father and mother are worried sick for me and Tony, and everyone else. If I'm taking charge of anyone, it'll be the members of my family," said Rahel.

"All the more reason to come with us, then," said Karras. "It's not going to get better, it's going to get much much worse."

"It's a fallen world, Michael. It's doomed to get worse and worse, until the Day of Judgment. My family's already been through war, Communism, poverty, racism, the church shooting, you exposing us to all sorts of Satanic dangers and nonsense."

"But you have to come," Karras said. "I need you."

"Why?"

"In case you're right," Karras said.

"You didn't get dizzy after the teleport," Tony said.

"Because I'd already inhaled my share of brimstone!" said Rahel.

"I'm going with Mike," Tony said. "I want you to come with me, Rahel. If it's a trap or some weird long con, I want you watching my back, and I'll watch over you."

Rahel didn't say anything. She just lowered her head, and raised it, once.

26.

SHARON TOYNBEE'S VOLVO was pretty crowded, and for much of the trip nobody wished to speak, as there seemed to be nothing to say after Rahel's simple nod. Then Katrina Chu-Ramirez, sitting between the Alazars in the back seat, broke the ice.

"Ms. Toynbee," she asked. "What was that language you were speaking on the phone? Was it Enochian?"

"No, too many people in the intelligence community understand Enochian," Sharon said. "I was speaking to my twin in the language we share."

"You have a twin?" Karras said. "Identical?"

"Yes, but you can tell us apart pretty easily. He's a man," Sharon said. She turned on the car's blinker and rather suddenly turned off I-94. "The airport," she said.

Karras was surprised. They were nowhere near Detroit Metro. Then he saw the field and the tiny buildings at one end.

"Is your twin a pilot?"

"He is!" Sharon said, in that precise way a parent congratulates a normally inattentive child for noticing something.

"And we're flying from this little airport to another little airp—Oh, yes, yes, of course we are," said Karras.

"Yes, all sorts of things you don't know, but think you do from movies and newspaper articles about crashes. Flying VFR so no flight plan, Class D and E airspace all the way, and yes, the flight is going to feel like you're sitting in the bed of a pickup truck, driving over small boulders on a cliffside road."

"Oh, great," said Katrina. Rahel squeezed their hand. "Please don't say 'crashes' again."

"No promises," said Sharon.

Ann Arbor Airport was the sort of airport one only encounters if one is rich enough to afford a small airplane, or unfortunate enough to work at the bottom of the aviation barrel. Leonard was the latter, but he did have access to a plane. "Old new media," he explained after hugging Sharon—Karras had never seen Sharon hug anyone, or smile for longer than it takes to punctuate a sentence—and shaking everyone's hands. "Aerial banners and photography, mostly. Rarely skywriting. Marriage proposals, President's Day sales for used car lots, some graduation and football stuff for U of M. Keeps me in the air. Speaking of, this is my Cessna 206. Six seats, so it's kismet that there are six of us. I'll need you, Tony, in the left-hand rear seat, and Mike on the right-hand seat in the middle row, behind Sharon. No bags?" He gave Katrina the once over, noting the flakes of vomit on their jeans. "No change of clothes." Leonard was all business.

"We're going to the mall, Lee," Sharon said. "The Mall of America."

"One-way trip," added Tony.

"I hear you can live there if you keep moving," said Katrina. "It's like an internment camp, with stuff to buy."

Riding in the Cessna was like straddling the engine of a flying lawnmower. Even if it had been appropriate to speak in front of Leonard of plans for the Mall, for the confrontation with whatever mass-shooting event Viktor Surge had warned Karras of, conversation was just impossible. Katrina spent the entire flight with their head between their knees, occasionally weeping. The Alazars were mostly silent, save for episodes of snapping at each other in Amharic. Tony was clutching the armrests of his seat as though physically holding the entire plane in the sky himself. Rahel looked pale, and kept her gaze on the porthole by her seat. Leonard chirped at Sharon now and again in the language they had developed as children, and Sharon answered him in English; whether to try to include him and the others, or because the vocabulary of the twin language was too limited for a grown-up conversation, Karras couldn't tell. He was too busy trying to will his stomach to stay inside his body.

The flight was just under four hours long. "How annoying," he said after the Cessna banked and pointed itself at the runway at Flying Cloud Airport. "I didn't know I was going to have a one-time shot at teleporting until I'd already done it."

"Teleporting!" said Leonard. He laughed. "You have to send me comps of all this guy's books, Shar." She said something in the twin language and they both laughed so obviously at Karras that everyone else aboard laughed too.

Leonard rented an SUV, drove them from the tiny reliever airport to a nearby Hyatt, and paid for a single room with his card. It was Leonard who purchased a plane ticket for Katrina on his phone and announced that when they moved out in the morning to the Mall of America, which had a shuttle connection to the *real* airport, MSP, he would take Katrina there, and wait till their plane took off. Then he'd take himself back to FCM, fuel up, and fly back to Michigan. Left unstated: *by himself.*

"This room is very tiny," he finished up. It was true. The Alazars were seated on corners of one twin bed, Karras on the corner of the other. Sharon had taken the chair at the small corner desk, and Katrina had positioned themselves up against the wall, pretty keen, it was obvious to Karras, to be as close to Leonard as possible. "I'm going to go to the fitness center and swim a quick hundred laps. You guys do whatever thing you're planning on doing, and it was great to meet you all. Sweet dreams, enjoy Minneapolis when you get there. I can't wait to see the video." And with that, he left.

"Video?" Rahel asked.

"That was a lot of credit card and cell phone usage just now from your brother," said Tony. "We're gonna be tracked."

"His cards are probably still under his deadname," Katrina said. They had commandeered the recliner in the corner the moment Leonard left, and now curled up on its cushion like a sleepy puppy. "That might buy us some time."

"Sure... but surname?"

"We have different surnames," Sharon said.

"But you're twins!" said Rahel.

"Toynbee is my married name."

"You're married?" asked Karras.

"You changed your name when you got married!" Katrina said, less asking than spitting.

"It was a strange long weekend," said Sharon. "I kept the name to remind me of my mistakes."

"This is a pretty strange long weekend too," said Katrina. "You comrades should all get tattoos when you're done. When I'm of age, I'll get a matching one. I always wanted to get my thighs tattooed," they said, patting them lightly where crusted vomit wasn't. "That way I can look down and admire the art whenever I want."

"Travel really makes you loopy, doesn't it, dear?" asked Rahel, only somewhat impatient. "Me too. I need to shower and I guess change back into these clothes. We all do; we smell. This room smells like a foot with us all sitting here. And how are we to sleep? I propose that Sharon and I share a bed, and that my brother and Karras share one. Katrina, you seem okay where you are, yes?"

Katrina was asleep already.

"That one smells most of all. I want to polish her up with baby wipes before tomorrow."

"They're not a girl—" Sharon started.

"Yes, yes, I'll start a Twitter account just to apologize tomorrow, if I survive," said Rahel. "So, 'comrades,' what is the plan?"

"Sleep," said Sharon. "And dream. And if you're desperate for a change of clothes, the gift shop sells those comically oversized sweatshirts with an outline of the state made to look like a beer mug."

"I'll pass, Ms. Toynbee," said Rahel.

"I'll be right back," said Tony.

27.

SLEEP CAME EASILY to Michael Karras, which was insane to think about. Tony snored, and sleeping next to him was like sleeping next to an open furnace operating at full blast. *Do all men run this hot?* And there was more than ever to process. That Tony, now snoozing inches away from him in a new shirt and no pants, had pointed a gun at him, and that having weapons pointed at him was becoming distressingly common. Then there was the book club at the core of Little Round Bombs; that Viktor Surge, whom he'd only met once years ago, had died but also communicated with him, and with Dennis, of all people; the fact that he, Michael Karras, had violated the laws of physics, and had plenty of semi-reliable witnesses and even physical evidence that he'd done so. But still, Karras fell asleep in five minutes. He dreamt the tiniest microdream of Jesus Christ in a televisual heaven— thick shag clouds, golden gates, a blue sky scored with a platinum shimmering—pointing a finger at him, and two wingèd angels approaching with handcuffs and truncheons to arrest him for his crimes. They flew at him, lost coherence, transformed into spinning wheels festooned with a hundred unblinking eyes, wings like infinite birds fluttering to earth after being shot out of the sky; they were everywhere, filling all heaven, the entire universe. That woke him up.

Sharon had done something to everyone that made sleeping and dreaming possible, even reasonable. It was the way she breathed, as she spoke to them after Tony came back with his shirt and Rahel out of the bathroom, a towel wrapped around her head to protect her hair. They needed to sleep, and so they would. Their bodies had been through a lot. Sleep, sleep, said Sharon, and they all had toddled off to bed.

Now Katrina slept hard enough to look dead, the way infants do. On the women's bed, Rahel practically clung to the far side, to leave as much empty space between her and Sharon as possible. Her arm hung off the bed. The towel around her head had come half undone and also spilled over the edge. Karras put his head back on his pillow and tried to think of what Sharon could do, what might happen, but his brain rebelled and he fell asleep, hard, into an infinite blackness. It was as though endless angel wings had extinguished the stars.

Later, he felt moisture on his cheek, and smelled something that wasn't his own funk, or Tony's. He opened an eye and saw the curve of a naked breast. Sharon was kneeling over him, her hands on her knees, a weird smile on her face. She licked her lips and kissed him again.

"Hello, Michael. Would you like to go to the washroom with me and fuck?" she said. She was cute, her gold and silver hair catching what little light there was in the dark, her breasts hanging low, the cutest little two-roll pooch of a belly, hips like a cello, the tiniest patch of pubic hair. No tattoos on her thighs, but there was plenty of room for them.

"You're not dreaming," she said.

"I had a weird dream," Karras said. "It was about God."

"Why don't you come into the bathroom with me? I'll give you a little bath and then we can fuck," Sharon said.

"Are you the devil? Is this a trick?"

"It's no trick, Michael. If Leonard had a higher credit limit, we could have gotten two rooms and fucked with a little privacy." She smiled a second time, wider and more weirdly than before. She had a little snaggle tooth that Karras had always admired, but never got to look at so closely before. A moonbeam was coming in through the vertical blinds, striping Sharon with light. He was sure she had spent a little bit of time shuffling back and forth to find the exact right spot to stand in.

"Is this something your coven would do—have sex with each other before some major magical operation?"

"It was a book club," she said. "A revolutionary book club."

"Sharon, any other time, I'd jump at this chance, but it's been a hard couple of weeks."

"Any other time, I wouldn't be offering, Michael," she said, and she kissed him on the mouth. "Once in a lifetime. Get it?"

Karras nodded, and smiled, and winked, and hoped she could see the wink in the dark. "Well," she said, "the future lasts forever."

That line from Althusser, the incomprehensible Marxist turned incomprehensible murderer, probably meant something, but Karras was too sleepy to contemplate it. Sleep came quickly again, and nobody licked him awake a second time.

28.

SHARON ROUSED THEM all early, before sunrise, before the Hyatt's complimentary breakfast, even. The mall's many stores usually opened around 9am, but the mall itself opened to the public at six to allow people to simply walk around for exercise, or to get out of the region's often horrifying weather. Everyone was grumpy. The vending machine in an alcove behind the lobby provided Strawberry Frosted Pop-Tarts for Karras and Tony. Rahel chose three different flavors of potato chip, and Katrina a slim pack of Oreos, which they explained were vegan, though that they themselves were not vegan. Sharon wanted nothing but a cup of the cucumber–and-orange-flavored water in the lobby. "Acid for my batteries," she called it, standing by the water jug as the others slipped into the ambiguously comfortable lobby chairs.

"I don't get it," said Katrina. "If your book club were revolutionaries, why didn't you just organize the masses? Why all this, I dunno…?"

"Black magic," said Rahel.

"The two of you," Sharon said. "Just organize the masses. As if it's so easy?"

Katrina peered at Sharon, shrugged like an adult might.

"Hmm, well yes, you managed it to a certain extent."

"I'm in eighth grade," Katrina said.

"In 1968, the world was on fire. I'd say revolution was in the air, but the fires of rage and rebellion consumed all the oxygen. If you don't win, you lose, and hard. Vietnam, civil rights, the student rebellion, women and gay liberation, the Panthers, Prague. All of it was—"

"*Tuhn tuhn dadada dun tun tun tan tan*," Katrina sang. "I've seen the montages, lady, heard that song they always play. My parents are very into television documentaries."

"Was that supposed to be 'Redemption Song'?" asked Tony. "'Kiss the Sky'?"

"'In-A-Gadda-Da-Vida,' I think," said Karras.

"But anyway, when you organize the masses, you're as likely to get Stalin… or the Derg," Sharon said, glancing at the Alazars and hoping for support their tired expressions did not grant, "as anything else."

"Is that true?" said Karras. "I mean, are we comparing the efficacy of mass movements to whatever..." He gestured at his body. "I mean, is there a spell—?"

"A spell?"

"Just admit that they're spells. Not Surrealist mind tricks, not revolutionary mathematics invoking superstring theory to fold space, it's magic. You know some magical theory, and I'm able to perform magic. So, why not both? What's the spell for the general strike, for planting soviets in workplaces and growing them like seeds?"

Sharon poured herself another cup of the fruited water, and knocked it back in a gulp. "You want to know it? It's very powerful. Here it is, Michael: *Two, four, six, eight—Organize to smash the state.*" She crumpled the cup in her hand and tossed it across the entire empty lobby and into a wastebasket by the reception desk. The check-in clerk sleeping at the counter didn't raise her head. "When you are on a stage in front of an international workers' congress or on every TV channel and social media app at once, just say those words, and you'll have your revolution, sans contradictions or brutal necessity or anything that might make a liberal blanch. But you're not exactly a people person, are you, Michael?"

"No, Sharon, I guess I am not," Karras said. Would Sharon have been more forthcoming had he fucked her a few hours ago, Karras asked himself, bitterly, before realizing that no, had they hooked up, leaving her well-disposed toward him, she would have been *less* forthcoming. "I even became a writer just because I wanted to work from home. I'm not cut out for street politics. I learned that years ago. Even shoeleather reportage, this old New Journalism shit, isn't for me. I learned that about myself over the past few weeks. Ah, here's your brother." The automatic doors into the lobby slid open, and indeed there was Leonard with an armful of pastries and freshish fruit he'd sourced from a food truck. They descended on him like half-starved apes, incapable of speech.

THERE WAS AN unconscious collective decision not to talk about politics, or the murder of America, or even the sleeping arrangements in the cramped hotel room, while in the car with Leonard. Sharon, sitting shotgun, hadn't briefed anyone on the video cover story she had clearly fed him in their private twin language, and didn't speak to him now. He obligingly filled the silence in the rental SUV with the sounds of the local NPR station. The Alazars bookended Katrina Chu-Ramirez in the middle row. None of them had slept as well as Michael Karras, and they leaned sloppily against one another. The broadcaster was discussing an important novel that examined middle-class social mores through the prism of adult children returning to their hometown upon the occasion of the sudden death via erotic autoasphyxiation of the family patriarch. Karras, in the rear of the SUV by himself, had half a mind to tap Tony on the shoulder and ask for the Makarov.

It was morning twilight by the time the SUV made its way to a parking garage the size of a major city hospital and to the Metro Transit station at one end of the Mall of America. A handful of people were already milling about the entrance. A bus steamed a few yards away. Leonard pulled up to the curb and put his hand on the keys in the ignition. "Ready, Katrina?" His voice was bright and raspy, like a grapefruit spoon.

"Uhm," said Katrina.

"We can't idle here," said Tony, looking out his window. "It's a bus stop. The Minnesota people are already smiling at us to leave."

"Okay, I guess I'm ready," said Katrina. "I'm sorry, everyone. I ran away because I was afraid and because I wanted to talk to Michael, and I've just been a burden."

"Katrina, you've been great," Michael said. "You're pretty much the only one here who hasn't pointed a gun at me, or threatened me, or nearly broken someone's arm tussling over a gun." Leonard turned around in his seat, inhaling sharply to ask a million impossible questions, but Sharon said something in their odd chirpy-froggy language that calmed him.

"And I, uh, gave you all a free plane ride and

brought danish this morning," said Leonard.

"Thank you, Leonard," the Alazars said in unison.

Karras nodded. "Yes, thanks so much."

"Can you tell me what you're going to say…?" Katrina said. "In the video."

"Guys…" said Tony.

"It's just a trailer for my book, filmed with our phones," Karras said, hoping that was the lie that Sharon had told Leonard, or close enough. "You know, amusing ourselves to death, but also so thoroughly online that we make the real world experience of shopping and entertainment more like a virtual world. That's why we're gonna just, uh, use our phones, record 8k, make it feel organic."

"What's the line, Mister Karras, what's the once-in-a-lifetime line!" Katrina shouted.

"I…" A bus pulled up behind the SUV, bumpers nearly kissing, and honked loud enough to rattle the rear windshield. "I'm not sure yet. We're just going to improvise."

"Kid, we gotta go," Leonard said, opening the driver's side door.

"It'll be okay, Katrina. We'll send you the video, text you the line. By the time you land, it'll all be over and it'll all be fine," Rahel said. She reached out and squeezed their hands. "It was wonderful meeting you. You do wonderful work—God bless you."

They hugged and Katrina wormed over Rahel's lap to get to the door Leonard had just opened. Tony said his good-bye as well and Michael shrugged and waved at Katrina's angry back. In the front, Sharon unbuckled herself, slid into the driver's seat, and strapped herself back in. She said something in the twin language and Leonard responded almost identically, so it was probably just an exchange of farewells. The bus behind them honked again. Sharon put the SUV in drive and pulled away from the curb, muttering what was obviously a twin language curse. Tony laughed.

"So what is the plan?" asked Rahel. "What does 'murder America' even look like? We're just guessing that it'll be phantoms with AR-15s, and that somehow we could stop them. What if it's a bomb that brings the whole place down around our ears?"

"This place is a whole neighborhood on its own. A bomb couldn't do that—it would take months for a demolition crew to even do preparatory dismantling, take out the load-bearing columns, the internal walls. It would—"

"Violate the laws of physics?" Tony interrupted Karras.

"Be too obvious to carry out in secret, is what I was going to say," said Karras.

"All bets are off now," said Rahel.

Sharon pulled into the parking structure and found a reasonable spot only two stories up. It was dawn.

29.

WHATEVER RUDIMENTS OF a plan Karras had been preparing in his backbrain collapsed into ruin at the size of the Mall of America. Someone had just dropped a roof on an entire downtown, moved all the airline ticket counters out of O'Hare and replaced them with once-popular stores. There were four different instances of Foot Locker alone, five different but identical Lids stores—and yes, many of the men strolling about the promenades were wearing baseball caps, and khaki or denim knee-length shorts too. Karras and Tony stood out by *not* resembling enormous eight-year-old boys.

There was a water park, a small but energetic-looking roller coaster and other amusement-park rides somehow associated with the cable channel

Nickelodeon, and an entire IKEA that made Karras's head swim when he saw the name on the directory.

"I guess we're not splitting up to cover more ground," Karras said.

"We need more people," said Tony.

"Or fewer," said Rahel. "I didn't want to start a conflict while the child was here, but you, Sharon Toynbee, need to go."

"You pointed a firearm at me with Katrina in the room—how did you not want to start a conflict?" Sharon said.

"You started that conflict," said Rahel, jabbing at Sharon with her forefinger. "With your coven's spells. And now you're continuing it. You brought us here—"

"Michael divined the—"

"Easy to fake on a computer you have access to, and you just happen to have a twin who can fly a plane—"

"There are more than half a million licensed pilots in the US, more pilots than there are Ethiopian Amer—"

"And if your coven—"

"Book club."

"—is so powerful, so high and mighty, why do you need him?" Rahel demanded as she whipped her finger back and hiked her thumb over at Michael Karras standing behind her. "Why on Earth is he the center of the universe? Because he had some random dumb thought in his head as a child?"

"I admit I'm curious about that too," said Karras.

"Do you *feel* like the center of the universe?" Rahel wheeled on him. "What's it like?"

Of course he should deny it. Only the worst sort of person would truly consider themselves the center of the universe. The feeling went beyond mere self-involvement or narcissism; it wasn't like a mental illness, or the sort of religious sentiment that compelled his wizened grandmother to say, as she watched a news report about the flaming crash of TWA Flight 800, "This is God telling me that I shouldn't go to Greece next year." It wasn't Jesus betting on his football team, or an expectation that anyone would do anything for him, ever. It was just—

"It's mostly like reading about life in a book," he said. "Other people's lives. Their thoughts, how they treat other people, and going *Hmm, interesting*. And you get to re-read the passages you really like, and skim the boring bits, and sometimes if you don't like the story you leave it unfinished."

"We're dead," said Tony.

"We are not," said Sharon.

"Who else was in this book club?" asked Karras, suddenly. "I cranked out how many books for you? Six? And the first I heard of LRB's origin as a magic coven was... yesterday? And this once-in-a-lifetime magic, that's not the sort of thing a small group of three people *could* discover. You need more experimenters than that to get anywhere. And I can hardly be the only writer you recruited in the hope of finding someone who, as a kid, decided that they were inside their skeleton instead of vice-versa."

"Ah, Mister Bennett, he was in the book club!" said Rahel. "He talks about the holographic universe nonsense, and Michael, all the time."

"A Mister Bennett was, but not Christopher. His father, Roderick, was, and yes, Mike, you're right. A revolutionary book club is slow work. Add even one more person and the dynamic changes. Start a mailing list and try to recruit people in other cities, and you end up with splits, disagreements, *mutations*. Three years later, your New York cell are all Trotskyists, the San Francisco gang are Maoists, and then two people you managed to recruit in Houston declare themselves to be metaphysical Pabloites and either join some televangelist's megachurch, or, worse, declare that they're going to perform 'deep entry' on one another."

"They get married and have kids together?" asked Rahel.

"No, murder-suicide," said Sharon. "Almost as bad."

"You said there was an accident. What was the accident? When did it happen, for real?" asked Tony. "If Viktor Surge could log on to the internet from beyond the grave but also from before the grave, the 'accident' could have happened at any time."

"You're all so smart," said Sharon. "I hope the

three of you, if you live through this historic moment, can sit down with a couple of good books."

"If we live through the *moment*...?" said Rahel.

"We live *in* the moment," said Karras.

And in the next moment, the mall fell silent. All of it, the chatter and footsteps of the customers beginning to explore the open stores, the constant distant roar of the ventilation systems, even the roller coasters stopped mid-test run. Nobody blinked, nobody breathed. Then things faster than air stopped. The lights shifted color, electrochemical reactions in Karras's brain slowed, idled, and with a great quantum groan, time started again, crawling.

Sharon was still talking; it just took the words much longer to reach Michael Karras, as though he was at the opposite end of the Mall of America: "—the Lenin quote I manufactured."

"He whispered, 'There are decades when nothing happens; and there are weeks when *decade*s happen' in his son's ear when he was born, and that turned Chris Bennett into a famous lunatic with a microphone?" said Rahel.

"Yes, though he probably whispered it every day while the infant Christopher was still pre-verbal."

"Why is all this happening now?" asked Tony.

"Obviously, after decades where nothing happens, this is the week where decades happen, brother," said Rahel. "Try to keep up."

Karras had questions. He had objections. But

time was too slow. The controls in the hands of the homunculus in his skull were sluggish. Then he thought

Oh.

There was a shimmering entering the foodcourt.

A shimmering and the slight taste of ozone passed before him.

Oh, yeah.

On the second level, rounding the corner, a shimmering.

Karras turned around with an aching slowness, having to personally invite, then beg, each muscle in his legs, his torso, his neck, to please please fire, activate, flex.

Live in the moment.

More shimmering, the galleria was filled with shimmering, like the hand of God had reached down and given the snow globe in which He kept the Mall of America a very solid shake. What would Rahel think of that image?

Oh, yeah, 'live in the moment' was one of those '68 slogans. One détourned by Maxwell House, and Kodak and a dozen other brands.

In the distance a *pop-pop* sound, one more definitive than a pop-culture jingle.

Time snapped back into place. The shimmering ceased. No—Karras could no longer perceive it.

"Sharon! Remember when I was in Texas, and we were talking about the Dallas shooting and you told me about—"

"Invisibility cloaks?" Sharon asked.

Then her head exploded.

Tony tackled Rahel, shielding her with his body. Eyes up, Makarov in his hand. No way he knew how to shoot from that position. Karras ran. The mezzanine erupted with gunfire.

He could still see the shimmerings, though the moment in which he'd been living had passed. They moved swiftly, threading through the surging, panicking, bleeding, screaming crowd, but they weren't perfect. One bit of dislocated ripple was slammed to the ground by a knot of white-shirted workers from the Johnny Rockets. Karras pounced upon it. Someone stepped onto his back and over it, crushing him into the flesh and bone under the cloak. Touching it tingled. It was easy to grab onto but hard to hold, like trying to cup a handful of agitated air over a charcoal grill. His brain wouldn't cooperate with his fingers, selecting instead to believe his lying eyes. Karras just mounted the figure in the cloak and pressed down with his sternum. Beneath him, the shimmer warped, took on streaks and curves of darker coloration. Something to grab on to! Karras searched with his hands, seeking a seam, a zipper. The colorations shifted, ink in water, and he saw a face.

His own face, warped and distended. The reflection in the bottom of a glass, or a funhouse mirror. The other Karras was smiling, a toothy Steeplechase grin, a nose like rising brown bread, then from nowhere a real fist closed the real Karras's eye and sent him reeling into the legs of someone running past. The 'oof' sounded familiar.

The funhouse effect vanished, but not quick enough. Tony's big hand reached out and grabbed where a neck would have been and then fell atop the nothingness.

"Get the gun!"

Through his tear-filled squint, Karras could see a slit in the cloak, the small Uzi submachine hanging off a broken trigger finger. He snatched it away, and the shooter howled. That was enough for Tony to find his mouth and deliver three, four right hands to the jaw and eyes.

"Oh, shit," Karras said. "Thanks! Here!"

Tony threw up his arms. "Where'd you get *that?* I meant get the Makarov out of my waistband." He pulled his pistol from the small of his back and offered to it to Karras.

"But wh—?"

"Police are coming! I'm black, and all the real gunmen are invisible!"

Karras stood there, stunned, his eye swelling shut, noise overwhelming him.

"Idiot!" snapped Tony, and shoved the gun into his free hand.

"Rahel?"

Tony grabbed Karras by the shoulder and dragged

him back to Rahel. She was okay, but parts of her were missing at first glance. A teen boy was twitching at her feet, face red, jeans wet with piss and something else. Rahel waved the cloak at them with invisible arms.

"How'd you do that?" Karras said.

"He tripped over us. I kicked him where it hurt till he stopped yelling about it," Rahel said. "Get under this, we gotta get out of here."

"No, we have to stop this!"

"How?" the Alazars said. That unison trick never got less disconcerting.

"LensCrafters, where is it?"

Rahel glanced at the directory. "Not far!" She found the edges of the cloak and tossed it over Tony's head, ducked under it herself, and with a free-floating arm pulled Karras in too. It wasn't perfect—their shins were still visible—but at least they didn't have to learn how to walk without being able to see their own legs. Inside the cloak was like looking at the world through a remarkably persistent soap bubble. Oil-slick rainbow haloes wrapped around them, furniture and people stretched and then shrank at the border. A phalanx of police in blue, helmeted, shielded, mustered some yards away. They weren't charging yet, just building a quick cordon to kettle the chaos, protect some of the more valuable real estate.

"What's the plan? Conga line walk!" Rahel barked.

Tony put his hands on his sister's waist. Karras shoved the pistol awkwardly in his pocket and snagged Tony's belt.

"I can see them through my black eye a bit, because it's watering. Let's get glasses, smash the lenses, see what we can see!"

"And then?" She sounded doubtful, but started off toward the LensCrafters, practically pulling the men behind her.

"And then *we'll see!*"

Sharon was dead. Was it purposeful? Bennett must have known what she looked like. But it hardly mattered. Someone ran right into the three of them, but bounced off Tony's body, arms flailing, expression scrambled. Tony muttered "Sorry" too softly to hear outside the cloak. Sharon had known what to do— why had she been so cagey about telling Karras what his role was in stopping this murder? Rahel nearly slipped on a puddle of soda—no, Karras realized when he stepped in it too, blood. Did Sharon know about the cloaks in the first place? Was that why she had planted the idea in Karras's head, the way she had planted a suggestion to sleep last night? Last night, when she woke him up, naked—

The LensCrafters had been abandoned, and nobody was looting it, unlike most of the other stores they had passed. Who was going to take the time to grab a random prescription pair when the Mall of America had two Sunglass Huts, an Oakley Store, a

Solstice Sunglasses, and something called Eyebobs? Karras gave the shopping floor a quick once-over with his squinting eye and saw nobody lurking in a corner like a white-sheeted ghost, then nudged Tony forward.

"Good luck finding lenses that aren't shatterproof," said Tony as he whipped the cloak off the three of them. "I'm gonna see if I can hang this in the doorframe or something so we have privacy."

"So you can see the cloaks?" Rahel. "Because you're squinting? That's all it takes? I've been squinting too, I'm crying, I don't see a thing!" Rahel's eyes were cracked red, her cheeks glistening, snot hung from her nose. "I saw her die! I hurt someone. Tony nearly shot someone!"

"I gave him the gun, sister." He was working over some lenses with the heavy base of a mirror, every few seconds a sharp thunk followed by a muttered 'Nah.'

"I'm sorry," Karras said. "I mean, I saw Sharon die too…" It felt real, not like the deaths in the newspapers, on TV, or even the deaths of his grandparents. In their coffins they looked fake, dried apple dolls laid out in outfits the men and women he knew had never worn. Thinking about it was awful, and his head was pounding. It was just so meaningless.

"Ah, got one!" said Tony. "Rahel, see if you can find a radio somewhere. This is supposed to be happening all over the country. Maybe we can send a message…"

He squatted down behind the counter where he'd been working, duck-walked to the window, raised himself slightly, moved the hanging cloak to one side, and then looked through the cracked lens he held between forefinger and thumb.

Sharon hadn't died confronting a shooter, or manning the barricades surrounding the White House on the day of The Revolution. She hadn't even died slowly enough to say some final, dramatic words, or bring closure to her loved ones. She'd probably been mourning, on some level, the suicide of Viktor Surge. His death at least had some meaning attached to it. He freed up the possibility of using the slogans as a form of direct praxis.

Tony thumped away at more lenses, derailing Karras's train of thought. Rahel turned on a small clock radio she had found, turned the volume up all the way, and searched through the fuzzy AM band. "It's all local, reporting on our situation—just, you know, behind. They think it's a single shooter."

"Reports will come in," said Tony. "Michael, do you want me to make you a pair of glasses? The smashed lens idea kinda works. I mean, I can see the cloaked figures now, just not anything else."

Why did Sharon want to fuck him last night? Tony was more attractive by every measure, and Sharon was so casual in her nudity and her offer that she couldn't have cared so much about personal connection. She didn't seem like a demisexual, or whatever a Katrina

Chu-Ramirez might label her, at least not six hours ago.

"I don't want to use the guns," Rahel told Tony as he fitted her for frames. "I'm not going to commit the sin of murder. I don't want either of you two to do so either. The witchcraft is bad enough."

"I'm keeping Dad's gun; I won't shoot it and I'm not going to carry it out of here, but I'm keeping it. Mike, you'll keep carrying it, okay?"

What did Sharon mean—*the future lasts forever*? Even in its original context, it was more of an aphorism than a slogan. Althusser's great big idea was that ideology was an imaginary relationship with real life. He killed his wife, supposedly in a fit of madness, certainly was found to be insane. So much for him as a thinker.

"Michael, we have to go," said Rahel. "This was a mistake. We can't do anything here. We're going to try to get to a freight elevator, a loading dock."

"Yeah, the consumers down there are sitting ducks, because they're thinking like consumers, rushing for the doors, hoping the cops save them, you know," said Tony. "We have to think differently. I made you some smashed-glasses. They work. We'll have an advantage. The guns are yours."

What else had Sharon said? Ah yes, at the center of the Spectacle is the void. At a place like the Mall of America, that's obvious enough, even when there isn't a massacre happening. The Alazars were right, it was too late to do anything. No, it wasn't too late. Karras had already messed with space. Viktor Surge had messed with time, and had jumped into the void to give Karras the power to transport himself. And now Sharon was dead too. What magic she had done could also be reset. Anyone with the right frame of mind and performing the correct actions could make the world a place where for decades nothing happens and in a week decades happen.

"Sure, I'll take the gun," Karras said. "Let me just find a pen and paper. I want to write something down."

"What, a will, or a suicide note?" said Tony. "Come on! We have the glasses, we have a cloak, let's just get to the loading dock."

"Rahel, did you mean it when you promised Katrina you'd send them the slogan that could save the day?" Karras asked.

"I keep my promises, Michael," Rahel said.

"Even though it's 'black magic'?" Karras asked. He found a prescription pad and a golf pencil, scribbled a note. "Witchcraft?"

"I'll pray for Katrina, and for myself, and for Sharon and Viktor Surge," said Rahel. "And also for you. But I'll do it."

Karras had been hoping that Rahel Alazar would say something like that. He did not think she was right about God, her faith, the way the universe functioned. And he should know—he was the center of the universe, after all. And at the center of the universe was a void. But only someone as sure as Rahel would keep her promises. And Karras needed the example of someone as sure as Rahel right now.

He remembered a slogan that had tickled him back when he first started engaging in street politics, when he had first started writing. It was the '90s, when the World Wide Web was new enough that people called it that, as if it were distinct from the world instead of limning it. He was in Seattle, with the Teamsters and the turtles, a naïve Ralph Nader and the diabolical Pat Buchanan. One more body in a city clogged with them, trying to wrestle the abstraction of neoliberal globalization to the ground as if it were stored in the marrow of men. It was a fool's errand, and that realization was what birthed the slogan all but spontaneously, from a thousand skulls, but from Karras's first. From there, the slogan had electrochemically replicated itself in 999 primed brains, socio-spooky action at a distance. Then, laughing, he shouted it, and it was picked up in waves by the masses surrounding him, making it echo across the canyon streets.

Karras wasn't just thinking anymore, he was speaking aloud, in the third person.

He found a sample case under the counter, shook the sample frames out of it, and put the Makarov in it, then handed it to Tony. The paper he folded between his fingers and handed to Rahel. Then he said that he would be fixing all this now. The trick wasn't to take an action, it was to change a person—don't *do* magic, *be* magic.

"Three! Word! Chant!" said Michael Karras as he put the Uzi to his head and pulled the trigger.

ONE YEAR LATER

"Can I just ask again, please, please," said Dennis, except for that second 'please,' which was more of a sob. He could have done better had he the means to just wipe the tears from his eyes, but his wrists were bound behind him, to an eyehook drilled into the wall of the shipping container he was in with Jerry, who was similarly tied, and Djimon Melaku, whom Dennis was addressing.

"Of course, friend," Djimon answered. "You can ask anything you want, and I'll answer honestly, as I have been."

"You can ask over and over again, Logan." Jerry said. "The answers won't change."

"That's right, Columbo," said Garn Nibley. He was going through a large paper sack full of gas station snacks—triangular half-sandwiches sealed in plastic, yogurt, energy drinks.

"I've got a question for you, actually," said Jerry to Garn. "If you're back here with us, who the hell is driving now?"

"Wait, who's Columbo?"

"That's a TV detective. Before your time. He was annoying," said Djimon.

"The computer's driving," said Garn.

"Are you going to untie us, or feed us like baby birds?" asked Dennis.

"Then why are you even here, if the truck doesn't need a trucker?"

"I'm management," said Garn.

"We'll untie you if you swear to God to behave. You two are fairly resourceful. We saw you on *Year Zero* last year," said Djimon.

"Yeah, last year, Year Minus-One," said Garn, so amused with himself he opened up a lemonade and drank a celebratory gulp.

"Your resourcefulness is why Rahel recommended you for this mission."

"What mission? Why didn't you just ask us to do the mission instead of kidnapping us?" Dennis said.

"Mission's classified," said Garn.

"As I've already explained, if we describe the mission, it may fail. You may have refused. We may have been overheard. You know there are spy drones everywhere now," said Djimon.

"Invisible ones," said Garn.

"Habeas corpus suspended, the camps in full swing for native-born as well as immigrants," Djimon said. "We must be the players who take no chances."

"You think plucking two teenagers off the street and stuffing them into the back of a truck—" Dennis said.

"A truck that shouldn't have even been on a residential street!" Jerry said.

"—wasn't suspicious?"

"Given the current political juncture, two grown men arbitrarily hauling away two young men is the least suspicious thing the drones could capture on video," said Djimon.

"You guys look like shooters. No offense," said Garn. "Nerds."

"So it's the perfect cover. Two more probables being profiled and carted off to a detention center," said Djimon.

"Which is exactly where we're taking you," said Garn with a laugh. He had all the food laid out on the floor of the container and was separating it into two piles.

"What?" said Dennis.

"Please, he's joking," said Djimon. He turned to Garn. "Please stop joking."

"The day I can't make a nerd cry is the day freedom in this country has truly died," said Garn. "Why don't you two kids imagine that meme of a bald eagle crying a single tear while beneath it the Twin Towers collapse?"

"You're a fucking dick, dude," Dennis said. "How did you two even end up working together?" he asked Djimon.

"We belong to the same book club," said Djimon. "I for one, actually read the books. He attends mostly for the snacks."

"And where are you taking us, if not a detention center?"

"We *are* taking you to a detention center."

"You said he was joking!" Dennis cried.

"But it's not a falsehood," said Djimon. "It's just—"

"Funny because it's true?"

"It's funny because it's classified," said Garn.

Jerry pointed at the two piles of snacks with his toe. "Don't worry about it, dude," he told Dennis.

The boys were untied, and fed, and given the sleeper to rest in, and the container was filled with crates of food, and in the morning the truck stopped for fuel at a dusty gas station far from the highway and the heavily monitored truck stops. Dennis and Jerry were given a bag of food to absolutely not eat and told to walk a while through a brief wood till they came upon a large and obvious fence.

"And if we run?" asked Jerry.

"Go ahead," said Garn. "Good luck getting home without us and without getting arrested for loitering near a camp for real."

"And if we eat..."—Dennis looked down into the bag—"ah, never mind, this is all shit anyway."

"Let's go, Logan."

They began their walk. The woods were dark, and dense, and old. Roots and branches tugged at their boots, their jackets.

"Don't leave the food," said Jerry.

"It's all vegan," said Dennis. "Are we being hazed?"

"Kind of. But I don't think the food is for us."

Jerry was in the lead, confident in his ability to navigate, but he managed to turn himself around a couple times, then passed it off to Dennis as a tactic he was using to throw off pursuers or investigators who might comb the area in the morning. Even with all that, it didn't take too long to find a break in the woods, a patch of grass illuminated by stadium lights, and beyond that the high fence and brutalist architecture of one of the new detention centers. Since the coordinated ten-state 'murder of America' spree at the Mall of America, in Manhattan's Times Square, inside San Francisco's Salesforce Tower, on the campus of Brigham Young University, and other public gathering spots across the country, these centers had become commonplace. This one appeared to be a repurposed big-box store, blocky and squat and with fewer windows than even an ordinary maximum security prison. The sky above it was busy with the insect buzz of drones of various sizes, from a sparrow that could be crushed in a fist to a child's snow sled.

"Now what?" Jerry asked himself. A step out of the woods and they'd be spotted. Perhaps they already had been. "They've got killer Rosebuds up there."

"Find a vegan and fuck off?" suggested Dennis.

"You found 'em," said Katrina Chu-Ramirez, their voice a little deeper now, raspy. They were wearing the camp-issue light brown prison jumpsuit and slippers. They sat on a log where they hadn't been even a moment earlier. "I'm not a vegan. I just like vegan food. Hand it over, I'm starved. They keep trying to slip me cold cu—Oh, fuck you, kid," they said at Dennis's smile. "I'm not here for your juvenile humor."

"Katrina Chu-Ramirez! I knew it. Well, I had a sense of it. Do you remember us? We spoke to you during Middlesex," asked Jerry.

"Of course I do," said Katrina. They held up one finger, and pushed a whole gas station onigiri into their mouth. "Mm-mmm," they said. Then a swig of lemonade. "Did somebody drink out of this already?" Katrina said, then swallowed.

"It was the white man," said Jerry.

"Figures," said Katrina.

"Let's go! We got 'er!" hissed Dennis.

"Not a her, and I can't go. I'm under arrest. I'll be an escapee if I leave," said Katrina.

"You've already escaped!"

"Nah, I'll go back in in a few minutes, after we're done talking," said Katrina.

Dennis had more questions, opened his mouth to gaping, but Jerry held up a hand, and patted the air. He was right, of course. People want to talk.

"Let's say I have a cloak," said Katrina. "And a drone-pilot comrade, three states away, but piloting one at this facility. Can you believe the government still thinks that local ties matter more than ideological ones? Half the kids in my tier were dropped off by their parents, and only ever get Zoom visits from their social media friends. Anyway, my pilot pal can unlock my pod, and heft me over the fence when I need to have a private meeting. Not everyone enjoys working for a police state, not even all the police. Just 99.99 percent of them. But there's always someone to help. Don't you agree?"

"No," said Jerry.

"Yes," said Dennis. "I do agree, and I want to help." He and Jerry exchanged bewildered looks. "It's true!"

"It is true," said Katrina. "Actually, almost everyone wants to help. Imperialist armies are full of people who just want to help by dropping bombs on apartment buildings full of sleeping 'bad guys.' The problem is that most people don't know how to help, so we end up with"—they gestured to the camp with the bag of Takis Fuego they were holding— "this. The company that built this store donated it to the government to help prevent another six thousand people from being murdered in one day. You know the slogan, 'Okay, Forget 9/11. Never Forget 18/22.'"

"I still don't know if there's always someone here to help, but I guess we're here to help, but not to help you escape?" Jerry said.

"Yah, exactly." They dug into their shoe and removed a small piece of paper, the sort of thing one would tear from a pocket pad, and extended their arm. Dennis shuffled forward, claimed it, opened it up, read it, and made a noise.

"Uhm, here, Jer," he said, handing it over.

Jerry read it too. His eyebrows twitched. "Well, why not just announce this on Chit-Chat or something?"

"Why not just give some random person their own nuclear weapon and see what happens?" Katrina asked. Dennis inhaled sharply, and emitted a single phoneme. "That's what we call in the prison system a rhetorical question," Katrina said.

"Will it work?" asked Jerry.

"For someone it will," said Katrina.

"I mean, there are lists of these things online, tons of people trying them every day, and every possible reason," said Jerry.

"I've never seen that one online," said Dennis.

"Yeah, it's not online, it's not published," said Katrina. "I mean there are an infinite number of potential sentences out there; maybe it is published, but not in a context anyone would recognize. It could be on a movie poster somewhere, of the front cover of some novel. Anyway, for it to work, there are objective conditions that must be met, and subjective conditions. Nobody knows what the subjective conditions exactly are, but they exist somewhere, in someone's brain. But there's the objective condition, right there. That's what our mutual acquaintance created." Again they gestured toward the detention center.

"You mean Bennett?" asked Dennis.

"Yeah," Katrina said. "You know how Nazis pretend to be anti-Nazis and the victim of the 'Real Nazis' of the left. Bennett spent his career warning his listeners about false flags and concentration camps, but he was just worried that another brand of camp would be founded before he could get his personal franchise off the ground."

"How do you know anyone alive has the right, uh, subjectivity to make this work?"

"Our mutual acquaintance created the subjective condition," said Katrina.

"You mean Karras?" asked Dennis.

"You're clever," said Katrina. "If you ever want an internship…"

"When should we try it?" Jerry asked.

"When it feels right."

"Does that mean now?"

"Does it feel right now?"

"No, it doesn't," said Dennis.

Jerry looked back down at the paper, and read the words written on it aloud. The three of them waited for a long moment, silent, only half-expectant.

"Do you feel any different, Katrina?" Dennis asked.

"No."

"Oh, well," Jerry said.

"It's okay," said Katrina. "Try again, any time. You too, Logan. If you go back down to where you were left, there will be a smaller, less comfortable truck waiting for you."

"If it worked, would we get a nicer truck?"

"No, Logan," said Katrina. "Hey, thanks for the grub."

"You're welcome," the boys said, not quite in sync. They waved and walked off into the woods.

Katrina waited until they could no longer hear Dennis and Logan crunching through the twigs and branches in the woods behind the prison. Maybe they *did* feel a little different, this time. Then they pointed the thumb and forefinger of their right hand into a gun shape, held their right arm steady with a grip on the wrist, but no, that wasn't quite right. *What was it meant to be?* they thought, and then realized. They reset their hands, forefingers extended and at right angles to make crosshairs, took aim at one of the larger Rosebuds circling the prison, and whispered to themselves, "Pew pew!"

The drone jerked suddenly, spun out of its normal flight path as if struck, and corkscrewed to the earth, dead.

Katrina smiled and put another drone in their sights.

ACKNOWLEDGEMENTS

The Second Shooter was a long time coming, and the first novel born out of my head, instead of someone else's, in many years. I'd like to thank Michael Curry for his patience in representing *TSS*, and David Thomas Moore for his patience in receiving it. Robert Swartwood was vital for reminding me that I never learned how to count. Sarah Langan made time for me that she did not have to. Rob Hart was extremely surprised, and that was good to see. Cara Hoffman keeps it real and surreal simultaneously. Thank you all.

ABOUT THE AUTHOR

Nick Mamatas is the author of several novels, including *Move Under Ground*, *I Am Providence* and *Sabbath*. His short fiction has appeared in *Best American Mystery Stories*, *Year's Best Science Fiction and Fantasy*, *Tor.com*, and dozens of other venues. Much of the last decade's short fiction was recently collected in *The People's Republic of Everything*.

Nick is also an editor and anthologist: he co-edited the Bram Stoker Award-winning *Haunted Legends* with Ellen Datlow, the Locus Award nominees *The Future is Japanese* and *Hanzai Japan* with Masumi Washington, and the hybrid fiction/cocktail title *Mixed Up* with Molly Tanzer. His short fiction, non-fiction, novels, and editorial work have variously been nominated for the Hugo, Shirley Jackson, Stoker, and World Fantasy Awards.

FIND US ONLINE!

www.rebellionpublishing.com

/rebellionpub   /rebellionpublishing   /rebellionpublishing

SIGN UP TO OUR NEWSLETTER!

rebellionpublishing.com/newsletter

YOUR REVIEWS MATTER!

Enjoy this book? Got something to say?

Leave a review on Amazon, GoodReads or with your
favourite bookseller and let the world know!

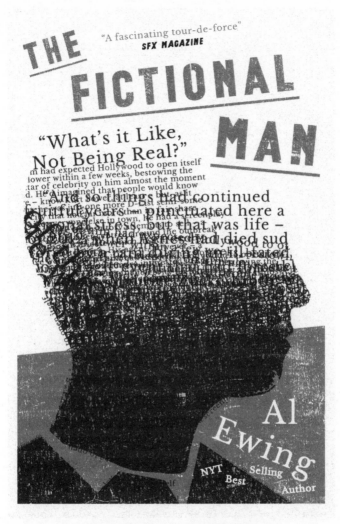